PART 0

AFTER THE BREAKING

THE BEYOND THE HOSTILE SKY CYCLE

PART 0
AFTER THE BREAKING

KAREN J. LAAKKO

atmosphere press

Published by Atmosphere Press

Cover design by Kevin Stone

atmospherepress.com

FOREWORD

Welcome to the *Beyond the Hostile Sky Cycle*—my life's work. It represents many years, many revisions and reimaginings, and a great many influences and inspiration sources, all working together to tell a story about worlds colliding.

Part of what makes fantasy and science fiction so great is that they confront readers with something new and different, and this series will blend the two genres to confront even the characters with something new. Methods will change from book to book, and each one will also present new imagery and settings. I hope this approach will make these adventures relatable—and, most importantly, fun!

This series is a *cycle*; it will start with some very important events (Part 0), reset itself (Part 1), and then slowly make its way back. And yet, in certain respects, it is also a *puzzle*. Follow the colors, other imagery, and even names and chapter titles, as some of these are clues about what is going on. Or, just follow the plot and see how things unfold. It's up to you!

I'd like to thank my "beta readers" over the years, who read drafts and offered feedback and helped me correct my missteps; you know who you are. :) But whether you're reading for the first time or the fourteenth, I hope you enjoy exploring the worlds of Vilse, Aktinos, Tetrachtha, and... beyond....

-*Karen J. Laakko*

For those who would like guidance with the pronunciation of this series' unique names, some suggestions are provided in the glossary at the back of the book.

TABLE OF CONTENTS

PART 0
AFTER THE BREAKING

*And so it came to pass that the fourfold
world was further divided into two, and the gods
vanished unto the firmament, to be replaced by new
gods who came from the firmament to guard the
land and dwell therein. At their coming worlds
were subdued, and the order of things was
rearranged so that the world's number was not
four, nor six, but two; for it was half of what it once
was. These gods, whose attribute was lightning,
whose weapon was the wrath of heaven, were
known as the Ouranothen....*

-fragmentary text discovered in the
ruins of Aktinos, now called "Vilse"
by most. Believed by many to be from
An Early History of Aktinos—though,
of course, there are numerous scholars
who dispute this claim.

PROLOGUE
DARK AGE

VILSE, THE LOST REALM

The realm was completely destroyed.

Buildings had been torn apart, some all the way down to their foundations. Huge blocks of amorphous stone lay strewn about—some near the ruined buildings of which they had once been a part, some not, many of them scorched a deep black as if by some otherworldly fire. If any vegetation had once flourished in this lofty, mountainous region, it was gone now, and even the brown and barren ground had a scorched appearance. Thick black clouds hovered stagnant above it all, making any clear view of the dark sky above difficult.

This must have been a wondrous realm once, but now it looked like some immense creature had chewed it up, spat it out, and then set fire to it. And yet, as Brinna stood near the top of the mountain trail and gazed on the dimly lit devastation, she could not help but feel a sense of relief, even of fond nostalgia: the wave of emotions experienced by one who has finally returned home after a long time. Those, she knew, were extremely dangerous feelings—especially here.

"We finally made it," Ljuset said beside her, and she turned to look at her fellow traveler: a fair-haired woman who, if she was experiencing similar mixed emotions, was hiding them well.

"Yes, we did," Brinna agreed absentmindedly, turning

back to cast a glance down the narrow trail which, at a now-unseen spot many hundreds of yards below, connected to the world's major plain. "I thought the trip would never end—though you have more reason to complain than I, for you magic-users tend to lack endurance. Now, let's get going so we can make it *out* of here in one piece."

"We will, we will," Ljuset stated, pivoting away with a startling suddenness. "Be patient."

Brinna frowned; it seemed this magic-user was as brusque as they come. And quite unruffled. She opened her mouth to protest the other woman's tone, but stopped when she saw the very serious glint in Ljuset's eyes. There had to be a reason why the authorities had considered her the best choice for this exploratory mission: their country's single most talented magic-user in an era in which magic was incredibly hard to tame. Angering her would not be a good idea—and might even endanger Brinna's unstated objectives of observation and planning.

Sighing, she put her hand on one of the steep cliff walls that bordered the trail, inhaled the smoke-tinged air, and thought of the rumors she had heard back home. Of the many scruffy-looking people who had called this place *svarthål*—a word of unknown origin and unofficial usage, which somehow conveyed that this region of the world entrapped and devoured anything that came within its reach. At the time, she had found those theories laughable, but looking out at her surroundings now, she could believe everything that had been said. Even now, the clouds of smoke were billowing toward the center of the destroyed area while the streaky, purple-and-black sky above them rippled in the same direction, as if responding to some force that wanted to drag its new prey into the monster's maw...

In the next moment, the fluctuations had given way to a blinding flash of light, which lanced downward for a terrible half-second before vanishing as quickly as it had appeared. On its heels came a low rumbling that rippled down the trail, sent rocks tumbling down from above, and nearly knocked Brinna off her feet.

She staggered, grabbed the cliff wall again for support, and blinked to clear her vision. When she could finally see again, she caught sight of Ljuset, who was on one knee beside her, head bowed in reverence.

"What are you *doing*?" she asked sharply.

Ljuset waited a few seconds and then lifted her head calmly. "Paying my respects. What we saw just now originated up there." She pointed toward another mountain that loomed, towering over their own, so tall that its peak was lost among the roiling black clouds. "That mountain is the highest place in our world—and, according to legend, the seat of the gods' power. As I'm sure you know, the heaven-fire is their wrath. If we're seeing it now, it would seem the gods need to be appeased before we go any farther."

"Maybe they wish for us to leave this place and not disturb the dead," said another voice.

Instantly, both Brinna and Ljuset turned to look at the third member of their party: a dark-haired young man who seemed younger than their twenty-two and twenty-six years, though this only made the circumstances of their original meeting all the more incongruous. He was nervous, too, and aloof. After coming upon the other two in their travels and expressing a desire to join them, he had barely spoken ten words to them. Nothing had been said about what he had been doing prior to meeting them, or how he had come to be traveling alone in a dangerous world. Just about all they knew about him was the name of the country he came from— Kevättären Valtakunta—and his own name, Salainen. The foreign-sounding words were all the more irritating to Brinna because she had no idea what their meaning or origin might be.

"Then why did you join us in the first place, if that's what you think?" she snapped at him.

"I desire to see the ruins," he replied, though he did not look at all sure of himself. Almost immediately he turned away, face faintly pink in the dim light, obviously ashamed that he had spoken.

"Then you must not be as concerned about this as you claim," Brinna concluded, and soon followed the statement up with a contemptuous snort. "Heaven-fire! Wrath of the gods! You read too much. Both of you."

"Actually, I hardly ever read at all," Salainen said softly, his gaze still averted.

"Well, *something* destroyed this realm," Ljuset cut in. "I'd rather show the gods the proper respect than run the risk of getting destroyed myself. Shall we move on?"

Brinna looked around: everything had stopped again. The black smoke-clouds hovered near-motionlessly once more, the visible portions of the sky were as still as the surface of a calm lake, and the ground beneath her feet felt stable. Back to relative normalcy, then.

Her mind raced to find possible alternative explanations for the flash of light—some release of energy, or a simple deflection of sunlight off something on that mountaintop—and stopped only when she noticed that Ljuset was regarding her with the same serious look as before. With a small sigh, she nodded her acquiescence to the magic-user's idea, and Ljuset whipped around in a flutter of robes and started up the last small segment of the trail.

Slowly, the group of three picked its way through the remnants of the vanished kingdom. Whoever had built it must have chosen a good location or somehow cleared away chunks of the mountainside, as the terrain was remarkably flat for such a high altitude. The whole area formed a vast plain, nestled comfortably in the middle of the mountain range. Once it must have been secluded, tranquil, impenetrable. Now it was isolated and eerie, and despite the passage of so many years, it still stank of death and destruction.

On they went, with Ljuset in the lead; she seemed to be using the decay-like stenches as a guide, steering away from them whenever they became too strong. This went on for minutes, and then tens of minutes, with no slackening in Ljuset's pace, and although Brinna kept up with her easily, Salainen did not. The young man lagged behind, his pace erratic—now becoming slower as he navigated rough terrain or paused in apprehension at what lay ahead, now speeding up again as he tried to put distance between himself and something unpleasant.

For all that he had journeyed to this plain *"to see the ruins,"* he spent almost no time looking at those ruins. His gaze was often fixed on the ground, and whenever he passed one of the huge, black-scorched boulders that littered the area, some of which were giving off unpleasant smells of their own, he would look away and edge around it cautiously. How could he have survived traveling alone for any length of time?

At last, Ljuset stopped at a point near the plain's left edge, between traces of a collapsed wall and what looked like the huge façade of an enormous building. The latter, too, had a scorched appearance; the entire wall of rough-looking stone bricks was an unnatural purplish-black in color. Even the massive, arching double doors, which felt cold and smooth like the blade of a sword, were burned and blackened. Unlike the other buildings, however, this one appeared mostly intact. Remnants of towers and battlements could be seen rising above and beyond the main wall, along with a few tattered fragments of decorative flags: their bright yellows and whites likewise stained purplish-black in places, hanging limply in the still, stale air.

Ljuset let out a sigh—perhaps of awe, or dismay, or both.

Placing her right hand on the wall, she rubbed it along the uneven surface to determine whether the purplish-black color would come off. It did not; it appeared permanent.

Sighing again, she shook her head. "It's difficult to believe that this was once called the 'Palace of Light,'" she muttered.

"Really?" Brinna asked, very much despite herself.

"Indeed. This building housed the rulers of the realm that we call 'Vilse'—once the realm of light and splendor, but now lost. When it fell, shadows covered our world and plunged us into a dark age. Or so the legend goes." Walking up to the right-hand door, Ljuset pointed to a spot on it that was just over her head. "This right here is the realm's symbol."

Curious, Brinna looked where Ljuset was indicating. There, carved into the metal of the door and partially obscured by wear, was a circular design depicting a mountain whose peak was being struck by a bolt of lightning. The peak was being blown apart, chunks of rocky debris flying through the air on both sides. At the center of the carving, straight lines that may have symbolized rays of light could be seen emanating from the point where the lightning was hitting the mountain—as if something, perhaps the realm itself, was being born from the impact. An identical carving could be seen in the same position on the other door.

"But if this was the realm of light," Brinna mused, "and if it was destroyed by the gods as you implied earlier—why would the gods destroy a force for light and good, assuming that they themselves are also a force for light and good?"

Ljuset frowned. "I don't know. But lightning is the province of the gods. Perhaps"—she nodded toward the faded, blackened carving—"this realm was destroyed because its people grew too powerful. Perhaps they became blasphemous, believed that they *were* the gods. That would bring divine wrath down on their heads, I think."

"Maybe," Brinna said thoughtfully. "But—" Cutting off

abruptly, she pointed upward. "Look at that."

The circular mountain-and-lightning insignia was not the only decoration on the large double doors. There was also, near the top of the left-hand door and situated slightly off-center, a drawing that looked like it had been made with chalk or some chalk-like substance. In crude white outline, it depicted what seemed to be some kind of winged being. The figure itself, though tall, was drawn only vaguely, perhaps to call attention to its massive, spreading wings. In one hand the figure appeared to be holding something long and thick, but the object had been smeared beyond all recognition. The rest of the drawing showed no such smearing, and the lines stood out sharply against the dark background, so crisp that they might have been drawn only the day before.

Brinna stared at the rough drawing for a long time; it was vague and indistinct, irrelevant to all of her goals, but she found herself unable to look away. Even when an unexpected breeze ruffled her clothing and sent a brief chill down her spine, she did not move a muscle. "What is it, Ljuset?" she whispered. "Have you ever seen anything like it?"

"No," Ljuset replied. "It's not mentioned in anything I've read about this place—not that even our most learned scholars claim to know much. But whatever it is, I suspect we're going to discover it for ourselves. What we seek is beyond these doors."

"*'Beyond these doors'*?" Brinna repeated in dismay. "You mean—in the palace?"

The very word "*palace*" was dangerous; it meant that the building was the realm's metaphorical center, the accursed heart of a darkened region that stood under darkened skies. It stood to reason that the worst of the evil would be behind these huge double doors. No matter how important Ljuset's task was, seeking answers here was likely to get all three of them killed... and yet, even as these doubts were running their course, Brinna did feel a desire to venture deeper, to enter the former Palace of Light. From the way Ljuset was slowly edging forward, her gaze suddenly vacant, she was experiencing the same sensation.

Maybe Ljuset's mission has nothing to do with it, Brinna thought to herself. *Maybe this place is playing tricks on us, manipulating our memories and driving us mad if we don't go farther into the darkness. Then, once we're within its grasp, it'll suck us in and swallow us whole.* Svarthål, indeed.

The cold touch of metal cut into her reverie: she had advanced all the way to the doors without knowing it. "Well, if we're going in, we might as well get it over with," she heard herself saying. And, with that, she began to push one of the doors open.

At once, something wet splattered against the door from the other side—and then a slimy tentacle curled around the edge and began to pull on it. To pull it open.

Brinna jumped, but a second tentacle had already wrapped itself around the area of her long sleeve that covered her forearm. Slowly it dragged her forward—she struggled to break free, but it was too strong—until she was face-to-face with the essence of shadow itself.

That was what it seemed like, at least. The creature that stood just inside the partially open door was not tall—only about half her height—but so amorphous and indeterminate was its form that even that fact was left in doubt. The creature... oozed. Numerous tentacles could be seen, along with curved claws and only the dead souls of this realm's inhabitants knew what else. Even as Brinna watched, sharp yellow fangs appeared from within the oozing mass of dark-purple shadow and seemed to arrange themselves in the shape of a dreadful grin at having caught a piece of prey. The tentacle's grip on her arm tightened...

In panic, she cast about for some way to defend herself.

Her bow was slung over her shoulder, out of reach, and it required both hands anyway; she brought her free arm down hard on the tentacle, with no effect; her upper body was bowing steadily forward as the monster tugged at her with incredible force. In one last-ditch effort, she set her feet firmly, prepared to lean backward with all her might—

Just as she had begun the maneuver, something silver flashed through the air in front of her, and the tentacle that held her was severed in a spray of dark liquid. It dropped, writhing, to the floor as the silver object—a sword—zipped past again, this time to bury itself within the shadow creature. A couple of quick cuts, and it was over. The creature collapsed and promptly began to disintegrate.

Shaking, Brinna worked to regain her balance, turned away—and found herself looking directly at the young man, Salainen. It was his sword that she had seen, now held in his hand and soaked in the dark blood-like substance. "You... you saved me," she stammered. "Thank you."

He merely nodded. He was holding the sword a bit awkwardly, she thought, and was looking at it with wide eyes, like he was unsure what he had just done.

So. This place was changing all of them, and in different ways. It might be best not to write him off just yet—at least until she found out what he was really after.

With a quick shake of her head, she turned her attention to her tunic's two long sleeves, which were dripping with a liquid that was distinct from the blood but—somehow—even more disgusting. Thicker. She shook both arms experimentally: her sleeves were nearly soaked through.

Turning to Ljuset, she shot the magic-user a pleading look. Ljuset raised one eyebrow questioningly, but stepped forward after a moment and held out a small scrap of cloth. Brinna wrapped it around one hand and then the other, carefully cleaned both sleeves of the thick liquid, and then let the cloth fall to the floor inside the doorway, whereupon she kicked out with her foot to send it into an adjacent corner.

"Why didn't you use magic against that thing?" she muttered to Ljuset as the group—having filed inside and closed the half-open door—began walking down the palace's first dark corridor. "It would have..."

"As I've said many times," Ljuset interrupted, "even those who have mastered the magic cannot expect it to obey their every whim. Too many restrictions. I would have tried it if your life had truly been in danger, but Salainen had things under control. His reaction was quite fast, actually."

Brinna snorted softly, but held her silence otherwise.

As they walked on, she held her bow at the ready, firing at anything that moved. Not that there was much in the way of movement; the corridors were eerily empty as they passed by. Where they might have expected to find rats, spiders, or even other monsters in this long-abandoned palace, there was nothing. There was not even any dust on the floors, a fact which was particularly odd because whatever servants had once labored to keep the building clean would have died or fled when the realm fell. Only the flickering remnants of a few yellow-white torch-flames on the walls countered the overall appearance of lifeless, austere stone hallways being held in some deadly thrall.

Or...?

As they were approaching a point where their corridor intersected with another, there was a distinct tapping sound far to the right. Brinna raised a hand to signal her two companions to stay put and then crept down the crossing corridor, her bow raised. After about a minute of this, she caught sight of a tall, yellowish blur, flashing across yet another intersection of hallways; there was a vague glint of silvery light.

She stopped in her tracks, lowered her bow, and considered how this sighting might mesh with her existing knowledge of the realm's current state. *...Interesting.*

Her initial temptation to investigate further was quickly quashed when she detected a strong sensation of cold in the hallway: far beyond anything she had felt since leaving her home country several weeks before. Numerous puddles of the same slime that the shadow creature had left behind on her clothing were just barely visible in the dim light, some almost as far away as the solitary door that stood near the hall's end. She shivered and turned back.

Upon her return to the corridor where she had left the others, she found them both looking at her expectantly. "It's fine," she said with a shrug. "Nothing of interest to our present goal. Ljuset, you lead from here. Based on what I saw, this palace is very large, and I'm worried that I'll get us all lost."

The echo of their footsteps from the walls was the only sound as they continued on their way. Ljuset walked several paces in the lead, and she often stopped to study the tattered wall tapestries that hung in this part of the palace. There were a great many of them, but even more numerous were the torches, which hung on the walls here as they had near the entrance. The ones in this area were weaker than the others and offered meager yellowish light at best—feeble, flickering, a poor defense against the surrounding shadows—but some illumination was better than none at all.

Brinna and Salainen, meanwhile, walked in the rear, almost side by side. On one occasion, she glanced sideways at him; he was also looking at the tapestries as they passed by, though he did not stop to investigate them closely. It was likely, she reflected, that he was going to be a difficult one to figure out.

Finally, after an almost interminable walk, Ljuset stopped in front of yet another tapestry, and this time she did not resume walking when Brinna and Salainen caught up. "We're here," she said. "There's a hidden door behind this tapestry.

What we seek should be beyond it."

Brinna did not reply right away, for despite some annoyance and inner self-chastisement, she was studying the tapestry. This one, however, was interesting: it depicted what was obviously a battle. Two armies were spread out on a bright plain, one surrounding the other. The surrounding army was clearly arrayed in ranks based on the weapons wielded by the warriors—swords in one area, bows and spears in another, and who knew what else—and the figures were rendered in colors as bright as those of the large, yellowish-brown building, probably this very Palace, that stood off to one side. As for the other army...

"Look at that," she commented, tugging on Ljuset's sleeve. "There, toward the middle. Those purplish things—don't they look like the monster we fought before?"

Ljuset gave the tapestry a long look. "Yes, you're right. It seems we may be one step closer to finding out what doomed this realm. We'll have to see if the knowledge that rests behind this door supports that conclusion."

"Why?" asked Brinna. Grabbing a piece of the tapestry— the fabric started to give out at her touch, but did manage to hold together—she moved it away from the wall and peeked behind it. There was indeed a door there, half-rotten but more or less intact. "What's behind this that is so important?"

"The Palace's secret library, of course," Ljuset said, her voice swelling with pride and excitement.

Brinna groaned. "Library?" she repeated in dismay, but it came out sounding half-hearted, for she was studying the tapestry again. There was no sign on it of the strange winged being she had seen drawn at the entrance, and that fact left her oddly disappointed. "We came all this way and risked life and limb for—a *library*??"

"This is the best way to obtain the information we need!" Ljuset said in exasperation. "Would you rather kidnap one of those monsters and hope it talks? Now, hold the tapestry for me while I check the door for traps. There would have been a protective spell on it once, long ago, and the fact that it's unguarded now makes me quite suspicious."

Brinna and Salainen held the tapestry over their heads—not evenly, as Salainen was quite a bit taller—to keep it out of Ljuset's way as she examined the door. A faint yellowish glow surrounded her as she stepped forward and stretched her hand out in the same direction. More yellow, brighter and purer than the glow and arranged in a diagonal, X-like pattern, appeared on the door, bit by bit, as she passed her hand over it. She frowned at this, and then she was reaching out even farther, to touch the door.

At once there was a crackling sound, and she jumped backward, clutching her hand and grimacing in pain. "The protective spell," she said, a bit breathlessly. "It's still active!"

"But I thought you said..." Brinna began. Whatever was going on with the door, she wished Ljuset would hurry up and take care of it. Her arms were beginning to ache from holding the tapestry over her head.

Ljuset nodded. "I said it would have been placed here long ago. It shouldn't—can't—be here still! Magic spells remain in effect for a good long time—hence, one reason why we need restrictions on their use—but they fade away when their caster dies."

"Then—could someone still be alive in this place?" Brinna prompted, watching the magic-user closely for a reaction or suspicion, given the noises in the corridor she had explored earlier. Her arms really hurt now. Opposite her, Salainen stood as motionless as a statue; *he* was obviously having no such trouble.

"Unlikely," said Ljuset. "This realm fell at least a century ago. Even if someone survived the initial onslaught, that person would have had to live much longer than the normal lifespan. It's impossible."

Brinna observed that Salainen, while still motionless, now had an odd light in his eyes, and one corner of his mouth was curved into a tiny smile as he looked on at the magic-user and the door with its crisscrossing yellow lines. There, finally. A possible clue.

"Then this is a mystery requiring further study," she told Ljuset loudly. "However, such further study can wait until you deal with that spell so we can let *go* of this thing!"

Instead of replying, Ljuset frowned at the door for a few more moments, then gave herself a small shake and made a visible effort to focus her mind. Soon thereafter, a strange, yellowish symbol appeared on the ground at her feet, situated so that she was standing at its center. Light emanated from the symbol, and another glow surrounded the magic-user as she stretched her hand out once more.

This time, a beam of what might have been light shot forth from her fingers to sever the yellow objects that held the door bound. The yellow objects fell apart just like ropes, and they disintegrated and vanished before they hit the ground.

The spell finished, Ljuset lowered her hand, and the symbol at her feet—which Brinna knew was called a "rune"—slowly faded away. "There; it's safe now," said the magic-user. "Let's go in."

With that, she opened the door, which creaked alarmingly when she moved it, and entered the library. The other two struggled to keep up with her.

As soon as they had all walked through the doorway, a breeze rose up in much the same fashion as the one out on the plain had. Clouds of dust swirled, and when these had settled back down, the group saw brown bookcases and desks and chairs that looked like they would crumble if someone breathed on them. The typical musty smell of old books mingled with the stenches of rot and decayed wood, to sickening effect. It appeared that this secret library, enclosed by plain, tapestry-free walls of stone, had never been cared for as thoroughly as the corridors outside.

Brinna could not wait to leave.

Ljuset, however, was already moving among the book-cases, muttering to herself as she examined the books—or what was left of them. The hem of her long brown magic-user robes dragged along in the dust behind her, but she paid it no heed.

Not finding what she was seeking, she left the bookcases and began to wander through the rest of the room. A large book sat open on one of the less dusty desks, and it was there that she headed next. The book was turned to almost the last page, and a quill lay on top of it, its tip still pressed against the right-hand page beside the last word that had been written.

Carefully, almost reverently, Ljuset moved the quill aside, closed the book and picked it up, then brushed some dust from its cover. Based on the cry of triumph that immediately followed, she had found what she was looking for.

"Come over here!" she called to Brinna and Salainen, and when they had joined her, she showed them the book. It bore the title: *Being a History of the Wars with the Skiai and the Consequences Thereof, Recorded by the Most Renowned Scribes in All of Aktinos.*

"Ak...tinos," Brinna said slowly, testing the foreign-sounding word on her tongue. "But the official name of this place is 'Vilse,' right?"

"It's both," Ljuset replied. "More has changed besides custom in all these years. Language changes, people themselves change, and different groups often give their own names to things, as we can see even in the naming conventions of our own time."

"And those are not the only names by which this realm is known," Salainen said quietly beside her. "Some exist in my country as well, though most people these days call this place *Ikipimeä*—a word that refers more to the lingering darkness in the sky than to the area itself."

"What did people call the realm in older days?" Ljuset asked.

"Mostly *Valonvuoret* and *Ikuisuudentorni*," Salainen answered, "but the first one was only ever used in reference to the very distant past."

Ljuset nodded, but Brinna, whose head was already beginning to hurt from the effort of processing the long names, merely shrugged. "I'll take your word for it, both of you. So what do we do with this *wondrous* text, now that we've found it?"

"We read it, of course," Ljuset replied in a condescending, "*that-should-be-obvious*" tone that seemed to be typical for her.

"*Read* it?" Brinna echoed in dismay. "That huge thing? We'll be here forever!"

Brown robes billowed as Ljuset rounded on the younger woman. "Just what are your priorities here, Brinna?" she snapped. "Is the darkness not spreading to other regions of the world? Can you deny it?"

Brinna gazed at the magic-user sullenly. She could not deny it.

"I was sent to stop it, to put an end to this dark age once and for all," Ljuset barreled on. "The first step toward that goal is finding out exactly what created the darkness. If you truly want to help, then you can have no problem spending some time with this—a historical text, written in their scribes' own hands."

"I agree," said Salainen, with much more force than before, and the two women turned again to look at him. "My people have theories about what happened, and this is the best way to confirm them."

Brinna could feel her heart pounding in sudden panic as she glared at him. "What are you *talking* about? I thought you said you never read—"

But no one was listening to her; Ljuset and Salainen had already sat down at the nearest table and opened the book to the first page. Due to this development, would they deduce her intentions before she could even figure out how to proceed?

After a moment, however, she sighed and closed her eyes to calm herself. *Oh well. The text deals with the realm's struggles, nothing farther back—and it should at least be interesting, being about a war and all.* Reluctantly she pulled up her own chair, sat down beside the others, and soon found herself lost in a story of past and future ages.

CHAPTER ONE
MORNING

AKTINOS, REALM OF LIGHT
FIELD OF VICTORY

THE WAR HAD gone on for a long time, just as it had before and would have again. The tides of darkness had broken once more upon the land, unleashing the Skiai, who came to do battle with the forces of light. Combat was joined, and streams ran red with Aktinan blood, but the shadowy ones were always repelled—always, until that day which was destined to change everything. All of this was happening—the war still going well—when, in the midst of a battle under the bright sun and pale, rosy sky of early morning, a young warrior named Makheteon detected trouble.

The Skiai had descended, as usual, upon the aptly named Field of Victory from places unknown. Also as usual, the Ambushers had attacked the invaders from afar to drive them away from the Palace and civilians' homes and force them into a vulnerable position. This had cleared the way for Makheteon's own Elites to swoop in and take the brunt of the Skiai assault, with the squad of Finishers coming later for the final cleanup. Even now the Finishers' leader, a man named Ateles, stood at the most chaotic spot in the center of the fray, rallying his troops with fierce battle cries as his sword flashed in the sunlight to mow down one slimy, purple creature after another. If he was involved, then the battle truly was near its end.

But something else was different, Makheteon realized as he crept away from the fighting to a minuscule incline and surveyed the flat, dusty, pale-brown field. Something was wrong.

Normally, when the Finishers appeared, the Skiai would gather their forces for a last desperate charge against the Palace of Light, or begin an orderly retreat, or else feign a retreat and *then* charge on the Palace. As Aktinos' largest building and the seat of its rulership, the Palace was always their ultimate goal; and though they seemed to be unusually intelligent for monsters, they had never once changed their tactics. Now, however, the area by the Palace was largely clear. Photizousa, the leader of the Light-bringers with her dark-blonde locks and yellow mage robes, could be seen attempting to heal wounded Aktinan warriors beneath the Palace's lofty, yellow-brown outer walls while others from her squad formed a largely unnecessary perimeter. If the Skiai were still fighting but not charging on the Palace, then what were they up to?

A closer look at the battle's periphery revealed the answer. About a third of the remaining Skiai forces was withdrawing, slowly squelching past the Finishers who were distracted by their current battles, in order to surround and isolate another of the Aktinans, who was locked in combat a short distance away. Nor was this just any Aktinan warrior; he was the leader of Makheteon's Elite squad, even more important than Ateles or Photizousa. If he should fall, all would be lost.

Frantically, Makheteon cast about him for some way to help. Not for the first time, he cursed his leader's tall stature, along with the ridiculous black cape he insisted on wearing. It might have been a marker of high rank, as he claimed, but what it really did was make him stick out as the most obvious target on the whole field. And now he was in danger, and no one else appeared to have noticed. The other Elites, and the Finishers as well, were still occupied with their own clashes;

there would be no help from them.

A sword flashed by to Makheteon's left, to take out a Skia that—he realized too late—had come uncomfortably close to him. A few more seconds, and it might have attacked him.

Startled, he turned and saw the sword's owner: another Elite. The warrior looked at him quizzically as if to ask why he was just standing there away from the main battle, but he merely shook his head. Other than their considerable fighting skill, Elites were famous for one thing: loyalty, both to one another and to their commanding officer. Everyone would understand, once the full story had been told. The Elites' first priority in battle was to protect their leader....

But it was rapidly looking like there would soon be no leader to protect. The man in the cape was busy fighting two Skiai, seemingly oblivious to the fact that another one was creeping up behind him. This one was taller and stronger than the others, and it had on the top of its head a circle of what might have been spines or spiky fur, arranged so as to resemble a grotesque crown. This was one of the Skiarchoi, the leaders or officers of the shadow monsters, who were known to be impervious to all but the strongest magic attacks. Makheteon possessed some magical skill, but it would not avail him anything here. Against a Skiarchos, he would have to rely on his sword....

As he edged closer, wondering from what angle he should attack and watching with some trepidation as the line of other Skiai began to fence the Elite Leader in, something slimy slapped against his armor-protected forearm. Before he knew it, a purple tentacle had wound itself around his gloved hand and broken his grip on his sword. The weapon fell to the ground, only to be snatched up at once.

Cursing mentally, Makheteon turned once more—and found himself looking into the grinning face of another Skia. The creature knew exactly what he was thinking, what he was trying to do. It bared its gruesome fangs in an even wider grin and then, almost casually, broke the blade in half and handed it back to him.

Makheteon was furious. Letting the useless weapon fall, he wasted no time before drawing one of the simplest runes he knew and calling down the fires of the sun to attack his enemy. Weak yellow-white flames broke out on the Skia's body, flickered briefly and then spread as the blaze took hold, but he had no intention of waiting to see if the spell finished the job. Instead, he looked around briefly, then—seeing a sword lying beside a wounded Elite—picked it up and whirled around. The Skiarchos was very close to the Elite Leader; if it merely reached out, it could touch his cape....

Unfamiliar sword in hand, Makheteon sprang into action. He charged as fast as he could, right through the wall of sizzling, purplish-black flame that now stood between him and his target—he thought he felt it singe his leather armor, but did not slacken his pace. Soon he burst through the isolating line of Skiai, swatting his left gauntlet to the side to beat back one of the creatures, and proceeded to plunge his sword into the unsuspecting Skiarchos. The higher-ranking Skiai normally put up a bitter fight, but this one had been so intent on its target that it never noticed its attacker. Makheteon had no trouble finishing it off.

"...Well done," said a quiet voice behind him, and when he had turned around, he found himself face-to-face with the Elite Leader. Now that the two of them were under the lurid light cast by the Skiai's flames, it came to him again how very odd-looking his superior was.

His name was Psephos Anolethros—the second name was a title of sorts, which he had assigned himself for some unknown reason—and he was extraordinarily tall and thin, with short, nearly black hair and sunken-looking, dark eyes. Those eyes, despite the deep shadows beneath them, were sharp and clear, seemingly able to look through almost anything, and they were his most intimidating feature, even more than his height. For all that, though, his complexion was unusually pale for an Aktinan, and this paleness only made his eyes look even darker, as did his short-sleeved suit of yellow-and-white armor, which did not suit his coloring in the least. His facial features possessed the symmetry and slightly rugged character that women might consider handsome—Makheteon had indeed heard one or two of the female Elites express that sentiment—but his appearance only frightened everyone else. All things considered, he was a competent, if reserved, leader, universally acknowledged and respected, and clearly not a man to be trifled with. From the way his great battle-axe was dripping dark blood, more than a few Skiai had learned that last fact during this fight, to their severe detriment.

"Thank you, sir," Makheteon said presently, trying to resist the urge to back away. Those eyes were shining now, reflecting the light of the unnatural fire that surrounded the two warriors, and the effect was quite unnerving. "When I saw that you were in trouble, I just had to—"

"Come to my aid," Psephos interrupted, finishing the thought. His pale lips curled upward into what might have been an attempt at a smile. "Loyalty. Very admirable."

"Y-Yes, sir," Makheteon replied. "S-Shall we... return to the battle?"

"Ah, but there no longer is a battle to return to," Psephos said. "Look—already the Skiai are retreating, no doubt intimidated by how quickly you dispatched one of their leaders. Their new tactic failed to work, and now they must withdraw and regroup."

A glance over the Field of Victory proved the truth of what the Elite Leader was saying. As Makheteon watched, the dark fire winked out and the Skiai began to move away, to return to wherever it was they had come from. Soon, only Aktinans remained on the plain.

"Now that that is all finished with," Psephos continued, walking toward the area where the other Elites were gathering, "we have other matters to discuss. I am pleased with what you have done today, Makheteon. I believe that you may be worthy of a promotion."

Makheteon gaped, and stopped in his tracks so abruptly that he almost fell. "A—*promotion*, sir?"

Before either of them could continue, a scraping noise signaled that someone on the ground nearby was shifting position. "If it's not too great of an inconvenience," called out a stiff, indignant voice, "would you give me my sword back sometime before nightfall?"

Instinctively following the sound to its source, Makheteon blinked in surprise, then suddenly grinned. "Well, if it isn't my esteemed brother Khrusaoros! I didn't recognize you down there; you're usually the last one to fall in battle. How did you manage to be wounded?"

The injured man scowled; one gauntleted hand was pressed to an area of his side where the armor had been torn open, but the spread fingers could not entirely conceal the vicious-looking burn wound beneath. "Skiai—at least seven of them at once. Came squelching after me in their hideous way as if I was the only Aktinan around. Did they *not* see the masses of other warriors who were closer to the Palace?"

To battle at least seven Skiai alone and come away with only a single, non-life-threatening burn: it was quite impressive, but the requirements of a longstanding, mutual sibling competition prevented Makheteon from saying as much to his elder brother. Instead, he uttered a half-hearted "How unfortunate" and tossed the sword hilt-first onto the barren ground, careful to avoid the places where small puddles of Skiai slime glinted in the sunlight. "Here's your beloved sword. Rest assured that I *did* take good care of it, as would any Elite who is using a borrowed weapon."

Khrusaoros sat up—with an effort—and reached for the sword. "As long as you didn't bend or dull it..." he muttered, looking it over.

"That explains it," Makheteon said suddenly. "You were indisposed; that's why Lord Psephos was in danger! The task of protecting him fell to me instead of you, and now I may receive a promotion for it!"

Alarmed, Khrusaoros looked up from his inspection of the blood-smeared blade. "I must truly be delirious. A promotion? You?"

"That is correct, Khrusaoros," Psephos said behind the two brothers, and both jumped in startlement. "In fact, I have been seeking a second warrior for my personal guard, and I see no reason why I should not use both of you brothers in that capacity. Indeed, that seems the wisest choice; for there is nothing more loyal than a brother." His lips curled again into another small smile. Or a sneer.

"I would be honored to serve in your guard, sir," said Makheteon.

"Good," Psephos replied. "You will, of course, need to be tested for this promotion, but for now, you may attend me during the war council which will inevitably follow this battle. Tell the other Elites to disperse in accordance with standard protocol, and then you and your brother are to meet me just outside the Great Hall in half an hour."

Makheteon nodded and gave a very slight bow. "Thank you, Lord Psephos."

The Elite Leader's eyes flashed, but he showed no other reaction to the gestures of respect that had just been directed at him. Without another word, he turned on his heel and strode off across the Field toward the Palace, his cape billowing grandly behind him. Makheteon watched him go.

But, within moments, he heard a groan and a faint *creak*

of leather as Khrusaoros tried to stand up.

"No, don't strain yourself," he told his brother. "You may cause that burn to break open into a real wound. I'll call one of the Light-bringers to heal you."

Despite his words, however, he remained where he was, watching until the long black cape disappeared from his sight. Watching, in bewilderment.

Could it be true, what he thought he had perceived during the conversation? Had Lord Psephos Anolethros, revered and feared leader of the Elites, really looked... afraid?

THE PALACE OF LIGHT
THE GREAT HALL

Makheteon, just like any Aktinan warrior, had seen the Great Hall, the huge throne room situated at the center of the Palace of Light. He had even walked past it countless times, but had never been inside. Now, as he and the others filed into it, he marveled at how large and majestic it was. It was bright, too, but that was to be expected.

The Great Hall was a huge, rectangular room with a square table placed in the center and a raised platform at the far end. Windows high up on the yellow-brown stone walls and in the arched ceiling admitted large quantities of sunlight into the room. These were unadorned, as Aktinos was more concerned with war than with art, and a few colorful tapestries along the walls completed the Hall's decorations— except for the shining golden throne that stood at the center of the raised platform, almost blindingly bright in the otherwise austere room.

The symbol of Aktinos, commonly called "Lightning Striking the Mountain," was carved into the back of the throne, on which was seated Lord Eudianax IV, ruler of

Aktinos. His gaze swept imperiously over the entire Hall, leaving no doubt about who was in charge, but from his clothes alone, one could not have known who was the leader and who the underlings. He was clad in yellow-and-white leather armor like any warrior of the Elites, though *his* armor was bright and immaculate, betraying the fact that he had not been fighting any battles for a long time. By longstanding tradition, he was the only one of all the warriors who did not own or wield a weapon, having laid down all arms when he took the throne, though the general consensus among the lesser Aktinans was that this was not such a bad thing. A situation in which even their lord was called upon to fight surely would not bode well.

Behind and to the left of Eudianax, completely wrapped in dark-brown cloth, was his adviser, Eudrakes. Unlike most Aktinans, this individual preferred to remain in the shadows, and even now, he seemed to be seeking out the darkest corner behind his ruler's throne. He always kept himself cloaked despite Aktinos' mild to warm climate, with only a small patch of pale skin visible beneath his heavy hood, presumably so he could breathe. His advice was never wrong, however, and he even experienced visions from time to time, which led some to whisper that he possessed prophetic powers. Others could not decide whether he had been chosen for this position as adviser because of his remarkable foresight or his deep, booming voice.

Opposite Eudrakes, but concealed by a spell of invisibility, would be the leader of the Protectors, Eudianax's personal guard and a military faction kept entirely apart from the others. More Protectors would be keeping watch throughout the Hall, silent, unseen until some trouble should arise. All told, the area around Eudrakes and the invisible leader seemed to exude a certain darkness, which only made the golden throne and the lord of light shine all the brighter. Privately,

Makheteon wondered if the setup had been contrived to create such an effect.

Toward that shining golden throne the leaders of the military divisions advanced, one by one, to kneel formally and profess their allegiance to their ruler and realm. First came Ateles, who was known equally for his shock of short, unkempt blond hair and his fierce, savage fighting spirit; his mottled yellow-and-white Finisher's armor, similar to that of the Elites, was perpetually stained with Skiai blood. Next was the robed Photizousa, whose Light-bringers were essential to the Aktinan cause as scouts and battlefield healers, and sometimes as backups to other fighters. The third leader, a young woman with brown hair, was unfamiliar to Makheteon, but her tan-colored armor, designed to blend in with the largely barren Aktinan landscape, proclaimed her leader of the Ambushers. Judging by her age, she must be new to this position.

Last, of course, was Psephos himself, and Makheteon and Khrusaoros advanced on their commander's heels as he approached Eudianax's throne in his turn. Makheteon went down on one knee when the other two did, hand over heart, and murmured "My lord" when the other two did, and then they were standing up again to go to the large square table, at which the other three division leaders were already seated.

In the moment before Makheteon turned away, he thought he saw Eudianax frown a little, and the lord of light's eyes flashed. No doubt he had noticed that the Elite Leader had just acquired a second warrior for his personal guard. Surely, however, the frown was not one of anger; Eudianax was well-respected and widely considered a good and just ruler, despite being militaristic even by Aktinos' standards. Perhaps he was amused. Makheteon and Khrusaoros looked so much alike that few outside the Elites could tell them apart—if these were even aware that they were not the same person. Still, as Makheteon joined his brother in assuming a protective position behind Psephos' chair, he could not help but notice that none of the other division leaders was accompanied by a guard.

No sooner were they all settled than Ateles turned an almost sneering gaze on the Elite Leader. "Another bodyguard, I see.... Surely we are safe enough under the watchful eye of the Protectors, who will defend any Aktinan if necessary? Are you afraid... *Pseph?*"

Psephos glared darkly across the table. People were forever shortening his name, perhaps to poke fun at the perceived pompousness of the cape and the self-assigned title, and he resented it immensely. Most, after using a nickname to his face once, never did it again—but not Ateles. The two leaders were notorious for their dislike of each other, and the constant need for them to work together had not improved the situation in the slightest. There were whispers that Ateles had been promised the promotion to Elite Leader, but Psephos had been granted it instead; other rumors told of a competition over a girlfriend, in which Ateles had come out victorious.

It seemed that Psephos considered the promotion more important than the girlfriend, at least on this day, for his dark eyes held a bit of smug amusement as he responded to his rival's taunts. "These are dangerous times, Finisher," he said coolly. "I am twenty-nine years old, and we have been at war for every one of those years, possibly longer. On the day the Skiai unravel our battle plans, on the day they come after you personally because they know you are one of our leaders, you will weep because you do not have anyone guarding your back."

"By Water, Wind, and Fire!" Ateles spat, uttering Aktinos' second-strongest oath. "What kind of an Elite Leader are you? First, you lead a squad of mage-swordsmen—and yet you refuse to wield a sword, instead relying on that huge, *unwieldy* axe that anyone with half a brain can swing to destructive effect; and you must not have magical powers, for I have never once seen you use them. Then you insist on wearing that—that *absurd* cape, as if you are not already the most conspicuous target on the whole field, and now this—! And all you can say is, '*These are dangerous times*'? You are a coward, and a joke of a leader, and you should learn to face the dangers like the rest of us or—"

"May the three avenging goddesses take you," Psephos interrupted, his tone quiet but nearly a growl. The other military leaders, who had been attempting to calm the two combatants, fell into a stunned silence; for this was the strongest oath that an Aktinan could utter. Even Ateles looked taken aback. Suddenly, the Hall was eerily quiet.

"Silence!" thundered Eudianax. "The realm of light cannot afford such petty quarreling. Already we are under siege, with our enemies gaining on us every moment. Our light will surely be extinguished if we do nothing but sit here and bicker. You are to be civil with one another, on pain of demotion."

"And the Ouranothen are not to be invoked in vain," added Eudrakes. At this, Makheteon looked upward almost hopefully, but the divine visages of the three Avengers—the most terrifying figures in all of Aktinan mythology—did not appear. Eudrakes must merely have been giving a warning, then—and may the Avengers take anyone who did not heed it....

Despite the warnings, Psephos did not appear ready to back down. "I will have my bodyguards," he stated flatly.

"You will, of course, have the new one tested in the Hall of Warriors?" asked—not Eudianax, but Eudrakes. This was odd, and everyone turned to look at the cloaked adviser. "And you will give him a title such as befits his new rank? This promotion would leave him only one step below that of Division Leader, and his title must reflect that fact."

"Of course, my lord Eudrakes," Psephos replied. "All those

who are promoted must be tested, to make sure that they have the spirit of a warrior. This will be done as soon as possible after this council." After he had spoken, he finally appeared to subside, and he sat back in his chair—sullen, but at least he was silent.

Eudrakes nodded in the direction of Eudianax, who then turned back toward his underlings. "Very well. Psephos may keep the one bodyguard, and he may promote the other into the same position, provided that he passes his test. And the rest of you may take the same precaution if you feel such a need, for you have been no less dutiful and loyal than he in your service to Aktinos." He paused for a moment in case objections were forthcoming, though this was unlikely; he was not considered a good and just ruler for nothing. Seeing that everyone appeared satisfied, he continued: "Now, let us do what we convened here to do. I wish to hear reports relating to the battle just completed and its consequences for our war effort. First, casualty and damage reports."

Photizousa cleared her throat before speaking, and after the agitated tone of the preceding argument, her voice sounded even calmer than usual. "Casualties were quite low, my lord," she said—addressing Eudianax, but she also looked around at her fellow division leaders, her gaze reproachful, reminding them of the matter at hand. "The Light-bringers count ten killed during the battle, from all military divisions combined. Approximately two dozen warriors were wounded, some severely. While several of our strongest fighters"—she nodded across the table in Khrusaoros' direction—"have already made a full recovery, others have yet to do so. The Light-bringers are tending to the latter group as best they can given the limits of the magic, and a large proportion of them, including more than half of those with serious injuries, are expected to survive. There are no civilian casualties to report, and no damage was inflicted on any buildings, as the

Ambushers successfully led the Skiai away from all architecture. The battle was fought on the open field, and civilians were able to remain in their homes without disruption."

Eudianax appeared pleased. "Very good; those numbers are low indeed for a battle of this scale. The Ambushers and their battle tacticians deserve praise. Now, what of the Skiai? What were their losses?"

"That," said Photizousa, "is slightly more difficult to assess, my lord, since Skiai dead disintegrate without leaving a trace. However, we have interviewed several individual warriors, and their accounts suggest that perhaps as many as three hundred Skiai were slain."

"Including at least one Skiarchos," Psephos put in. "I myself saw it fall."

"A Skiarchos?" Eudianax repeated. "Excellent."

Psephos nodded. "Yes, my lord. They usually protect their officers well, but something was different this time. Without leadership, the creatures panicked, and the battle ended almost immediately with their retreat."

He appeared about to continue, but Eudianax cut him off. "Very, very good. I am pleased, division leaders. The battle turned out well, it seems—the best of any in recent memory. Now, how did it begin? Where did the monsters appear?"

At this, all eyes turned toward the young woman with the brown hair and the tan-colored armor; a quick whisper from Khrusaoros told Makheteon that her name was Enedra. Not being quite tall enough to reach across the table while seated, she stood up and tossed a small, flat purple disc onto a map of Aktinos that lay open there. There were other purple discs scattered over the map, marking places where the Skiai had descended upon the land.

"We spotted them here, my lord," she began, indicating the spot where she had placed the most recent disc. A second whisper from Khrusaoros told Makheteon that this was her first war council because she had been promoted very recently, but her voice did not shake as she addressed the others. "At the northern edge of the Field of Victory, close to the foot of the Mountains of Air." Those were mountains that rose even above the Aktinan plain, which was itself located in the mountains.

Not for the first time, Makheteon wondered why people had taken it into their heads to call the range by that name. Sure, the mountains rose high into the air, but so did the already lofty position of this realm, right?

Meanwhile, Enedra was still talking. "As you can see, there is no obvious pattern to where the Skiai appear. I have spent a great deal of time analyzing this information, as have my best tacticians, but none of us can make sense of it. Indeed, it seems that the places where they appear are chosen at random. All attempts to trace the locations back to a common source or circumstance have been unsuccessful."

The other division leaders remained silent for a moment as they considered this information. As Eudianax and the others had said, the war was going well, and the Aktinans had found solutions to most of their problems, but even after all these years, one issue plagued them still: the question of where the Skiai came from and where their headquarters was, if they had one. Much effort had been expended on attempts to answer this question, by warriors and tacticians alike, but all in vain: no one had the slightest notion where the enemy came from, or even what had started the war.

"It's extremely frustrating," Enedra went on, frowning at the map and the purple discs. She was rambling now, but seemed not to care; perhaps she liked to talk, or was unaware of the usual war council procedures. "There is never more than an instant's warning. They simply... appear, whenever and wherever it suits them. A sort of purplish darkness spreads, like a stain on the very air; it grows larger and larger, foglike, until finally it splits open and an army of Skiai descends to earth. We must be prepared for this, but we can neither predict it nor prevent it."

At this, particularly the word "*predict*," all eyes turned toward Eudrakes, who seemed to shrink farther back into his dark corner. "My eyes cannot see everything," he intoned—not for the first time in one of these councils.

"Have they tried?" snapped Psephos—rather belligerently, even for him. All eyes turned toward him next, but the other leaders did not have much time to indulge in their surprise.

"They have," stated Eudrakes. "The origins of the Skiai are lost in the mists, beyond the visible. That is past; the war is now, and the war is everything."

"And, surely, finding their stronghold is a part of the war?" Psephos persisted.

Before Eudrakes could make a retort, Eudianax raised a commanding hand. "Enough, Psephos. We will inquire about this calmly and peaceably, and if you do not cooperate, I shall have to remove you from our company. Photizousa, do you have a report for us on this subject?"

"I do, my lord," said Photizousa, "but, unfortunately, there is not much *to* report. As according to your orders, I have been sending out reconnaissance squads as often as possible, but my Light-bringers have found nothing—no camps, no outposts, no signs of any enemy presence. As far as we can tell, the realm of Aktinos belongs to Aktinos alone. We have searched everywhere, both outside and within doors, from the Mountains of Air to the Valley of the Gods and everywhere in between...."

Her voice trailed off, as if she had been about to continue talking but had suddenly changed her mind; and Psephos, it appeared, was the only one who picked up on it. Straightening in his chair, he asked sharply: "Have you searched *everywhere,*

Photizousa? Every location in this land?"

The normally serene Photizousa's eyes widened, and a few moments passed before she could speak. "Well... there is one place that we have not searched, that no one can be persuaded to search. The Lightning-Struck Mountain."

Psephos looked like he was about to say something, but Photizousa forestalled him. "No one can go near it. The path up the mountain is steep and treacherous, and a sort of power emanates from the cloud-obscured peak. Benevolent or malevolent, we cannot tell, but all of my Light-bringers have felt it, and they fled in terror and refused to go any closer. We strongly believe that the power is warning us away from attempting to scale the mountain. Whatever is up there, we suspect it is... divine."

"The Ouranothen themselves," murmured Ateles, his blond head bowed in a way that could not have clashed more sharply with his tough exterior.

Makheteon and Khrusaoros exchanged glances. When they had been growing up, they had heard stories of the Lightning-Struck Mountain, the tallest mountain in the world. There was a temple at the peak, the stories said, marking the place where the Ouranothen had descended from heaven and even now dwelled, a seat divine. Had other Aktinans been told the same tales, or were there different versions?

"Because of this power, this... divine aura," Photizousa went on, "no one has dared even approach the Lightning-Struck Mountain. It is the only place that we have not examined thoroughly."

"If our people cannot scale the mountain, then it is unlikely that the Skiai could have made it their base," Ateles pointed out.

"That works only if the power that resides there is friendly to Aktinos," said Psephos. The heat had gone out of his voice, perhaps because he feared being expelled from the Great Hall, but it remained in his eyes. The heat never left those eyes, ever. "If, as she said, it might be a malevolent aura, then it may very well be the Skiai themselves, or the source of their strength."

"Probably not, if the Light-bringers could sense it," Photizousa objected. "They said that it felt similar to our own power, and yet different at the same time."

"But if it were benevolent," Psephos countered, "then they should have no trouble approaching it."

"What are you suggesting, Psephos?" Eudianax cut in from his throne at the end of the room.

"I am suggesting that someone scale that mountain and examine it for a Skiai presence," Psephos said calmly. "It is the only place that has not been searched; surely it is the only place the enemy could be?"

"Preposterous!" Ateles burst out. "Do you know the power of the Ouranothen? They would *never* tolerate—"

"Then," Psephos interrupted, "once the Skiai stronghold has been located, a force can be sent to obliterate it, and there can be an end to this war."

For some reason, Eudrakes' hooded head bobbed ever so slightly at that statement: an expression of tacit approval that went unnoticed by the others in the Hall.

"We don't need to find any strongholds to obliterate the Skiai," Ateles tried again. Sour at having been interrupted, he was doing a poor job of hiding it. "Did you hear how many of them were slaughtered today? We are bleeding their forces slowly, diminishing them by attrition—"

"Attrition can affect either side of the conflict, and then there may be no Aktinans left to enjoy any victory," said Psephos. "Whether you realize it or not, Finisher, these are dire times. There is reason to believe that our old strategy may not be working anymore. During the battle today, the enemy changed its tactics, and droves of Skiai came after me and my guard personally—no charging on the Palace this time. If this war drags on much longer, perhaps they will also recognize the lot of *you*, come after you as leaders. It is imperative to strike at the enemy while you still have the upper hand."

Silence reigned in the Hall for a long moment following this pronouncement. Finally, Eudianax spoke. "We will consider your suggestion. In the meantime, Photizousa is to continue her routine reconnaissance, and the rest of you are to resume the usual pre-battle protocols—"

This, apparently, was not enough to satisfy Psephos, for he immediately rose to his feet, looking indignant. His dark eyes flashed. "I am fatigued," he said quietly. "I beg leave to depart."

Without waiting for an answer, he turned his back on his fellow leaders. A quick hand motion signaled to Makheteon and Khrusaoros that they should follow him, and then he turned on his heel, seized his battle-axe from where it stood propped beside his chair, and very nearly stalked out of the Great Hall.

As he followed his leader, Makheteon could not help thinking that something was going on with him. Something was odd, something was bothering him; and, somehow, Makheteon did not think that the recent run-in with the Skiai was all of it.

CHAPTER TWO
NOON

AKTINOS, REALM OF LIGHT
MOUNTAINS OF AIR

Slowly and carefully, Photizousa picked her way along a steep, pale-brown, rock-strewn mountainside. Her long mage robes did not make the going easy. Perhaps this undertaking had not been her best idea; but it had to be done. As long as she did not fall and break her neck on the way to her destination, she would be fine.

After this thought process had repeated itself a few times, movement a short distance up the slope caught her eye. A moment later, a figure stepped out from behind a large boulder, waving an arm in greeting.

Photizousa had to squint before she could identify the tan-clad figure as that of Enedra, the young leader of the Ambushers. Were it not for the movement, Photizousa would probably not have been able to tell that anyone was there; the Ambushers' camouflage was that effective. But there she was, and she obviously wanted to catch Photizousa's attention. Going up there would mean a delay and a detour, but it could not hurt to talk to her... to find out what she thought about recent events.

Her decision made, the robed Light-bringer changed direction and began to scale the barren slope. The climb was difficult but not overly long, and within a few minutes, she had reached Enedra's hiding place. "...Greetings, Enedra," she panted, sitting down on the boulder and turning to face her fellow division leader.

"Oh, it's you," said Enedra in feigned surprise. "You were bold, coming so close to our place of ambush. I nearly mistook you for a Skia and ordered my warriors to fire on you." She pointed to a spot behind the boulder where several long spears were propped and at the ready.

"Right, I can imagine," Photizousa said dryly. "Since I obviously have a Skia's fur and fangs, not to mention its vicious claws."

"Exactly!" Enedra agreed cheerfully. "In fact, although you claim to be human and have done good things for our realm as leader of the Light-bringers, I wouldn't be surprised if you were actually an enemy agent among us." She raised an eyebrow in mock suspicion.

Photizousa could not help smiling as she shook her head. This young woman had a decidedly odd sense of humor, but this was a forgivable fault if her fighting skill was anywhere near what rumor and reputation said. "I'm amazed that you can maintain such levity in a serious war situation...."

Enedra shrugged, and a frown obliterated her brief mirth as she sat on the other end of the boulder. "We need *something* to keep us sane, and there's nothing wrong with a little harmless humor. How goes the reconnaissance?"

"I don't yet know," Photizousa answered, her eyes involuntarily straying toward her destination, which still loomed distant on the horizon. "I'm on my way to the Lightning-Struck Mountain—not to scale it," she added hastily, seeing that Enedra looked startled. "My intention is to explore a little around it, investigate that power that my scouts keep mentioning. If their accounts are accurate, then I will know that we have no hope of making it up there."

The young Ambusher paused for a few moments, her head

tilted slightly to the side as she considered the information. "Did Eudianax put you up to this?" she asked finally.

"No; it was my own decision, made on my own initiative. I believe that we must investigate all options in this ongoing war effort. If the Skiai truly have been up on that mountain all this time, it would certainly be to our benefit to know it, don't you think?"

"It's an interesting idea, for sure," said Enedra. "I hope it sheds light on the problems we're facing. I trust you'll let the rest of us know what you discover?"

Photizousa nodded. "I plan to announce my findings at the next war council."

That mountain looked a little too close on the horizon now. Though she was not usually prone to weakness or cowardice, she averted her eyes from it and hastily changed the subject. "How goes the lying in ambush?"

"Boringly, if I may use such a word," sighed Enedra. "We sit around all day, our forces scattered, simply waiting for the enemy to come to us. Sometimes, Skiai appear and we have a battle, but most of the time, we have a whole lot of nothing. I find it extremely frustrating that we don't even know where or when they will appear—as I said in the last council. The war caters to their whim, and we are at their mercy, always on the defensive."

"Then you agree with Psephos? You think we should go on the offensive and seek out the Skiai?"

Enedra frowned moodily at some unknown object in the distance. "I don't know what I think—except that this war is endless, going nowhere, and tedious to no end. I was promoted to this position only last week, and already I hate it. Being the leader means more time on duty, you see, and my most interesting pastime when I'm sitting here is to think about the spectacular demise that my predecessor supposedly met. The war was interesting back then, even for the Ambushers."

"But the war doesn't cater to *your* whim," Photizousa pointed out. "It has no obligation to make itself interesting and exciting just for you."

Enedra was shaking her head impatiently. "Yes, I know this. I suppose my real problem is with the war in general. Sometimes I wonder… what the purpose of it all is."

Photizousa blinked. "…Purpose?"

"Yes, *purpose*. Why are we fighting this war? Who are the Skiai, and why are they here? And yet, to my knowledge, not one proposed battle plan has ever included asking the Skiai what they want."

"I should think that is obvious," said Photizousa. "They want to destroy us, and we must kill or be killed. This is a conflict of light versus dark, day versus night: the most… elemental… conflict there is."

"But the concept of day would not exist without night. Dark doesn't necessarily mean evil. For all we know, *we* could be the evil ones."

Photizousa frowned at her fellow division leader. "I don't know about you, but the Skiai don't strike *me* as particularly friendly and good."

"Because that isn't what we *want* to see them as," said Enedra. "No one knows what their true nature is. Perhaps it is such that they reflect our perception of them, and we want to see them as malicious and monstrous in order to justify going to war against them."

Again Photizousa frowned, more heavily this time. This conversation was taking a turn that bordered on treasonous.

"So much, then, for the war itself," Enedra continued. "What about the pre-war era? We know very little, and what scholars we have exacerbate the problem by confining their attention to warrior lineages and past rulers and battles— which means that this realm of ours has no *real* history to speak of, no reason for existence other than to perpetuate itself. If you look far enough back in time, you'll find a gap, a void in our knowledge. And yet, we're always being told that Aktinos is eternal, that the Ouranothen placed us here at the beginning of time to aid in the fulfillment of some divine plan—which, somehow, *always* involves militarism and war! As far as actual *evidence* for this claim goes, all we have is a fragmentary story about two great warriors fighting on a mountain, which somehow influenced the choice of location—"

"Ah, yes," sighed Photizousa, and she closed her eyes in reverence while she called up what she remembered of the tale. "*...And thus they fought, dark against dark amid a sea of white, and out of their shared darkness there came a light, and the light's attribute was wrath....*"

"See?!" Enedra said forcefully. Photizousa, opening her eyes again, saw the younger woman with both hands over her head, obviously in a state of agitation. "To me, the line about wrath was put in to justify our current way of life, but as for the rest of it... it makes no sense." She moved one of her raised hands in a circle to indicate the near-total ring of taller mountains that surrounded the plain, their dull, pale brown standing out strongly against the misty, pinkish sky above. "And this story that's been passed down over so many generations didn't even have the decency to tell us who the 'they' were?"

"I always thought... they must have been two of the Ouranothen," Photizousa said quietly. "Fighting a cathartic fight that left them both better off than they were before, though still with a bit of righteous anger in them."

"Really? Two *dark* entities?"

"Well, the Avengers must have dark hearts, in a way..."

Enedra sighed. "Think what you want, Photizousa, but you'll never dispel *my* feeling that this society of ours is something unreal in an otherwise real world—it's contrived, invented, like someone sat down and made it up and decided it was how we should live our lives. There are a lot of things that give me that feeling, and the gods—the 'Ouranothen,' as they're so often called—are some of the worst offenders in that respect. Think of all that we know about them; can you disagree with me on this?"

This was too much, Photizousa thought. "It seems what *you* know isn't enough," she snapped, "so let me educate you. The three Avengers are native to this world, Enedra; they are here, and they know all. They punish all types of wrongdoing, and their wrath may fall even on those who invoke them for *good* reasons; insult any one of them, and you will feel the force of her retribution. Your only recourse in such a case would be to appeal to the Wanderer, but she may not be native and travels regularly among many worlds, coming to the aid of those who need her most. If she isn't around when you invoke her, then, well..."

"So, four," said Enedra, who had been counting on her fingers as Photizousa named the Ouranothen in turn. "There are innumerable functions that deities could serve, countless roles they could play. Why, then, do we have only four deities, with only *two* different areas of responsibility?"

"There is something mystical about the number four," Photizousa mused. "Our world, Andikha, is said to have four major regions in all. Our military has four main combat branches. And now there are four Ouranothen. It is very neat, very symmetrical."

"Yes, neat and symmetrical, but that's my point; it seems artificial. And then, as you implied, they are four *goddesses*, with emphasis on the *ess*. Where in our otherwise-so-symmetrical system are the male gods—the fathers of the next generation of Ouranothen?"

This took Photizousa aback. "Enedra!!" she gasped, shocked at the irreverence.

Enedra shrugged. "Be scandalized all you want, but the

question remains, and I find it quite implausible."

"I'm sure there are male gods," Photizousa said stubbornly. "Maybe they are busy elsewhere."

"Or they're excluded from the pantheon so as not to *ruin* the beautiful symmetry, the symbolism, of four," Enedra countered, almost triumphantly.

"Here's some asymmetry for you," Photizousa snapped, now seriously annoyed at her colleague's lack of respect. "For as long as anyone here can remember, we've sworn '*By Water, Wind, and Fire*'—by three things, not four."

"Simple," Enedra said. "If the number four is so '*mystical*,' then swearing by it would be impious and blasphemous, would it not?"

Photizousa felt her eyes narrowing. "Well then, since you have all the answers that the rest of us don't, we might as well lump you in with Psephos in the 'dissatisfied and disillusioned' category. If you like, when I return to the Palace, I can inform Lord Eudianax of your resignation from your current post."

"No need for that," said Enedra, looking startled though not quite repentant. "It's just... interesting to think sometimes."

Perhaps you think too *much, then,* Photizousa thought to herself as she rose to her feet. That mountain was not going anywhere; there was no sense in putting off her task any longer.

"I'm off to find some answers of my own," she told Enedra brusquely. "If the legends are true and I encounter the Ouranothen on that mountain, would you like me to give them a message from you?"

Enedra smiled a little. "If you meet the Wanderer, ask her why she hasn't helped us at all in this war. After all, surely our need is as great as need ever gets?" With that, she dived behind the boulder once more, to all appearances the perfectly attentive Ambusher waiting for her prey.

Shaking her head, Photizousa set off once more toward her

destination. She could not figure out that young woman. To cast doubt on the gods themselves! But Enedra was good at what she did, and she was as loyal a servant of Aktinos as the best of the other warriors—hence the recent promotion to Division Leader. Still, given her propensity to think deeply, perhaps she would have been better suited to a position as a scholar... maybe as the first scholar of her kind if Aktinos really did have *"no real history to speak of"* beyond the vague story of the battle between the two dark entities....

These thoughts were all-engrossing, and in the end, Photizousa found herself feeling almost grateful that she had talked to Enedra—for the conversation, despite its strange and unsettling nature, had given her something to occupy her mind with during the laborious walk through the mountains.

The Lightning-Struck Mountain was located off the main range, situated so it could not be reached directly from the plain of Aktinos; one had to climb and cross other, smaller mountains on the way there. The path was so difficult that she wondered if the Ouranothen had planned it that way, to make their dwelling inaccessible to all but the boldest of mortals. Or the most foolish.

At last, she reached the bottom of another slope and found herself in a small valley. Directly in front of her, the Lightning-Struck Mountain reached up toward the firmament.

It was rocky and immensely tall, would come across as impenetrable even under the best conditions; and as it was, a thick cloud, like lingering smoke from a lightning strike, surrounded and obscured the peak. She craned her neck upward in a futile attempt to see through that cloud—nothing could be discerned except for some kind of soft yellowish glow on the other side—and then she felt it.

A power was indeed emanating from the mountaintop. It might have been noticeable elsewhere in the realm if someone were specifically looking for it, but here, it would threaten to overwhelm any magic-sensitive person.

Closing her eyes momentarily, Photizousa concentrated on that power, tried to determine what it was. If it was a type of divine aura, then it was stronger than any such aura she had ever felt in the sacred places of Aktinos. And yet, in a sense, it was also nothing more than raw power. There was no sense of welcome, or wrath, or anything in between: it was emotionless, and she wondered if its source was even sentient. Even if it lacked consciousness or awareness, however, it was dangerous. And as for benevolence or malevolence, either was possible, since power could be used for good *or* for ill....

This was startling. The power felt like light energy, like the magic of light that Aktinan mages wielded; it appeared that Psephos was wrong there, in suggesting that it could be related to the Skiai. How, then, could it be potentially malevolent? This might have been what her Light-bringers had meant when they had said that the power was both similar to and different from their own.

Frowning once again, she opened her eyes, squinted, stared at the peak in a futile attempt to will the obscuring cloud to dissipate. Somehow, she found herself taking one step up the huge slope, then another—

Without warning, a bright flash burst out of the distant cloud. She froze, one foot in midair, her eyes still fixed on the peak but her mind not quite able to process. The light was descending toward her with frightening speed, while her sense of the magical aura became so strong that it was almost painful. Every instinct told her to prepare a defensive spell, but her hand would not move to draw the runes.

Then there was a brilliant flare hardly two feet away, and before her stood a figure: ethereal and otherworldly, its color a dazzling yellow-white with a slight tint of purer yellow around the edges. It was too bright to look at directly, it all but exuded the power of the mountain, and it was definitely sentient.

At once the yellow-robed mage fell to her hands and knees, to abase herself, show humility. "...Ouranothen," she murmured. Her voice was steady, but she was trembling all over.

The figure, for its part, stood in silence, and though Photizousa was not looking at it—for she was looking at the ground—she was sure that it was examining her, scanning her. Its glaring yellow-white light pulsed, her head swam in confusion and disorientation... but then she felt a slight breeze, heard a soft *flap, flap* like the motion of wings. She clung to that sound, deafening though it was in the deep quiet. It was her only indication that what was happening was real.

At last, the being spoke—not verbally, but through a voice in Photizousa's mind, soft yet authoritative. *You are one of the warriors, young one?*

"Y-Yes, Great One," she stammered.

Her mind raced. Which of the Ouranothen was this: the Wanderer, or one of the Avengers? She thought there might be a way to tell; but something was odd. The mental voice was strangely dull—inhuman and genderless—although the legends always spoke of *"the four great goddesses"* with personalities bright and vivid....

But she could not think about that now, for the being was speaking again. *Yes, so you are. And your power is our power.* There seemed to be an approving tone in this; her heart lifted a little.

"Yes, Great One," she repeated.

You have come seeking answers.

"Y-Yes, I have."

Even as she spoke, a thought struck her more swiftly than lightning itself, and her heart sank again. If this being was one of the Avengers, it would probably not take kindly to being questioned by a mere mortal.

But, she reasoned after a moment, even one who was

about to be killed for impertinence could continue seeking the truth. "Please f-forgive me, G-Great One, but I am wondering—"

It spoke right on top of her. *You must not forget your duty. Your task is to guard, to protect. You warriors are the first line of defense. You* must *protect it.*

"Duty?... Defense?..." she asked uncomprehendingly. She raised her head to look more closely at the divine entity that stood before her—but then there was a great *whoosh*ing sound and more flapping of wings, and a powerful wind arose as the being soared away to vanish amid the mountain's cloud cover.

Numbly, Photizousa rose to her feet. Being so near an offshoot of that power had been most unnerving, and its retreat back to the peak left her feeling like an immense weight, the weight of the Lightning-Struck Mountain itself, had been lifted from her. But even so, she was still shaking as she turned around to begin the long trek back to Aktinos. The mental voice's last words to her reverberated in her head.

You must protect it.

"Protect what?" she murmured—only partly to herself. No reply, however, came from the mountain or the air. Perhaps she was supposed to know already; perhaps the other warriors were also supposed to know. Aktinos was indeed operating under a divine injunction; Enedra had been dead wrong on that account. But what if the Aktinans had lost sight of this divine commission?

Well, she would remind them of it. She now knew the truth... but at the same time, she did not know it. She knew that Aktinos was supposed to be on the defensive, protecting something; but she could not, for the life of her, imagine what.

THE PALACE OF LIGHT
HALL OF WARRIORS

Makheteon had always considered the Hall of Warriors to be a deeply mysterious place. Located in the Palace of Light's deepest basement, it was a huge stone room, many times longer than it was wide, so that it truly did resemble a hall. Narrow alcoves lined the walls to the left and right, along with torches in stone holders, one on either side of each alcove. The magical yellow-white flames were tall, but not quite enough to dispel the shadows that hovered on the room's fringes and inside the alcoves; the bright sunlight that was omnipresent elsewhere in the Palace could not reach this underground chamber.

Slowly and solemnly, he began his journey down the Hall. As was the case every time he came down here, strict ceremonial procedure could not prevent him from looking to the left and right as he walked, studying the larger-than-life statues that occupied the shallow alcoves. All were statues of warriors—the name of this place told him that much—but he did not recognize all the types, particularly those near the beginning of the sequence. He rather regretted this fact. The statues' stern, stony gazes seemed to follow him as he walked, to reproach him.

At last, the double line of warrior statues tapered off. The familiar Elite, Ambusher, Finisher, and Light-bringer were the final sentinels keeping watch over the next area, where the room widened out a bit. Psephos was there in this large rectangular space, flanked by Khrusaoros; the other members of the Elite squad were also present but standing at a greater distance, their expressions ranging from neutral to curious to envious. No doubt they had placed bets on what the result would be. Eudrakes would also be there, as an impartial observer and witness to what was about to take place, but he could not be seen. This came as no surprise; Eudianax's prophetic adviser had a talent for being invisible when he wanted to.

Nevertheless, these people did not draw Makheteon's eyes or thoughts for long. Instead, he turned his gaze downward until it landed on the huge runic symbol that had been carved into the floor directly in front of him. Located in the center of the open area with three mostly plain walls around it, the rune dominated this end of the Hall, and the assembled Elites had taken their positions around it but some fifteen feet away, to show it a sort of deference. It was dark now, colorless—illuminated only by the feeble glow of the torches on the walls—but this fooled no one. The carving was highly magical, and probably dangerous if used incorrectly.

"It begins," Psephos stated. He was standing very formally with his battle-axe held close to his chest and its long shaft slanted diagonally; the huge double blade was over one shoulder and perilously close to his head, but he did not seem to notice or care. Had he been standing in one of the many alcoves that stretched before him, he might even have been mistaken for one of the warrior statues.

"It begins," Makheteon echoed. Though his nervousness was increasing by the second, he made sure to speak loudly and clearly, as if by doing so he could ensure a positive outcome. "Lord Psephos Anolethros, Elite Leader, chosen warrior, I have come seeking higher rank and further advancement, if it pleaseth thee to grant me the opportunity."

"Very well," Psephos intoned. "Warrior Makheteon, you shall now be tested to determine whether you truly have the warrior's spirit, the spirit that seeks blood, the spirit that covets glory, the spirit that desires fame among the stars. Do you consent to this test and agree to abide by its ruling?"

"Yes, chosen warrior," said Makheteon, lowering his gaze as was expected of him at this stage. This test was held every time someone was to be given a promotion, to reaffirm that person's status as a true warrior. However, on every occasion when Makheteon had taken the test himself or watched someone else take it, the same thought occurred to him: Psephos was extremely formal in conducting the ritual, all the way down to the precisely-scripted dialogue, which in his mind was grounds for *de*motion if performed incorrectly by the candidate. The Elite Leader might be somewhat unorthodox in other aspects of his command, but when it came to this test, he clung firmly to tradition....

"Very good," he was saying now. "Remove your weapon."

Obediently, Makheteon reached over his shoulder and drew his sword from the sheath that was strapped to his back. There was no pang of regret as he stretched out and placed the sword near the far side of the carved rune; the blade portion was new, hurriedly forged for him to replace the one that had been broken in the most recent battle, and there had not yet been time or opportunity for him to try his reborn weapon out, much less to become attached to it. "Thus do I place my sword down," he said, "and only by the will of the Ouranothen shall I take it up again."

Psephos nodded, his expression blank and unreadable. "Let the test commence."

Stepping forward, Makheteon went down on his knees in the middle of the runic carving. As he did so, he bowed his head so that he was looking in the direction of his sword, which lay on the floor just in front of him. It did not take long for the rune's spell to initiate.

No one knew exactly what "told" the rune that someone had come to be tested. No human mage was directing the spellcasting, and the spell was not even a regular periodic occurrence; the rune was dark and lifeless most of the time— except for occasions when this test was held, which were unpredictable at best. And yet, despite that unpredictability, the rune's magic was completely reliable, which was little short of miraculous when one considered that the magic often failed to come to human mages who wanted it. It could be that the rune could detect when someone was kneeling on top of it. Or, perhaps—as was Makheteon's current theory—it sensed the power that resembled its own, the power of the light-based magic that, however weakly, was in him and all other members of the Aktinan warrior caste.

Whatever the source, however, whatever the mechanism, the rune filled up with energy almost at once. The lines and curves that made up the carving began to glow yellow-white, first softly and then brightly, brilliantly. That glow pulsed, brightening and vanishing and brightening again, as still more light rose up from the rune to swirl around the kneeling warrior like a wind and envelop him, obscure him from view. Yellow-white as the rune itself, opaque as fog, the light wrapped around him like an embrace, and he felt as though he were being watched by unseen eyes that were staring at him from within the misty light. If the light did indeed have eyes or eyelike appendages, he would not have been surprised; however, he could not raise his head to investigate this, for he would be committing a grave impropriety—and running the risk of blinding himself. Content to kneel there, his eyes fixed on his sword, he nevertheless wondered if his fellow Elites were watching as closely as *he* wanted to be watching...

The change occurred within the span of a heartbeat. One moment, the rune's light swirled around him while serving as a sort of wall between him and those watching the test; then, in the briefest of instants, that light flickered once. When it reappeared, it had changed color, so that it was no longer yellow-white but—

Red. Blood-red.

Dimly, Makheteon registered a smattering of applause from the fringes of the room, but he paid it no heed. This red glow was very mysterious, he thought. Mysterious, ethereal...

even foreign, as if it was not of this world, did not belong in this world. The runic carving was also glowing red now, he noticed; was it the source of the misty red light?

His reverie was broken by movement in the dense red fog that surrounded him. Some of the light swirled down into the sword that still lay on the floor, imbuing the weapon's entire length with a brief red tinge as it did so. Moments later, the sword rose into the air of its own accord and turned in a slow quarter-circle until it stopped and hovered in front of him: seemingly presenting itself to him, hilt-first.

Despite himself, he gave a small start. No matter how many times he had been through this ritual, this part never ceased to amaze him. It was not so much the lifting of the sword into the air—light was weightless, and so even the most ordinary magic could levitate objects—as the miraculous color change that the sword's hilt experienced. The T-shaped structure now gleamed a brilliant but deep red.

Its previous color had been yellow.

A sense of wonder stealing over him, he reached out and took hold of the hilt, plucked the sword out of the air. As soon as he did this, the red glow winked out, leaving the runic carving dark and cold once more. He was now visible to all, and all could see that he held the sword.

Lifting his head at last, he caught sight of Psephos, who did not seem to have moved a muscle during the entire test. Yes, he was very statuelike. Makheteon might almost have wondered if he had fallen asleep standing up and holding his axe in that pose—but then he spoke, his voice jarringly loud in the otherwise silent Hall.

"Makheteon, chosen warrior, you have passed the test set for you by the Ouranothen. To commemorate this day and immortalize your new rank, I hereby title you Khalkeonos: He of the Bronze-Forge. Together with your brother, Khrusaoros the Golden-Sworded, you shall be my personal bodyguard and the most elite of the Elite warriors. May your weapons and his shine brightly, lighting the darkness and showing all Aktinans the way to victory."

Standing up, the newly promoted Khalkeonos—the rank and title were bound together, such that everyone would now have to use the latter or risk coming across as impolite—sheathed his sword, retreated to his prior position in front of the giant rune, and then bowed deeply to his Elite Leader. "I thank thee for thy regard, Lord Psephos, chosen warrior," he said solemnly. "I shall not fail thee."

A few seconds too late, it occurred to him that he did not know what Psephos' title meant. He hoped that "chosen warrior" was adequate, since that seemed to be a generic title of sorts...

But Psephos did not seem to mind. "Very good. Come, then, Khalkeonos, and together let us seek blood, covet glory, and desire fame among the stars. For higher and greater goals now lie within your reach."

Those words concluded the ceremony, and the other Elites quickly came charging over: to congratulate their squadmate, try to reproduce the sounds of his new title, or tell him how they had known all along that he would pass. Khrusaoros wore a rare smile, Psephos' cape billowed as he turned away from the scene—and while this was going on, motion flashed unnoticed about halfway down the Hall.

Mostly hidden behind one of the warrior statues, which was serving as a source of cover, a young woman watched all that was transpiring. Watched, and planned.

CHAPTER THREE
AFTERNOON

"It appeared to me as I was approaching the mountain, but I am certain that it descended from the peak," Photizousa said wearily. "I am also certain that it is divine. It told me that I... that we... are to protect something."

"It was one of the Ouranothen, I tell you!" Ateles insisted. "We should listen to its words, abide by them, or suffer the consequences!"

The other people in the huge, yellow-brown Hall shuffled their feet or shifted in their seats, and some even fidgeted distractedly. The dust from the last council had not yet settled, the sun had not yet set upon the same day that had witnessed the most recent confrontation with the Skiai, before the leading warriors had convened again, this time by special request from Photizousa. Since then, they had faced the odd alliance of her and Ateles, both of whom maintained that a human of Aktinos had been visited by no less than a god. And now, though the sun had still not set, some of those present thought that this council, and the day as a whole, had already gone on far too long.

"Tell us again what this... being... looked like," Eudianax said from his golden throne. "Every detail must be clear and precise." As he spoke those words, his voice was calm. Advising caution, demanding patience.

Patience, however, was something Photizousa lacked just then, for she sighed in resignation before speaking. It was clear that the divine being's appearance was not the issue she most wanted to discuss. "As I said before, my lord, the entity shone too brightly to look at directly. I can tell you that it was fairly thin, perhaps similar in structure to a human, but taller than a human and not quite what I would have expected. It emitted a strong yellow-white glow, and I could sense a powerful, almost oppressive magical power in it. And it had wings."

Eudianax turned to his adviser. "Based on that description, Eudrakes, can you identify this being?"

"You are dealing with something highly magical," Eudrakes answered in his booming voice. "Related, even, to the root of all magic. I foresee that attempts to come to a greater understanding will lead to disaster. Its power is great, as is its benevolence, as is its wrath."

"That proves my point!" Ateles burst out, banging his fist onto the table in triumph. "'*Related to the root of all magic*'—what could *that* be, if not our deities? And attempts to understand them further will lead to disaster because it is not for humans to know the secrets of the divine."

The others were nodding in agreement—except Enedra, who looked at her colleagues incredulously. "Am I... hearing this correctly?" asked the young Ambusher. "Are we saying that this being which visited Photizousa, and gives us our undeniably useful magic, is one of the Ouranothen—who, as we've seen in our legends, are largely malevolent??"

"Eudrakes said that the being has great benevolence," Photizousa objected. "Perhaps it is the Wanderer, as opposed to the Avengers."

"And he also said that it has great wrath," Ateles added. "That may mean that the source of our magic is the Ouranothen in general. Benevolence coexisting with wrath—

the Wanderer coexisting with the Avengers."

Photizousa nodded emphatically. "That argument is good enough for me. Enedra, I'm afraid you are outvoted."

"Not quite yet," Eudianax cautioned, holding up a hand to forestall further talk. "What do you think, Psephos?"

All eyes turned to Psephos, who had been curiously silent up to this point.

The Elite Leader appeared startled, even uncomfortable, to find himself the center of attention, and he did not answer for a long moment. "I... can find no flaws in that argument," he said finally.

Now it was Eudianax's turn to nod. "Good. For my part, I am inclined to agree as well, since"—he dropped his hand and then nodded in Eudrakes' direction—"we have been warned against pressing the matter too far. For the purposes of this council, I will consider the debate closed: we were visited by one of the Ouranothen. Now, what are we to make of this occurrence?"

Photizousa spoke up at once. "If I may, my lord, I would like to call your attention to the words the deity spoke to me, or planted in my mind: namely, that we Aktinans have been tasked with protecting something. We are '*the first line of defense*,' it said. And yet, it did not reveal to me what we are supposed to protect, nor what we are defending *against*."

"This Palace!" Ateles declared. "We have always defended it against the Skiai—our primary task."

"Maybe not," said Photizousa. "If that were the case, then why were we called '*the first line of defense*'? What would the second line be—the ruling family, scribes, servants, and other non-combatants in this building? Somehow, I doubt it; for if that were the case, would they not be allowed to bear arms?"

"Regardless," Eudianax put in, "it appears that defense is to be our top priority in this war. Photizousa, did you receive any indication that we are currently performing this task well—protecting what we are supposed to protect?"

"I'm not sure," Photizousa confessed. "The deity also told me that we Aktinans '*must not forget our duty.*' Whether that means we *have* already forgotten it...."

"If we had, I think it would have said so," Enedra said dryly.

Ateles was nodding. "Yes, I agree. It seems that we are being told... to keep doing what we're doing."

"That statement is odd coming from you, Finisher," Psephos spoke up suddenly. "Does not the one who brings battles to their end wish to bring the war to *its* end?"

Ateles looked annoyed, but also bewildered.

"And the same applies to all of you," Psephos continued, looking around the room at each of his fellow leaders. His sweeping gaze even included Eudianax, who was still seated on his lofty throne. "Surely you wish to have an end to this wasteful and purposeless fighting, to wipe out the Skiai once and for all and be done with it? But defense will not win any wars. It is necessary to make a decisive strike, to face the Skiai on their home ground and defeat them; and yet, none of you are willing to do this. Of late, I have begun to wonder if you, in fact... *want* the war to continue."

At his final statement, the other leaders seemed to freeze. Enedra's eyes were wide and her mouth was twisted strangely, as if she agreed with his point but was afraid to say so. Ateles was obviously stewing in anger as he glared across the table at the Elite Leader. Photizousa, however, sat quite demurely, her hands folded in her lap and her eyes cast downward, determined to wait it out calmly until this stagnant argument went somewhere.

None of them spoke, and the silence dragged on, broken only by the loud beating of their hearts. When at last they heard a voice, it was an unfamiliar one.

"Please forgive the interruption, great leaders, but I have

come to discuss a matter of great importance."

Makheteon—Khalkeonos, he had to keep reminding himself—looked around in surprise along with everyone else. The angle was bad, as he was at his post behind Psephos' chair, and several seconds passed before he located the speaker.

Inside the plain, arching entrance to the Great Hall stood a woman who appeared slightly younger than he was; she had gone almost a quarter of the way to the square table without attracting the notice of the distracted leaders. Her shining black hair ran about halfway down her back, longer than most female Aktinan warriors wore their hair, and her cloth tunic was white, the color favored by Aktinan civilians. She was not very tall, either: even if she stood up straight, she might not reach his shoulder level.

She was captivating.

Most of the others, however, did not seem to share Makheteon's opinion. Although the newcomer had not advanced any farther and had made no threatening gesture, the three leaders who lacked personal bodyguards were fidgeting or looking toward Makheteon and Khrusaoros. Even Ateles, who had mocked Psephos to no end on the subject of bodyguards, had his hand halfway to his sword, and Makheteon found this oddly amusing. Here were these people who were beyond brilliant when it came to fighting the Skiai— the recent successes in the war more than proved this—but the arrival of an unarmed young civilian left them afraid and at a loss. Was it really that much of an imposition on their usual routine?

No one at the table moved, but a slight breeze and a few nearly silent footsteps signaled the presence of others, unseen but attentive. Perhaps they were already preparing to defend their lord....

"You may call off your Protectors, Lord Eudianax," said the young civilian, her voice calm and clear. Makheteon smiled:

they had been thinking along the same lines. "I mean you and your people no harm."

Eudianax raised an eyebrow, clearly not convinced. "We shall see if I will call them off. Who are you, young woman? Why have you come? How did you make it past the Palace's security forces?"

She smiled, unfazed by his intense scrutiny. "Very persistently and carefully, my lord. As for your first question, I am the last daughter in a family of blacksmiths. We have been faithfully making weapons for the members of the warrior caste ever since the reign of Lady Eudianassa II, when she came to us and said that the realm's stockpile of weapons from the old era had dwindled. We flourished in those days, even as a civilian family, thanks to her beneficence as Grand Light of the Realm and one of Aktinos' wisest rulers. Now I am the last of the line, and my family's trade will likely die with me, but I have decided that I would like to fulfill my service to Aktinos in another, more important way. I ask, great lord of light, for the privilege of joining your military forces."

Everyone stared at the young civilian in shock. Behind Eudianax's throne, Eudrakes stirred and edged forward a step.

"This is a most unusual request," said Eudianax. "What is your name?"

"I am called," the young woman replied, "Keraunia." As she spoke, she drew herself up to her full height and cast a haughty glare around the room; the name was obviously a source of pride for her.

"Very well, then," Eudianax went on with a nod. "Keraunia, what is your reason for wanting to join our military?"

The proud posture slipped a bit as a frown passed over her face. "Well, my lord, I said that I was the last of my line. The reason for this is that my parents were cruelly murdered by the Skiai—innocent casualties of war. I wish to avenge them."

"It grieves me deeply to hear this," Eudianax said, albeit in a mostly neutral tone. "We have tried to minimize civilian casualties, but the Skiai delight in bringing death and destruction, and we cannot prevent everything. Still, you are a *civilian*. It is not usual for civilians to break caste boundaries in this way."

"But it has happened before," Eudrakes put in quietly.

"True, it has," Eudianax conceded.

"Yes, my lord," said Keraunia, moving closer to the division leaders' table. "After all, your warrior caste has not existed forever, your line of Eudianaxes and Eudianassas has not existed forever. You had to have come from somewhere, and where could that be but from the 'civilian' population?"

Eudianax's eyes suddenly blazed, and he slammed his fist down onto an arm of his golden throne. "This is insolence!" he bellowed. "Aktinos is eternal and divinely sanctioned, an everlasting stronghold against the darkness of evil!"

Unperturbed, Keraunia looked her enraged ruler in the eye. "Divinely sanctioned it may be," she stated, "but eternal it is not."

The normally calm Eudianax had both fists clenched, and his face was turning red; Makheteon silently willed Keraunia to back down on this point, lest the first foes felled by his newly-reforged sword be his own people in an attempt to protect the girl from bodily harm. Meanwhile, Enedra was staring wide-eyed at Keraunia, as if she could not believe what she was hearing, and Eudrakes was creeping backward once more, returning to his dark corner. No one else moved.

"Even so," Keraunia went on smoothly, "Aktinos is here now, and I am willing and able to help it defeat its enemy. From the many years that I have spent around weapons, I have acquired proficiency with many different types: from the ubiquitous swords to spears and halberds, and even axes—"

Darting forward like a small blur, she seized Psephos'

battle-axe from its designated spot beside him and then backed up several steps. Despite the weapon's large size, she hefted it easily. She gave it a few expertly timed swings, as though she were hacking at an invisible enemy, and never once did she show signs of losing her balance. She was indeed, so it appeared, extremely competent.

Psephos, however, was not impressed. Spinning around in his chair, he glared daggers at the young woman. "...Give me my weapon back," he said in a low voice. Keraunia seemed to wither under his fierce gaze, but she remained holding the axe, unmoving save for a sudden fit of anxious trembling.

Yes, Makheteon thought. It made perfect sense: the girl had been calm in the face of Eudianax's wrath, but one quiet glare from Psephos made her quake in terror. Psephos tended to have that effect on people, to the extent that some of his colleagues often wondered if he had some secret magic spell to inspire fear in others... or, in private conversations when he was safely out of earshot, if he was something other than human.

Makheteon was willing to confess ignorance on the first theory, but he had serious doubts about the second. In his admittedly short time as an Elite—short because he had moved up in the ranks fairly quickly—he had seen his leader display many very human emotions. He had seen Psephos angry, pleased, dispassionate, envious, afraid... even smug. And the Elite Leader had his weaknesses. Known to few outside the Elites, for instance, was his odd vulnerability to fatigue. A long day's battle seemed to exhaust him, and he would always retire early. Even if the rest of the squad stayed up celebrating a particularly memorable victory in battle, he would extricate himself from the festive chaos and slip away into the night.

Whatever was causing Psephos' fatigue, two things were certain: it was real, and it was nearly crippling in intensity. It would drain his face of what little color it had, so that it was deathly white. Perhaps his affected fierceness was a way to compensate for physical weakness; after all, he was very thin, and his battle-axe was equal parts huge and heavy. No human could swing that thing around all day without experiencing fatigue. Did the Skiai get tired?

But this fascinating question was destined to remain unexplored, for a serious situation was developing in the Great Hall. Makheteon hastened to intervene.

"Please, give him the axe," he told Keraunia, taking a cautious step toward her. "He… doesn't like it when people take his things without his permission. If you want to join our military, the last thing you want to do is offend the Elite Leader."

The words seemed to break her out of her trancelike state, and she favored Makheteon with a smile. "All right," she said, and handed the axe over—not to the still-glowering Psephos, but to Makheteon, who propped it up in its usual spot against the table. Immediately, Psephos clapped his hand over the haft and held it there. Nothing short of his death would permit someone to take the weapon from him now.

"You wielded that axe very well," Makheteon continued quietly while the council resumed around him. "Few people in the realm know how to handle such a weapon."

"Thank you," said Keraunia. "By the way, what is your name?"

"Makh—" he began, but caught himself just in time. "…Khalkeonos," he amended. "Recent promotion, you see.…"

"Khal…ke…" she mused.

Just then, Khrusaoros glanced in their direction; evidently, he had heard the brief exchange. His eyes narrowed as he cast a rebuking look at his brother and a haughty glare at Keraunia, and from his expression, it was plain that he disapproved. Reluctantly, Makheteon—*Khalkeonos*, he told himself angrily once again—lapsed into silence, refocused his attention on what was going on in the council.

"Why should I grant this girl's request?" Eudianax thundered. "She is insolent, impertinent! The warrior's spirit belongs in the warrior caste, and let it stay there!"

In the shadows behind the golden throne, Eudrakes stirred again. "The girl deserves a chance," he stated.

Support from this quarter was unexpected, and Eudianax appeared momentarily startled out of his fury. "Is this a prophecy, Eudrakes?" he asked sharply.

"It is my opinion, my lord," Eudrakes answered mildly. "I am your adviser, am I not? I say, let the Ouranothen decide if she has what it takes to join the military. Occasionally, a warrior has been found among the civilian caste, and she may very well be one. Perhaps she will assist us in our war effort."

"But *will* she?" Eudianax persisted. From his tone, it was obvious that he would not tolerate a non-answer.

Eudrakes remained silent for a moment while he thought. "She may... contribute in unexpected ways," he said finally.

"Very well, then," said Eudianax, though he did not sound at all happy about it. "The girl will be granted a test in the Hall of Warriors. I command all division leaders to report there at once, so that we may be *done* with this business and move on to other, more important matters."

He paused, then abruptly rose from his throne and addressed his underlings in a louder voice, his words raining down among them like angry lightning bolts. "And I must say that I am quite disappointed in you, chosen warriors. Our light should have been burning more brightly than ever on this day when one of the Ouranothen appeared to us in divine glory. But, instead, you choose to bicker among yourselves and allow a mere civilian to besmirch our realm's reputation. The stain of the Skiai's influence spreads—even among you, I fear. If you do not wish to be swallowed by their consuming darkness, then obey me, obey the Ouranothen. Our task is one of protection, of defense, and I will hear no more objections. Dismissed."

Having said this, he apparently decided to dismiss himself as well, for he stepped down from the raised platform and stormed angrily past the astonished division leaders, then out of the Great Hall altogether. The *slam* of a distant door put the final seal on his departure.

The four division leaders, who had stood respectfully when Eudianax had stood, remained around the table for a moment and looked uneasily at one another. Despite their many tactical, personal, and philosophical differences, all of them were thinking the same thought: such an explosion was unprecedented for their current ruler. He had taken the throne during a time of war, when military and society alike had been in tatters, and he had restored Aktinos to glory by imposing order, discipline, and rigid militarism, yet through it all maintaining a reassuring calm and a sense of justice. Now, however, he exploded in anger and refused to listen to alternative opinions. It seemed that he was right: something was very wrong in Aktinos.

Finally, the division leaders pulled themselves together, and Photizousa and Ateles slowly began to make their way down to the Hall of Warriors. They looked worried, and Khrusaoros—standing off to the side with arms crossed—appeared disgusted more than anything.

Makheteon, it seemed, was the only Aktinan in the room who was unaffected by troubled feelings... for *his* dominant emotion was impatience. Standing near Psephos, he watched the Elite Leader talk soberly to Enedra and waited for the conversation to be over so he could volunteer to escort Keraunia to her test.

THE PALACE OF LIGHT
HALL OF WARRIORS

Only a couple of hours after his test for promotion, Makheteon was back in the Hall of Warriors; this time, however, he was a spectator instead of the candidate.

As part of the ceremonial formation around the huge rune, he stood behind and to the left of Psephos. His rigid stance mirrored that of his leader, as did the way he was holding his weapon: both hands grasped his sword's red-shining hilt at about the level of his stomach, the blade slanting upward across his chest and over one shoulder. The posture was uncomfortable, and it meant that he would run the risk of stabbing himself if he so much as twitched, but there was no getting around it; formality was part of the Elite way. On Psephos' other side, Khrusaoros stood in the exact same posture.

The other three division leaders were present also, completing the wide semicircle around the currently dark runic carving, but they did not look quite as formal as the Elite Leader and his bodyguards. They were there to receive the new recruit should she pass the test and elect to join their respective divisions, whereas Psephos—as Aktinos' highest-ranking warrior—was there to direct the ceremony. However, now that Makheteon thought about it, he realized that he did not know if it was possible for a new warrior to jump right into the ranks of the Elites. Having moved up through various ranks and divisions during his own military career, he had never thought about this question... but he suddenly hoped the answer was "yes."

Sudden footsteps echoed down the stony, statue-lined Hall; Keraunia was beginning her approach. She, too, held a weapon: an old-looking battle-axe that was similar to, but somewhat smaller than, the one Psephos held. Custom dictated that the person to be tested carry a weapon—even the

Light-bringers had swords that they carried during these tests, although they did not use them in battle—and so Keraunia had been forced to hurry home and take something from her family's collection of forged weaponry that the ancient Aktinans had rejected. Makheteon had escorted her there, and during the walk, he had told her as much as he could about how to behave during the test and what to say. Now, he could only hope that she had absorbed enough of the information to do everything correctly.

She stopped directly in front of the runic carving, at the precise spot where he had stood during the first phase of his test. For a brief moment, she reached out with one booted foot and poked at the rune as if curious about it—or afraid that it would shock her when she touched it. Nothing happened, and she soon pulled her foot back and rearranged her stance to be formal but slightly deferent, her head bowed a little. But for the fact that she was holding an axe, her posture was an exact replica of the one Makheteon had adopted when he had been in her position a few hours before.

As soon as the young would-be warrior had stopped moving, Psephos began the ritual dialogue. "It begins."

"It begins," answered Keraunia, in the same clear tone that she had used when addressing Eudianax. "Lord Psephos Anolethros, Elite Leader, chosen warrior, I have come seeking entry into the glorious ranks of Aktinan warriors, if it pleaseth thee to grant me the opportunity. May our light and splendor shine forever, illuminating both warrior and civilian, strong and weak."

"Very well," said Psephos. "Civilian Keraunia, you shall now be tested to determine whether you have the warrior's spirit, the spirit that seeks blood, the spirit that covets glory, the spirit that desires fame among the stars. Do you consent to this test and agree to abide by its ruling?"

His voice was very level and calm, Makheteon thought,

despite his recent anger over the temporary theft of his axe. It seemed that he truly was a stickler for rigid formality, before which even eternal grudges had to fall....

Meanwhile, Keraunia was answering the question. "Yes, chosen warrior," she said, lowering her gaze just the right amount. Thus far, she was doing everything perfectly—even better than some who had grown up among warriors and warrior customs. If the Ouranothen were watching, even they would surely be impressed.

"Very good," Psephos went on. "Lay down your weapon."

Stretching out as far as she could, Keraunia placed her axe atop the runic carving. "Thus do I place my axe down, and only by the will of the Ouranothen shall I take it up again."

Psephos nodded. "Let the test commence."

From this point onward, Makheteon felt as though he were reliving his own test from a distance. Keraunia stepped forward and knelt at the rune's middle, as he had; the rune began to glow yellow-white and projected bright light of the same color into the air, as had happened for him; the light swirled like thick fog, as it did for everyone. The wall of light, limited to the borders of the carved rune, obscured everything within its bounds, so that no trace of the young woman or her weapon could be seen. Thus it remained for several long moments—longer, Makheteon thought, than it had during his test.

Just when he was beginning to wonder if something had gone wrong with the rune's spell, the light flickered and changed. This time, its new color was a deep blue.

Seconds later, there was a bright-blue flash, like lightning coming from the blue fog or from the rune itself, and Keraunia's battle-axe went skittering away across the room. Hitting the base of a far wall, it came to rest as the blue light winked out and everyone could see Keraunia kneeling there with her head bowed. Weaponless.

It was all too obvious to Makheteon what had just occurred.

Apparently, however, it was not obvious to Keraunia, for she raised her head in bewilderment and began scanning left to right, looking for her axe. She had not yet located it when Psephos spoke and sealed her fate with loud, stern words.

"Civilian Keraunia, you have failed the test set for you by the Ouranothen. You do not possess the true warrior's spirit. The blood, the glory, and the fame among the stars shall belong to others, and you must be content with that decision, for it is the will and judgment of the Ouranothen. In accordance with their ruling, the warriors will take your weapon and give it to one of their own, for the greater good of Aktinos. Please rise, and leave this Hall of Warriors in humility."

Slowly, Keraunia rose to her feet; she looked crushed, even piteous. "As you wish... chosen warriors," she said brokenly.

Somehow, she managed to give each of the assembled leaders a respectful nod without breaking down entirely, but tears were beginning to roll down her cheeks as she turned and began to shuffle back down the Hall, her eyes fixed on the stone floor in front of her. Suddenly she seemed very small, and the warrior statues that lined both side walls seemed to loom over her, tower above her. And then, she was gone.

The others left the room soon afterward, one by one. Psephos, however, lingered, and even sent Makheteon and Khrusaoros to wait for him by the distant staircase. This done, he headed for the room's farthest corner on the pretense of retrieving the weapon that had belonged to Keraunia.

Picking it up on his way, he looked it over grimly, compared it to his own weapon. Except for the size difference, the two were very similar indeed.

Too similar.

Unconsciously, his gaze traveled down the shaft of

Keraunia's axe. It stopped when it reached the handle, which had not received the Ouranothen's blessing in the form of a blue, green, yellow, or red tint. The handle was as dull gray as it had been when it was first forged.

As dull gray as the handle of his own axe.

Mentally berating himself, he shook his head irritably. *No*, he told himself. There was no way that they could know. He protected that axe with his very life, never let it out of his sight. And even if someone did manage to take it from him with enough time to inspect it, that person would not notice, would take it for granted that the Elite Leader's weapon should display the color of highest rank. Perhaps this hypothetical thief would even mentally supply the necessary red tint: to reconcile it, make it seem normal.

No; there was no way they could know, or even suspect. Any of them.

They could not possibly know that, but for what could only be called a miracle, their own Elite Leader would have been in the same position as that unfortunate young woman.

CHAPTER FOUR
SUNSET

METAL CLANGED, WITH near-perfect rhythmic regularity, and silver blades and red hilts flashed in some of the last rays of the dying sun. Another person might have found the display blinding, but Makheteon and Khrusaoros were so used to it, and so intent on their swordplay, that they did not falter as they continued their mock duel. Their boots crunched loudly in the pale, barren soil of the Field of Victory, just outside the Palace grounds.

This sword practice was a sort of ritual for them, one that they pursued at every opportunity. On a typical day, their busy lives as Elites prevented them from fitting in more than one brief dinnertime session, but this day had already given them copious amounts of practice time. The Skiai had not attacked since early that morning, which in itself was odd, and now Psephos had retired to the Elites' barracks, claiming exhaustion from the battle and all the excitement that had followed. Until he should wake up, or until there should be some emergency, his soldiers were free to do as they pleased. Makheteon and Khrusaoros had started this, their second practice session of the day, right after Psephos had dismissed them, and they planned to continue for as long as they could. The sun would set within the hour.

"You shouldn't become involved with that girl," Khrusao-ros said as he parried his brother's attacks and waited for the opportunity to make some attacks of his own.

"What girl?" Makheteon asked innocently.

"You know *quite* well," Khrusaoros returned. "The Keraunia girl. I saw the way you were looking at her during the council."

"And?"

"And the Ouranothen rejected her," Khrusaoros said testily. "You are a warrior; she is a civilian. It is not for us to consort with such non-combatants. I should think the Ouranothen have made this quite clear—for, otherwise, they would have given us a different social structure."

"Civilians are people, too," Makheteon objected. "True, they don't carry weapons into battle, but their way is no better or worse than our way—just different." Even as he finished the sentence, a sudden, inexplicable anger seized him, and he glared at his brother over their locked swords. "Somehow, I don't think your real problem with this is in the area of caste differences. Just because *you* could never have a girlfriend, Khrusaoros, doesn't mean that no one else should have one."

Khrusaoros recoiled, and his defenses dropped for a full second before he could recover, but he could not deny the truth of what Makheteon had said. Though he was handsome enough, there was something about him that, in recent history, had led to three rejections for three different reasons. The first woman, none other than the division leader Photizousa, had turned him down gently but firmly because he had been only a middle-rank Finisher at that time; the second had fancifully decided, contrary to normal Aktinan practices, that she wanted a man who was *not* a warrior; and the third had mistaken him for Makheteon when she agreed to go out with him. After that third disaster, he had appeared to give up, and now he openly frowned on anyone's relationship as though it were personally offensive to him.

"This is nothing to do with me," he was saying now, stiffly, "and *everything* to do with you. You are my brother, Khalkeonos, and I care what happens to you. I fear that she would be a bad influence on you."

With a great effort, Makheteon managed to refrain from laughing as he reset his combat stance. "Why? Because she's a civilian and might induce me to neglect my warrior duties?"

"Because I believe that she's up to something. Think about it. A civilian suddenly shows up and requests to join our military? Eudrakes said that things like this have happened before, but exceedingly rarely. The civilians have their sphere, and we have ours. There must be some extraordinary motivation behind this attempt to break down those boundaries."

"Not extraordinary," Makheteon protested. "The Skiai killed her parents! Isn't that a 'normal' motivation to get back at them?" *He* certainly thought so—though, admittedly, Keraunia had not said anything more about it.

"There is no way to prove that what she said is true," Khrusaoros answered calmly, in the tone of one lecturing a child. "It could be nothing more than a pretense, while her real motives are more sinister. If you ask me, there is already one piece of evidence that favors this theory: the Ouranothen did not grant her admittance into the military. Obviously there is some flaw in her story, and the Ouranothen wished to forestall trouble."

Makheteon shook his head. "Then it's their loss that they didn't grant her request. If you ask *me*, she seems to have more of a 'warrior's spirit' than any of us! Did you see how skilled she was in wielding Lord Psephos' battle-axe?"

"Skill and power are not always beneficial," Khrusaoros said in that same infuriatingly calm tone, flexing his sword arm before he moved in to attack again. "In the wrong hands, they can be used to destructive effect. Perhaps her goal was to infiltrate our organization and use her skill and power to undermine us from within."

Makheteon stared at his brother in disbelief. "Are you insane, Khrusaoros? Undermining us would do her no good, nor her fellow civilians. They rely on us to protect them, to *keep them alive!* No matter how much they resent us, if in fact they do, undermining us would mean that *everyone*, warrior and civilian alike, would die."

Khrusaoros merely stared back and grunted noncommittally.

"In fact," continued Makheteon, his eyes narrowing and heat entering his voice, "I'm ashamed to hear this from you, and *you'd* be ashamed if you deigned to talk to civilians as I have every now and then. You might even have an easier time finding love, since young civilian women adore men who are warriors. But you refuse to do this, and then you go above your head in rank and wonder why you're rejected. Sometimes I think you're a little too haughty, too bitter, for your own good."

With an abrupt movement, he pulled back from the mock duel and sheathed his sword. Khrusaoros, who had been about to test his brother's defenses, was forced to halt mid-swing or risk stabbing him through the heart.

"Am I to infer," said Khrusaoros, "that you are showing me a new kind of rejection? That you are allowing a mere civilian to pit brother against brother?" Unlike Makheteon, he kept his sword out. Whether the reason was that he hoped to continue the practice session, or that he intended to fight his brother for real, was anyone's guess.

"Infer whatever you wish," Makheteon replied. His was the calm voice now, but it was a false calm. Anger boiled anew within him, and not even he was certain of its source. "However, this session is over—unless you can find someone else who is willing to put up with you."

Khrusaoros did not even blink at the obvious insult. "And the other Elites? Will you reject them as well? You were promoted only today; your new title makes that quite clear. Will you neglect your new duties so soon after Lord Psephos showed so much faith in you? This is not who you are, Khalkeonos. Come off it, and remember what you really stand for. You stand for loyalty. To be Elite is to be loyal."

Makheteon shrugged. "Loyalty is overrated, my dear brother. It leaves you no options. You may be supporting an unjust or deceitful cause, but you're far too shortsighted to see it. *I* can see it, though, and I am beginning to think that Aktinos itself is overrated."

Khrusaoros gaped, and the sword in his hand trembled. "Aktinos is...? What are you talking about? I know strange things have been happening recently, but surely this reaction is extreme?"

"How can it be '*extreme*,' when this realm can do nothing right??" Makheteon demanded. This was it, the main root of his anger; and now that he had identified it, the words kept pouring out. "The war dragging on and on isn't much of an issue for me; I think we need the war to keep us occupied... and so we can be good at *something*. Look at us, Khrusaoros! We oppress the civilians, turn away undeniably skilled fighters who are *willing to help*, fail to find our enemy's base, and more. All while Eudianax bungles every decision, and the supposedly all-knowing Eudrakes either claims that '*his eyes do not see everything*' or makes predictions that turn out to be false! He said that Keraunia would contribute, and what happened to her? Rejected, not given so much as a chance, even if she were the only one who could save us!"

"The Ouranothen said pretty clearly that she is not," Khrusaoros pointed out.

"Something is strange in that," Makheteon fumed. "Why

say that someone who is eager to fight doesn't have 'the warrior's spirit'? What makes a warrior? Why am I one while she is not? It makes no sense."

"Still, you *are* a warrior," Khrusaoros persisted. "And as such, you have certain duties to fulfill. As you have said, we protect those civilians of whom you think so highly. Will you abandon them? Will you abandon your loyalties?"

"Perhaps. Perhaps not. As I've said," he concluded grimly, "loyalty is overrated." With that, he turned his back on his brother and walked off, leaving Khrusaoros standing there bewildered.

As he moved away from the Palace and its grounds, his mind raced in frenzied circles. Maybe he had overreacted; maybe he should return to Khrusaoros and take back what he had said before word of his comments reached Psephos. He was an Elite, not a civilian, so he should act like an Elite... but doubts about the Elites' role and mission were beginning to creep into his mind. Certain of Aktinos' recent decisions and actions made him almost ashamed to be part of the realm's ruling military, and yet he could not imagine laying down his weapons....

Absorbed in these circular arguments, he did not notice when he crossed into a residential area that was located just off the Field of Victory. His thoughts continued to spin around futilely like a trapped squad of Skiai, and several moments passed before he looked up long enough to take in his surroundings. When he did, the confused thoughts dissipated at once, as if the trapped Skiai had escaped back to wherever it was they came from.

He was standing in the middle of the area in which the civilians lived—only the civilians, since the warriors lived in and around the Palace; evidently, even the regulations that guided their behavior expected them to want no contact whatsoever with the other caste. Situated at a distance from several civilian homes was one nondescript-looking, rectangular stone building. A few steps led from the slightly elevated front door down to the ground, and atop these steps sat Keraunia in her white tunic: her eyes following a vague, brownish-clad figure as it strode away toward the gap between two other houses, her frown and vacant gaze revealing that she was deep in unpleasant thoughts.

Before Makheteon knew it, he had walked to the foot of the small staircase. "I'm sorry about what happened, Keraunia," he said—softly, so as not to startle her.

It had not worked, for she jumped in fright and jerked her head toward him. She stared at him for a few seconds without seeming to place him. "You are Khal...keonos?" she asked finally.

He made a face. "You can call me 'Makheteon.' In fact, I'd prefer it if you did."

Now it was her turn to frown. "Is that your old title? I don't want to seem rude."

He shrugged. "I could never get used to the new one. I don't think it suits me."

"I see," she said. An awkward silence fell, with both of them looking at each other but not knowing what to say.

"Anyway," Makheteon ventured at last, looking down and shuffling his feet, "I'm truly sorry about what happened in the Hall of Warriors. It's not fair. I really thought the Ouranothen would grant your request."

"There's no need to feel bad about it," she replied with a dismissive shrug of her own. "Perhaps I didn't want to be a warrior as much as I thought I did."

"Still, if there's anything I can do for you—either now or later—please let me know."

She paused thoughtfully before answering. "Actually... there *is* something you can do."

He looked up in surprise. "...Really?"

"Yes. You see, my petitioning Lord Eudianax was not merely a matter of wanting to join the military. I had an... additional goal, as it were. That could be why I ended up being rejected—I was not motivated solely by love of war."

As he listened to her, Makheteon could feel his eyes widening. An additional goal? Could Khrusaoros have been correct in theorizing that she had some malevolent objective? If that turned out to be the case, Makheteon did not know what he would do. He wanted to help her, but he was not interested in working wickedness. By Water, Wind, and Fire, he was not *that* displeased with Aktinos!

"This goal of mine," she continued, "required me to have some connection with the military, and so I sought entry into your people's organization. What I failed to realize at the time was that that connection need not be myself."

"And so, now, you want *me* to be the connection," he supplied.

Suddenly, she looked a bit uncomfortable. "In a word... yes."

"I will *not* help you destroy my people," he said with a sudden stiffness that surprised even him.

"No, I never said '*destroy*,'" she said vehemently, shaking her head. "You misunderstand me. I want to help your people."

He stared at her, unconvinced. "And how will you do that? Please don't take offense, Keraunia, but you're a civilian. We warriors may not make the best decisions at times, but we are doing everything in our power to defend this land against the Skiai. What do you have that we don't?"

"I have something very big," she said in a low voice—so low that he had to move closer in order to hear her. "It's bigger than you can imagine, and it might be our only hope. This war has been going on since before either of us was born, and there were other wars in the distant past, but I know how to break the cycle. I know how we can put an end to this war, to all wars, and save Aktinos. All I need is your help."

"Do you know where the Skiai's base is?" he asked in bewilderment.

She shook her head again. "No; no more than you do. If I did, I could have just given the information to your leadership and hoped that I would be believed. But, in a way, we don't need to know this. What I have can end the war and banish the Skiai—forever."

Makheteon considered the information for a moment. If she was right, and if they could accomplish together what Eudianax and the others had failed to do...

She must have sensed that his mistrust of her was faltering, for she swooped in immediately. "Will you help me, Makheteon?" she asked, fixing him with an intense gaze that would not let him escape.

"I'm considering it," he told her. "Can you tell me what this world-saving and war-ending thing is?"

"No," she said bluntly. "Not until you are fully on board. And once you've been told, you cannot back out of the mission. If you do, I might be forced to kill you"—she smiled unnervingly—"and I don't want to do that."

Despite himself, he felt a small shiver at her last statement. This girl might be only a civilian, and she might be significantly shorter than he was, but none of that meant that she was any less formidable. There was much to be feared even in people like her—indeed, perhaps more than there was in people like him, for people like her were not expected to display such strong and dangerous qualities. When they did display them, one knew that the feelings were sincere and the danger real.

"I will help you, Keraunia," he promised. Even as he spoke, he knew that he would not back out of whatever she asked him to do... and he had a feeling that she knew it, too. There was the fact that she had just threatened him, but that was not all. She was strong, and he had always liked women who were strong. That fact was probably written on his face so clearly that even the Skiai could understand it.

"Good," she responded, nodding approvingly. "Now, before I can tell you what we're doing and why, I need you to go and recruit some people for me."

"*Recruit* people?"

"Exactly. This is part of the reason why I needed a connection to your military; this task is too big for one person to do it alone. I need you to recruit two of the best warri… no, three. Three is better."

"From which military division?" he asked. "And why warriors? Wouldn't civilians be easier to convince?"

"The division doesn't matter," she answered. "All I ask is that they be courageous, competent, willing to run dangerous missions, and able to keep a secret. That's why they must be warriors; how many courageous civilians do you know?"

"One," he said at once. "You."

She gave him a brief smile that never seemed to reach her eyes. Those eyes remained either emotionless or sad; he could not tell which. "In that I am not typical, I assure you. Anyway, if you bring these three warriors back here, I will explain everything. Please make haste. Time is of the essence."

"All right," he agreed. "What should I tell them?"

She shrugged. "Convince them to help without truly telling them anything. Didn't I just do the same to you? I'm sure you'll think of something."

The young Elite nodded, and without another word, he turned and began walking back the way he had come. Keraunia, still sitting on her house's front steps as she watched him weave through the maze of other dwellings, smiled and felt a certain sense of satisfaction.

Then she raised her gaze to the darkening sky overhead, and she experienced a sudden and nameless dread.

✳✳✳

THE PALACE OF LIGHT

Slowly, each step seeming to carry a ponderous weight, Ateles made his way down the short stone staircase that led to the Palace's first basement. No other warriors were wandering these corridors, which was no great surprise. The Ambushers and some of the Light-bringers had long since reported outside for maneuvers, other Light-bringers were still tending to those who had been wounded in the most recent battle, and even the Elites were out practicing after a fashion. Ateles' own soldiers would also be somewhere on the plain, awaiting orders. But there was nothing to be done about that now.

Having reached the door that led to the Finishers' barracks, he yanked it open, and as he walked through the austere, mattress-strewn main area and found it deserted as well, he began to hate himself more and more. He was all too aware that his present actions were a sign of weakness and hypocrisy, an indication that—despite all his brave words—he was no better than Psephos. However, no feeling of rivalry with the Elite Leader would change the facts. It felt like eons had passed since the battle that morning, and now he, Ateles, needed quiet, time to think... and a few minutes of rest.

A second door led from the main sleeping area to the leader's private quarters. He opened it and paused on the threshold to look around.

Located just beneath ground level, the warriors' barracks were generally dim, but not these rooms. To his knowledge, he was the only one to have chosen a decor similar to that of the Palace's upper levels, with the same brownish-yellow color, like gold stripped of much of its shine, for the walls. Small torches with magical, carefully controlled, yellow-white flames provided some illumination, even if they winked out occasionally and had to be replenished by the Light-bringers.

At the moment, they all still burned.

The right side of the sizeable living room held a single, pale-brown couch with two huge tapestries, both of which depicted scenes of war, hanging on the wall behind; the left side had a large bookcase with four shelves of carefully arranged texts. On the top two shelves were books about war and tactics; on the bottom two, tomes on history and philosophy and religion and language. Already the bookcase was full to bursting, with the most recent acquisitions sitting horizontally atop the others since there was no more room on the shelf itself. Soon, it would be necessary to enlarge the bookcase or obtain a second one.

Ateles advanced wearily into the room, stopped in front of the bookcase, and studied the rows of battered books: some of which had frayed at the edges or showed faded, barely legible lettering on the spine, and all of which emitted a musty but pleasant smell. He had long known that this was the reason behind his energetic, merciless fighting style, which had made him deeply feared even among his own soldiers: he believed in Aktinos, was passionate about the need to combat the Skiai, and was confident in the power of the Ouranothen. His readings had imbued him with a deep respect for Aktinos' history and traditions—but, now, he was all too aware that that same respect was the reason behind his present state of disquiet.

A civilian had come perilously close to breaking down the caste boundaries that had held firm for so long. The other leaders questioned orders and divine injunctions in a way that came close to sedition. And even Eudianax himself, embodiment of the realm's light, had lost control and yelled at his underlings instead of fostering unity. It was doubtful whether he and the others were capable of acting as the Ouranothen would want. It was as if no one was listening anymore.

Perhaps, Ateles thought, he agreed with Psephos more than he had been willing to admit during the council earlier that afternoon.

Shaking his head, he turned away from the bookcase. These misgivings were nothing that a short nap could not fix. Once he had gotten some rest and eaten something, he would know what to do, would have some idea of how to steer Eudianax and the others back to the right path without defying protocol—and as for *why* this would be so, the reason was simply that it *had* to be so. A military-ruled realm could not flourish for so long if its decision-makers trembled and withered at the first sign of adversity. Even if the specific problems and solutions generally did not make it into official history texts.

His decision made, he set off for his bedchamber; but he had not gone five steps before the thin, physically fit figure of his girlfriend stepped out of the doorway ahead. Slightly above his shoulder in height, probably close to his own thirty years in age, and clad in the pale-brown uniform of an Ambusher with her posture perfectly straight, she had a demeanor that seemed to dare others to take her lightly. From the first moments of their meeting, he had thought that there was something almost regal in her bearing; this had, in fact, been one of the main causes of his initial attraction to her, alongside her beauty. Her dark-brown hair was pulled into a single braid that spilled about a foot down her back. Only her eyes had a strange emptiness that counteracted his overall impression of her confidence.

She offered no greeting when she saw him, just watched silently as he came to a sudden halt in the middle of the living room. This was not surprising, as neither she nor he was particularly fond of talking, and their relationship was not founded on a need for verbal interaction. Most of the time, they did not speak at all.

A few purposeful strides, and she had planted herself directly in front of him. Her gaze rose to his face before drifting downward again, taking in his entire figure from head to toe, and one corner of her mouth rose to form a tiny smile. The empty eyes had taken on a faint light. Stepping closer, raising her hand, she placed it on his shoulder and ran it slowly down his chest, and her touch was like that of lightning itself. He was unable to suppress a gasp as a jolt shot through his entire body.

With an effort, he shook his head. "...Not now, Erroguia," he said tiredly. "The other Ambushers will be waiting for you outside."

But it was quite apparent that she would not accept any such response. One hand quickly went behind his back, pulling him to her with surprising force, while the other went behind his head, seized a clump of his blond hair, and pushed downward until his face was at a manageable height. As her lips closed on his, it was as if more sparks flew, and their call was as inexorable as the call of the Ouranothen—cutting through his many distractions to remind him how much he cared for this woman. In a flash his fatigue was gone, replaced by affection and eagerness, as he put his own arms around her and held her tightly.

Yet, right before he moved to respond to her kiss, a vague thought arose. In the past she had occasionally ambushed him in much this same fashion, but he had never before seen her so... insistent.

CHAPTER FIVE
DUSK

AKTINOS, REALM OF LIGHT
FIELD OF VICTORY

Less than an hour after leaving Keraunia's house, Makheteon was heading back there. The sun was now totally gone from the horizon, with its afterglow in the starless indigo sky the only light leading him to his destination. He could only hope that it would linger long enough for him to get there, or he would be in danger of becoming lost in the maze of civilian homes with only unreliable light spells to help him find his way.

Behind him trailed three warriors, all women. He had had these three in mind from the moment his earlier conversation with Keraunia had ended, and recruiting them had proved to be less difficult than actually finding each of them. They were the result of a task he had undertaken on a challenge from one of his fellow Elites: to have a successful date with at least one girl from each of the other military divisions. And so there was an Ambusher, named Aglaë; a Finisher, Ganaï; and last of all came Selaä, of the Light-bringers. To convince them to go along with the current task, he had merely approached them away from their squads and asked them to help him with something, and a little charisma had gone a long way. He was convinced that they would be reliable helpers, for his sake if not for Keraunia's—if they did not kill one another first out of jealousy....

Luckily, however, everyone was still alive upon arriving at Keraunia's house. She had gone inside but must have been listening at the front door, for as soon as the group of warriors started up the small staircase, she opened the door practically in their faces.

"You came," she said in tones of obvious relief. "Thank you."

Makheteon shrugged as if to say it was no big deal. As the three recruits filed past him, he introduced them to her—and for people who had grown up in the elitist Aktinan warrior culture, they were surprisingly polite to this stranger civilian.

"Are you the one who interrupted the leaders' council earlier today?" asked Ganaï. "I heard about what happened in the Hall of Warriors, and you have my sympathy. I don't know what I would have done if *I* had been denied a place among the warriors."

Keraunia looked suddenly uncomfortable, and she shuffled her feet and muttered something to the effect that the issue was closed now and there was no point in dwelling on it.

"I was sorry to hear about what happened to your parents," said Aglaë.

"I'm sure that the Ouranothen will help you through this dark time," added Selaä. "You need only ask for their aid, and they will grant you comfort."

It might have been Makheteon's imagination, but he thought he saw Keraunia frowning slightly at the yellow-robed mage, her brow furrowed. Guessing that she wanted to return to the task at hand, he cut in: "Anyway, we're all here. What's this task that you wanted us to assist you in?"

"Right," she said, giving him a grateful nod. "If you four will come with me, I will take you down to the basement. What we are about to discuss must not be overheard."

With that, she led them down the small house's sole staircase into the basement, which was surprisingly chilly.

This was probably the location of her family's forge, but the prevailing darkness was too deep for anything to be seen other than vague, amorphous shapes wrapped in the shadows at the room's distant edges.

The five of them sat in a near-circle on the floor, and as Makheteon looked around at the others with only the torchlight from the upper level to illuminate the scene, it came to him again that he was the only male in the group. This could be either very good... or very awkward.

"You are all warriors," Keraunia began, "and so, you know better than anyone the extent of the current war against the Skiai and the devastation it has wrought. You and your people have been trying for many years, but none of your best tactics have succeeded in defeating the Skiai or driving them out of this realm. In times like these, when the present cannot accomplish a goal, it may be useful to consult the past; and in this case, it is the past that will deliver the desired result."

She paused for a moment, and when she resumed, her next words appeared to be addressed directly to Makheteon. "What I said in the council today, the statement that so enraged your ruler, is true. No matter what your legends and myths say, or how they try to cover up the fact, they are wrong. Your realm of Aktinos is not eternal. We civilians remember our past, and we will not allow it to be forgotten."

The three new recruits had been sitting in placid silence, but now they stirred agitatedly. "What do you mean?" gasped Aglaë, while Ganaï glared at Keraunia and Selaä looked scandalized.

"I mean what I said," Keraunia snapped, almost belligerently. "There was a time when your dear Aktinos did not exist. But you deny this inescapable fact, and then you wonder why you can't remember anything beyond the last few wars or series of wars. The truth is that you can't bear to face the truth, to imagine what lies beyond the reign of the first

Eudianax and Eudianassa in the annals of your history. Even just the *possibility* of a time when you warriors didn't reign supreme is abhorrent to you."

"Easy," Makheteon cautioned. "If you want to enlist their help, you don't want to anger them." Even as he spoke, though, he wondered if he was too late. Selaä's hand was twitching as if preparing to draw a rune, Ganaï looked like she was reaching for her sword, and Aglaë appeared seriously offended.

Keraunia closed her eyes momentarily, and the brief action appeared to calm her. "Yes, you're right. I'm sorry, all of you; it's just that we civilians have our grudges against you warriors, just as you have your grudges against us. My purpose in calling you here was *not* to offend you, but to tell you how this nearly-forgotten past can be of use in the here and now. Will you hear me out?"

The three female warriors were obviously wary and unconvinced, but they nodded in perfect unison.

"Good," said Keraunia. "First, I want to tell you something of that former age. It was what one might call a golden age, for it was almost entirely peaceful. No one was considered better or worse than anyone else on the basis of birth or occupation, and there were few distinct categories of people. There was, as it were, only a single caste, and all residents of each region of the world enjoyed the gift of magic, which was granted to them by what you might call divinities."

"The Ouranothen," Selaä guessed at once.

Despite her best efforts not to, Keraunia chuckled. "No, not them. It was you, not we, who invented those particular mythical figures."

Selaä gasped audibly. "'*Mythical*'? '*Invented*'? I will have you know that the Ouranothen are real, and unless you acknowledge that fact, the lightning of their vengeance will fall upon you!!"

Unfazed, Keraunia shrugged. "Let it. I have nothing to fear, for the power of my divinities will protect me."

This silenced everyone for a long moment. Finally, Makheteon managed to stammer: "Your... divinities? Do you and the other civilians have your own set of gods?"

"Not gods in your sense," Keraunia corrected him. "The people of the past did not revere them as you revere your Ouranothen. Instead, they were thought of more as... distant, impersonal guardians. Guardians of the magic."

"What exactly were these guardians?" asked Aglaë.

"Spirits, non-corporeal entities. Their exact nature was a mystery, but it was known that they represented the elements: fire, air, water, earth. This place where we are sitting, the region known as Aktinos, used to be the domain of the air spirits. Accordingly, the magic used here was aligned with air, rather than with light as it is now. In addition, this region was cold, and the mountains were perpetually covered in snow and ice. The people took refuge from the chill and the biting wind by creating their settlement within the mountains, in a labyrinth of caves and ice caverns."

Now that she was lost in the details of her people's past, all aggressive tones dropped from her voice, which instead took on a detached, absentminded quality. It seemed likely that not even a Skiai attack would break her out of her voiced reverie. "But then... something happened to the world. It was so long ago that no one remembers exactly what it was, but everyone remembers the effects it had. The sun shone more brightly, and the snow and ice melted. The caves collapsed in on themselves, leveling some of the mountains to form a plain, and the winds ceased to blow. Within a short time, the Region of Air had gone from a snowy, windy, and cold place to the barren and scorched wasteland it is now—and these events were accompanied by, or perhaps were the signals *of*, the air spirits' departure from the world. The other elemental spirits left as well, and with them went the gift of their magic."

Abruptly, she seemed to awaken, and her next words were not dreamlike, but sharp and direct. "It is on these elemental spirits, and on these old forms of magic, that we must now rely. Only they can save us from defeat and death."

"But you just said they're gone from the world," Ganaï observed.

"They are gone," Keraunia agreed, "but is their power? Let me show you something that may help answer that question. First, we need some more light...."

There were brief sounds of someone moving around and doing something, though the lighting from above had dimmed and each seated person could not tell precisely who was moving, or why. Then, all around the group and all at once, magical flames lit up torches that had apparently been hung on the stone-bricked side walls for this purpose.

Curiously, the flames were bright blue.

The new light afforded the four warriors some measure of visibility, and they gradually became aware of the basement's nature—dark-gray, rectangular, and surprisingly large—as well as that of the surface on which they were sitting. The floor was of hard stone, as was usual for Aktinan buildings, but it was strangely uneven, and now they understood why. They were literally sitting on top of a runic carving that was just like the one in the Hall of Warriors, except for the fact that the symbol—or what they could see of it—was shaped differently.

"Now you begin to see," said Keraunia, and her listeners spun around in surprise. Her white-clad form was now standing in front of some shallow niches at a far end of the room; this in itself was odd, since no one had heard her rise to her feet.

She was holding one hand behind her back, and as the group watched, she raised the other and slowly began to trace a rune in the air. The process was the same as that used by

Aktinan mages, yet every stroke she drew appeared not in yellow-white, but in a deep and pristine blue. When the rune was complete, the carving also began to glow blue as she spoke again.

"This room, my basement, was once an entire building, one of two with the name 'Shrine of the Air Magic.' As you can see, there is another magical tradition in the history of this place, and the elemental power is still very much alive here. It needs only someone to use it, to awaken it."

She allowed her rune to dissipate, and the carving's blue glow faded as well, but not before it had made its point. The four Aktinan warriors could do nothing but sit there in a state of stupefaction.

When, at last, someone found a voice, it was—predictably—the mage, Selaä. "That power, Keraunia—what is it? It feels like our magic of light, but then again, it doesn't. Something has been... added..."

"Nothing has been added to it," Keraunia said firmly. "This magic isn't derived from your magic; it far predates yours and is much stronger, being one of the original four. What you have witnessed here is something that outsiders haven't seen in centuries: a display of the water magic." As if anticipating the next question, she paused only briefly before continuing: "And the power's source is... this."

Bringing her non-rune-drawing hand out from behind her back, she showed the group what appeared to be a fairly large glass sphere—but further investigation indicated that it was much more than that. An ordinary glass sphere would not be emitting a faint blue glow, nor would it have swirling light within it. The light, which was in countless shades of blue, moved about with the serenity of a calm sea and provided an emphatic complement to the blue torch-flames on the walls.

"This," said Keraunia, sitting down once again among the thunderstruck warriors, "is the Essence of Water: the source of all water magic, back then as well as now. As long as it's safe, the magic can still be used even with the water spirits gone, although there is enough power for only one person at a time to wield strong spells. When the elemental spirits dismantled the old magical institutions prior to their departure, they left the Elemental Essences here in the realm: to ensure that the magic would never die, or to promise that they would return someday. Eventually, my family was given this Essence by a great woman from the Palace—one of the few allies we've had from your side. For many generations since then, we've been responsible for protecting the artifact from evil ones while awaiting the right time to use it. This task has been difficult, and dangerous at times."

"Then your parents...?" asked Aglaë.

Keraunia shrugged—carefully, so as not to drop the sphere. "This is a secret that would mean bad news for the forces of evil if it were let out. Draw your own conclusions."

Makheteon frowned. He had a feeling he knew where this discussion was going, and he was not sure if he liked it. "You said that your family has been waiting for '*the right time to use*' this Essence of Water," he said to Keraunia. "Now that you are the last of the line, is this '*the right time*'? Do you really think it would be a good idea to bring a foreign form of magic into the present war?"

"I don't just think so," Keraunia replied; "I *know* so. Along with this Essence—which, remember, is only one of four—there is a small verse which has been passed down in my family. A prophecy, if you will. It goes like this..."

She appeared to take a breath, and when she spoke again, her words carried the mystical aura of prophecy and the powerful ring of historicity.

> "*Runes rule the ruins.*
> *Runes ruin the rulers.*
> *The rune-ruler shall ruin.*
> *The rune-ruiner shall rue.*"

"'*The rune-ruiner shall... rue*'?" Ganaï repeated, blinking in confusion, after the last echoes had died away. "I think we'd expect '*shall* rule.'"

Keraunia shook her head. "No; the original text, and the oral tradition thereafter, definitely say '*rue*' there. It's a startling choice, maybe, but it makes perfect sense. We must not destroy the runes that are left over from the old culture, for they are our only hope of salvation."

Meanwhile, Makheteon was still frowning. "We warriors don't much care for riddles," he said with no little impatience. "What does it mean? And how do you derive the conclusion that elemental magic must enter into the war with the Skiai?"

"Here is my family's traditional analysis," Keraunia answered. "The first line is obvious: there are runes in the old ruins of the Region of Air, many of which are now incorporated into new structures and used for various purposes. The person who '*rules*' these runes—that is, uses them, activates them, places them under his or her command—will cause destruction. But to whom? '*The rulers*'— which opens up two possibilities. First, this could spell doom for the rulers of the Skiai, the same beings who are '*ruling*' the war by dictating its course, deciding when battles will be fought, and so forth. Or, if we adopt a more metaphorical interpretation, the runes are '*ruining*' the leading warriors in that the leaders don't know what to do with them, and if they are misused, they could cause real destruction."

"And if they are used correctly, they could wipe out our leadership and inaugurate a new era of elemental rule," Makheteon added. "You cannot ignore that possibility."

Keraunia did not appear the least bit fazed. "Well," she said coolly, "does it look like you have a choice?"

Makheteon had to concede that fact. Current strategies were leading only to a destructive stalemate, so it was preferable to break that pattern by any means available. And if Aktinans were to be in charge of this effort, then, surely, all would turn out well.

"Finally," Keraunia went on, "consider the prophecy's structure: four lines, each with four words in it. In many respects, our world may be said to be 'fourfold'—four old magics, four main Regions, four sets of spirits, and so on. Similarly, our approach to fulfilling this prophecy must be fourfold. Four people, carrying four Essences, activating four runes, reviving four groups of elemental spirits. It makes perfect sense."

"What do you mean, *'reviving'*?" Selaä asked, more than a little suspiciously. "Are the spirits dead, and we're bringing them back to life? I thought you said they were gone altogether—had *left*."

"Right; it's more that we'll be reviving their power and catching their attention. If we're lucky, the spell may even allow them to come back personally; there was an old relationship by which humans' using their magic strengthened and empowered them, just as their magic strengthened and empowered humans. But, essentially, our job is to call their power down to banish those who don't belong here."

"Namely, the Skiai," Makheteon supplied. A "*stain*" on Aktinos, Enedra and Eudianax had called them....

Keraunia gave a brief nod.

"I don't understand," Aglaë cut in suddenly. "Why all this trouble to revive a dwindling, obsolete magic? It seems simpler to use currently existing magic to accomplish the same goal."

"She has a point," Makheteon confessed. "Maybe it's your elemental power that doesn't belong here."

"Maybe so," said Keraunia, "but your magic isn't going to do the job. Are there spirits of light for you to call upon?"

At this, all eyes turned toward Selaä, the resident expert on the Ouranothen and all things ancient.

"No," Selaä answered shortly, "unless you count the Ouranothen. Our magic comes from them, but they aren't guardians of it in the way you described your spirits, and I doubt that they rely on our using magic to strengthen them. They are so powerful that they don't need such a setup."

"And yet, even at the peak of their power, they have not yet been able to help you in your struggles," Keraunia pointed out. "The magic that you use is weak—don't deny it—I've witnessed its failures many times when I've observed battles from this house. For this task, we'll need as strong a magical power as there is. Besides, the prophecy works not in ones, but in fours. Unless your magic of light comes in four types, there's no escaping the conclusion that elemental magic is the answer here.

"What I want you four to do," she continued, loudly so as to forestall any objections, "is divide up the magics among you. Each of you is to take one Essence and travel to a specific location where there is a rune like the one here. For instance, the person who gets Water will take my Essence and come here when it's time to cast the spell. This person will have the easiest task. Which one of you wants it?"

A tense silence followed the question. Makheteon looked nervously at the other three warriors, who were obviously displeased with Keraunia's comment about the magic's being weak. Selaä looked ready to unleash an attack spell, and even the two non-mages, Aglaë and Ganaï, were scowling and had crossed their arms over their chests. The leather armor of the latter two Aktinans creaked softly as they shifted about in restless annoyance.

This scene of thinly veiled hostility continued unabated for an endless minute while Keraunia waved the Essence of Water to and fro in front of the others' faces. Then, finally, the group seemed to come to a silent consensus that Keraunia *had*, after all, spoken an undeniable truth. The crossed arms were uncrossed, placed in a relaxed position, and the three female warriors looked at one another with inquiring gazes.

After another moment, Aglaë held her hand out in Keraunia's direction, palm up. "If no one else minds, I'll take it. The duties of an Ambusher are very time-consuming and demanding, and there's no guarantee that I can free myself from them long enough to go on a major quest. Luckily, the others are currently in a transition period, moving into position for the evening, or I wouldn't have been able to come here for this meeting."

The others nodded their assent, and Keraunia's expression showed both satisfaction and relief as she handed over the Essence of Water. "Excellent. Now, for the others. Air and earth are available for choosing, but I believe the fire spirits have already chosen their champion."

"Really? Who?" Makheteon asked, puzzled.

She beamed at him. "Why, you, of course. Surely you remember your test in the Hall of Warriors? The rune shone distinctively red for you, and you'll notice that for me it shone blue. The connection is obvious."

Memory crashed down on him, and he shook his head. He had no idea how she knew the details of his test, but he *did* know that she was wrong. "No, Keraunia; the colors aren't meant to signify elements. The rune was red for me because red is the color of high rank, and it was blue for you because blue is... well, it's the color of low rank or no rank. The colors help us determine whether a person passed the test."

"Colors can mean many different things, Makheteon," she countered, her tone almost condescending in a way that reminded him eerily of Khrusaoros. "It may be that fire magic, because of its powerfully destructive nature, was highly respected in the old days, and because of this, its color became the color of high military rank. In any case, I stand by my theory that you are meant to wield fire magic. Will you seek out the Essence of Fire?"

He shrugged. Fire, air, earth—which one he adopted as his did not make much of a difference to him. "All right," he said. "And the rune—where is it?"

"In the Hall of Warriors, naturally," Keraunia replied. "It's the one that turned red, right?"

After that, the focus shifted to the other two magics. Those had just been assigned to their future wielders—once Selaä had learned that the ancient magic of her homeland was air magic, she would not be denied it, and Ganaï agreed to take the earth magic—when the same thought occurred to each of the fire, air, and earth people, seemingly all at once.

All three of them opened their mouths, but it was Ganaï who spoke first. "This is all well and good, but we have no power without the Elemental Essences, and I'm guessing that you don't have the other three sitting around in this basement. Where are they?"

"That's a good question," Keraunia said. "I do know that, in accordance with the new order of the world, the Essences of Water, Fire, and Earth were brought here; this must be obvious from the fact that my family held the Essence of Water. So, all four are somewhere in Aktinos. Presumably, there were three more families charged with protecting the other Essences, but this was so long ago that they have probably already died out as mine is on the brink of doing. However, there is someone who may know something regarding the Essences' fate. The current Eudianax's adviser, Eudrakes."

This was unexpected, but the four warriors did not have much time to be confused before Keraunia continued speaking. "When I was in the Great Hall earlier today, I felt something strange. The power of the water magic—in *him*. Sometimes I felt it, sometimes I didn't, but it was definitely there when I did feel it. Without a doubt, he knows about the elemental magics, and of course he would have been able to sense the water magic in me as I sensed it in him. Makheteon, Selaä, Ganaï—I recommend that you talk to him, ask him for the Essences, steal them from him if you have to… if he doesn't foresee your arrival beforehand. Then, once you all have the Essences and can use your magics, go to your respective runes and activate them simultaneously. This should strengthen the spirits, and then you can proceed with a summoning spell. You should already know the spell in question, since runic symbols are the same today as they were back then. Only the alignment of the magic has changed."

This topic concluded the meeting. Keraunia closed the discussion with an exhortation to her helpers to finish their task as quickly as possible, preferably during the coming night. Makheteon was mildly surprised that Aglaë, Selaä, and Ganaï had agreed to go along with the mission—especially given their anger at the beginning of the meeting—but then he noticed how skeptical they looked still. Even Aglaë, who held the glowing Essence of Water in her hands, was frowning as she glanced from it to the points on the walls where the blue torch-flames, now gone, had been burning a few minutes before.

Perhaps the three of them were merely playing along, hoping to prove Keraunia wrong about her various claims regarding magic, history, and the divine. Oh well; as long as they handled their three magics properly and accomplished their goal, what did their precise motives matter?

As he followed this line of thought, he found himself reminded of a question that had been troubling him for some time. Turning to Keraunia when they had all reached the top of the long, steep staircase from the basement, he spoke quietly to her. "Why did you have me recruit *three* extra people? It would have been just as easy, if not more so, to recruit me and two others and have yourself be the fourth person."

"I may not have much time left," she answered matter-of-factly. "It may be known that I am the last one left in my family, and if it is, our enemies will come after me quickly. They will not, however, be expecting Aktinan warriors to hold the Essences. This will add a level of security to the present endeavor."

"Don't talk like that," he said firmly. "You can defend yourself! Even if you can't cast powerful water spells with the Essence gone, you're more than competent at wielding weapons—"

"There's another reason," she interrupted. "If there's one thing I've learned today, it's that I'm not a warrior; I'm a descendant of blacksmiths. The blacksmith doesn't use weapons, merely makes them and furnishes them to the true fighters. That is my duty here, and I've fulfilled it. Don't worry about me, Makheteon. Just get this done, for me and for all of us."

He nodded reluctantly and headed for the door, but as he walked past her on his way outside, he was certain that he saw a strange sadness in her eyes.

✳✳✳

AKTINOS, REALM OF LIGHT
MOUNTAINS OF AIR

In Enedra's opinion, no activity was more tedious than making her thrice-daily rounds to check that the members of her squad were in position. And that was especially true on this day, when the rounds followed endless, aimless hours of waiting and would have only *more* waiting as their likely reward.

The natural-fire flame atop her long wooden torch flickered, the areas it illuminated changing with every second, as she picked her way along a slope near the foot of the great mountain range that enclosed Aktinos. She was careful to move neither the torch nor her head toward the places where the Ambushers' night watch would be stationed—hidden by boulders, curves in a mountain face, or just the evening shadows—and the squad members themselves shared the same sense of stealth. Most of them signaled their presence and acknowledged her simply by tapping a spear or arrow against the nearest rock.

Yet, soon enough, the torchlight hit upon a large boulder much farther up the slope—her own daytime hiding place and the site of her conversation with Photizousa many hours before—and her fingers clenched around the spears that she held in her other hand as she found herself wishing for something to distract her from the memories. Photizousa's blind faith was troubling enough in itself, but all the more so because it seemed to be shared by almost all of the other leaders, Eudianax included. And to Enedra—young, newly promoted, eager to contribute—the situation was somewhere between frustrating and infuriating. To take her seat at the table in the Great Hall, brimming with the fire of ambition, only to find the others stuck in a never-ending loop of battling and defending... and *waiting*?

At least Psephos offered a different perspective. His statements on ending the war, which had been made for the first time on this day, still resonated with her, though she was not sure if *she* was blinded: namely, by her longtime admiration for him. Never mind that she had barely been a teenager when he appeared on the scene, or that the aftermath of the last council was the first time she had spoken to him for more than a minute; she had always liked his bravery and methods. Would the other leaders allow their biases—negative *or* positive—to drive their opinions of matters that would affect the entire realm?

In time she passed another Ambusher outpost, hidden amid a field of shadowy boulders; the warrior there was new to the squad and could not keep from murmuring the word "*Ma'am.*" And though her first instinct was to reprimand him for endangering his own cover, she kept walking and soon spun his utterance into the beginning of a new and vague resolve. From this point on, she would prove herself worthy of the title, and the journey would start at the next council. She would help Psephos if he welcomed it, or embark on tasks of her own if he did not, until—somehow—she had enabled Aktinos to break out of its stagnancy. And if those efforts removed all opportunities for battle? That would at least be balanced by a removal of the need to lie in ambush for hours...

Her boots crunched on the sloped terrain as she came to a sudden halt; her approach to this latest hiding place had brought no tapping, no spoken words, and the silence tore her from the trance of routine and repetition. Cautiously she edged up the slope, shined the torchlight in the same direction... but saw only a boulder standing beside a protruding wall of rock, all as empty as the promises of the Ouranothen.

"Where's Aglaë?!" she snapped—much more loudly than she had intended. The two words seemed to echo from mountain to mountain, carrying her location to all the listeners in the world.

"No idea," called the warrior who occupied the next outpost. "She was with us when we left the Palace, but then she fell behind."

Shaking her head, disgusted at Aglaë and herself in equal measure, Enedra carefully turned back, searched until she spotted the Palace—it was quite close by, the rear portion of its night-shrouded outer wall looming near the bottom of the current slope—and then began to descend. She had gone about half the distance when she heard a familiar *squelch*, a scant foot away.

Her heart just about stopped.

Something shot upward to slap against the wooden shaft of her torch; she recoiled instinctively, and the torch fell to the ground. Illuminating what looked like a giant, rippling mass of dark-purple matter, scrabbling down the slope toward a small iron gate that the Ambushers used for easy re-entry to the Palace grounds.

She had not seen the cloud of darkness that usually heralded their arrival. Yet they had long since arrived.

Foreign footsteps pounded down the slope above her, and someone shouted *"Raise the alarms!"*—but there was no need, for warriors from other divisions, who had no doubt been awaiting orders on the Field of Victory, were already pounding closer around the corners of the outer wall. And that was the last detail about the world beyond the wall that Enedra registered for some time.

She hurled one spear, and then another, to transfix as many Skiai as possible, but held on to the last one as she swung it around in blind rage and desperation—the battle begun in a heartbeat, but seemingly lasting for an eternity. Another Ambusher, her spears used up in the first moments of battle, tumbled down the mountainside, her arms raised to shield her head as she tried to steer her headlong roll away from the enemy horde. Bowstrings twanged; swords of Finishers or Elites flashed in the light of the fallen torch; droplets of blood and purple ooze flew through the evening air. Shouts from human throats mingled with the soft, enigmatic noises that Skiai warriors were wont to utter while fighting.

Enedra's armor was soon dripping with sweat and Skiai blood, and she was not the only one. Breathing hard, she stepped toward a spot of relative calm, careful to avoid wounded Aktinans and disintegrating purple shapes—and then she saw it. A subgroup of some dozen Skiai, even now squeezing their spineless, tentacled forms between the vertical bars of the nearby gate.

The contortion of the purple bodies was gruesome and made her gag, but even worse was the grim milestone that the sight represented. The Palace and its grounds had always been places of utter safety. Never breached by Skiai; seldom even approached, for battles would end before that could occur.

Not for a moment did she pause to think. Letting out a wordless shriek to distract the other Skiai, she charged back toward the place where she had stood at the beginning of the clash, seized her torch, and plowed downward through the melee. At the gate she lifted one booted foot and kicked at the metal—not daring to touch it for fear of Skiai slime—but though the gate merely wobbled on its hinges, there was a Light-bringer somewhere behind her. A dim, but sizzling light spell soon flashed by to knock the gate's two halves inward.

The path now clear, she threw the torch forward with all her might, for extra illumination—it showed the skittering Skiai still approaching the nearest wall of the Palace proper— then darted over the dry ground with other Aktinans hard on her heels. Her spear was slippery with substances both harmless and dangerous, but it was her only remaining defense, and she clung to it with both gloved hands as she stabbed it this way and that, her squad running up to form a half-circle around her. Somewhere to her right, another warrior's armor was breached and he went down with a powerful *thud*, his continuing, pain-filled cries shattering the night—yet her own attention remained fixed on the Skiai. A few of them had reached the wall and were beginning to batter it with their slimy appendages....

Some time later, a human hand fell on her shoulder, and she came out of a stabbing motion that—she only then realized—had no purpose. All around her was shadowy, disintegrating Skiai matter, scattered among fallen Aktinans;

a few Light-bringers were already beginning to tend to the latter. She knew she had not hit any of her own people in this final phase of the fight, but her knowledge in other respects was surprisingly sparse.

Panting, dropping the gore-spattered spear, she stumbled over to the place where her torch lay, picked it up once more, and came back to find that the person who had roused her from the haze of battle was the same Ambusher who had called her *"Ma'am"* during her earlier rounds. For some reason, although her vision was bleary and she was still breathless from her exertions on this endless day, that connection was able to conjure a tiny, momentary smile onto her face.

"We... got them all?" she asked her subordinate presently.

He nodded. "Nearly so, Division Leader—there's just one Skiarchos that we lost sight of partway through. Some of the others have already gone to try to track it. But it's true what you told us this afternoon, about comments that were made in the morning council: the Skiai are *different* today."

She felt herself blinking at him, and he pointed to a nearby stretch of wall, just above ground level. When she had shuffled over there, she immediately saw what he meant.

The Palace's towering wall was intact, undamaged as always... but her torchlight glinted off vast swaths of purplish slime, which dripped down large stone bricks and even a couple of windows. It looked like the Skiai had literally tried to break into the room beyond—and that idea, combined with the issue of location, would cause her to rethink much of what she had resolved while making her rounds.

For, unless she was much mistaken, that wall and those windows formed part of the Elite barracks.

CHAPTER SIX
EVENING

THE PALACE OF LIGHT
BARRACKS OF THE ELITES

*L*IGHT.

It assaulted his eyes, ravaged his soul. It alternately blinded him and revealed to him a place that looked like it had been burned. It was intolerable... but it had to be tolerated, for this was necessary. He was searching for something—something very important. She had sent him here to find it, and she would thank him when he had successfully recovered it.

If he could remember what it was.

Rising to his feet—it seemed he had not arrived cleanly—he took one step forward, and then another. All around him were bizarre, shining structures, each one reflecting a blinding silvery glare that seemed to pierce through his eyes and into his brain. He tried to look away from them, but knew he could not. They were a clue, related to his objective, and he needed to find out what they were....

And then he was outside the shadow of the largest such structure.

It beat down upon him at once—one sun with the fury of ten thousand. He staggered, sweat pouring down his face and dripping from there to the ground, where he was sure that he saw it sizzle and evaporate.

Strangely, no one else appeared to be having trouble. Vague figures wandered about, not so much walking as gliding over the ground, moving placidly in and out of the shining structures. Their white or yellow garb—a stark contrast to his own dark-colored clothing—served to intensify the glare that permeated the entire area. Even the hot ground seemed to reflect it back at him.

One figure, different from and a bit clearer than the others, suddenly passed him by, going the other way. It seemed to be a fair-haired man dressed in brown: familiar to him in a distant, detached sort of way, though seen only out of the corner of his eye and with foreign clothing to throw him off. He started to turn in that direction; dimly he heard a whooshing sound, and he completed his turn just in time to see the fair-haired man, his face averted, vanish into thin air.

He sneered. Were these beings such cowards that they had to hide themselves in invisibility at the very sight of a stranger? He turned around again to continue on his way...

But he could not turn around. He could not move. The light... the heat. It was too much. It scorched his feet, beat down on his head. He felt like he had been clubbed. Blinding pain seared the area behind his eyes, and white spots broke out on his vision as a feeling of lightheadedness spread. With a groan, he collapsed to his hands and knees and vomited violently onto the ground while the white- or yellow-clad beings continued to flit past him serenely. He had never encountered these beings before, but, somehow, he knew: none of them would stop to help him.

He had had enough. Let someone else run this mission; he wanted no part of it. Slowly he struggled up to a kneeling position, sour bile now burning his throat, and turned around to find the cool, comforting darkness from which he had come.

It was gone. The shadows had vanished now, at high noon. His starting point glared back at him, now as bright as the rest of the plain.

Despair consuming him, he collapsed again, but the searing ground offered no comfort. Far above him, to his fevered vision, the sun seemed to have multiplied. Two, then three, then four of them were burning him; the ground was burning him. Wracked by agony, he opened his mouth in a silent scream that he knew no one would hear as he waited to be burned alive—

Psephos jerked awake, his heart pounding in his room's semi-darkness. The memory of the dream lingered fleetingly and would have departed, but at this point, it was practically ingrained on his mind. Almost every time he had tried to sleep in recent days, it had come to him. A recurring dream... a recurring nightmare.

There was no way that he was going to be able to return to sleep. Reluctantly he rose to his feet, and his first movement revealed that he was bathed in sweat, as if the dream had been even more real than it had seemed. A quick look out a nearby window revealed that it was no more than an hour or so after nightfall.

At least he had managed to catch *some* sleep. Never mind that it had not been for very long, and that it had been anything but restful.

Seizing his battle-axe, he left his personal quarters and walked through the barracks' main area. Some of the Elites were there in the plain-walled and torchlit room, separated into several groups by gender and rank, also catching up on much-needed sleep. He walked around them, quietly so as not to wake them.

For a moment, he considered bringing his bodyguards with him on this impromptu excursion, but then he decided against it. He would not be gone long—or rather, he *could* not be gone long. It would be only a matter of time before the fatigue returned with a vengeance.

His first thought had been to take a walk outside in the cool and crisp night air, but as he left the barracks, he found himself heading down stairs and curving hallways. Heading for the deepest basement.

Before he quite knew what was happening, he had entered the Hall of Warriors. During his time as Elite Leader, he had been in this room too many times to count—but never had it disturbed and unsettled him as much as it did at the present moment. Now, on his third visit to the place in a matter of hours, the very sight of it made his heart sink down to his toes... but he could not turn and leave. He felt strangely drawn inside, almost as if he had been meant to come here on this night.

As always, the statues that lined the Hall stared stonily off into space, their expressions frozen and distant. They were lofty, silent, and as proud as the tradition they represented: the tradition of Aktinan warriors. They, and those who had sculpted them, would not be pleased to see that tradition sullied or marred.

Hesitantly, Psephos began to walk down the long passage that was simultaneously a reminder of history and a history lesson. His pace was slow, but his eyes were in constant motion as he stared at the various statues... studied them in the vain hope that they might hold the answers he craved.

At the beginning of the Hall, and presumably the beginning of history, was a warrior type resembling that of a mage, though its robes were plainer in design than the ones currently in use. One of its hands was raised to trace a rune for a spell, and its mouth was slightly open. The latter fact was another difference, as modern Aktinan mages cast their spells silently. In the war against the Skiai, a loud spell was a dead giveaway of location and—more often than not—resulted in a dead mage.

Next to that statue was another mage type, identical to the first one except for the addition of a sword sheath strapped to the mage's back. The sword's hilt could be seen protruding over one shoulder. This category underwent some evolution, with the next few statues showing the sword aspect increasing in prominence while the magic aspect diminished. The statues could be seen taking the swords in their hands and displaying them proudly, and the last of this type wore a belligerent expression and brandished a huge two-handed sword with a wicked-looking, curved blade....

And then everything changed.

The swords vanished; the magic vanished. In their place came a new warrior type, this one clad in something that looked like the mottled leather that most Aktinans used for their uniforms. The first example of this new class was unarmed, though no one could say that it was not a fighter. It wore the proud, haughty, and uncompromising expression that had come to define the Aktinan warrior. Carvings reminiscent of wind or air decorated its alcove, which also bore an archaic inscription reading, *"One of the Five."*

From that point on, the types were more recognizable as swords and magic made a comeback and seemed to vie with each other for dominance. Many different combinations were tried until the current categories emerged: Ambusher, wielding long spears; Finisher, wielding swords; Light-bringer, robed, hand raised for silent magic while stylized rays of light carved into the surrounding alcove emphasized the magic's nature; Elite, one hand raised for magic and the other holding a sword. Other weapons could be seen here and there in this final part of the sequence: bows, halberds, and even a crude-looking club.

Not one of the statues held an axe like the one he wielded.

Having reached the end of the Hall, he stopped and looked back at the entire set of statues. Only one of the dozens of larger-than-life replica weapons looked suspicious in any way: a spear held by a statue near the middle, its tip hewn much more roughly and sloppily than the edges of the other bladed weapons. This was also the only place in the historical sequence where two consecutive statues held the same weapon type.

He gave a start: he had walked back to the statue in question without knowing it. Craning his neck, he looked up at the spear—the top of its shaft also seemed wider than it needed to be to support such a small blade—and the face of the silent stone warrior above it, but no answers or insights came to him. No way to know if this weapon had once been an axe as he suspected.

And yet, the axe was his weapon; he had always known it. He loathed swords, could never learn to handle them. With the axe he was more than competent, and surely he had proven that it, too, was a legitimate and worthwhile weapon. His efforts, however, had been ignored by more or less everyone— to the point that the only other person he had ever seen wield an axe was the Keraunia girl, the civilian who had been denied the status of a true warrior.

A true warrior.

The words echoed in his head as he returned to the end of the double line of statues, only to find himself faced with an even worse sight—for there at his feet was the object which, perversely, he feared even more than the worst that the Skiai had to offer. The runic carving, lifeless though it was, seemed to stare back at him, to mock him. He was the only one of all the warriors who had never knelt at its center to be tested. Part of him wanted to try it, to see what would happen... but the other part thought it knew already.

Perhaps he had been deluding himself all this time, he thought. Perhaps he did not truly belong in this organization, with these people. He had bypassed their most important test for placement in the ranks of warriors, and his weapon of choice was not highly respected, or respected at all. And then there was the fatigue, the phantom sickness that had been plaguing him for as long as he could remember. No number of healing spells cast by the Light-bringers had been able to take *that* away.

He was weak, even sickly. What was he doing fighting in this war when he feared that, one day, he would be too ill to defend himself? After the last council, Enedra had said that he was a good fighter and a competent leader; granted, she had probably been trying to flatter him—and it was working, or he would not remember her saying it. But she did not know the full story. None of them did, and Aktinos would likely fall apart at the very possibility. Was their Elite Leader, the highest-ranking of all of them and the one who represented them in their most important ceremonies, even a warrior as they were?

You are not. Not as they define it.

That voice, soft and quite neutral, was not an echo in his head. Startled, he turned around—and found himself face-to-face with the fairly large, oozing and bleeding, dark-purple form of a wounded Skiarchos.

He brandished his axe at it, but only half-heartedly. The creatures, for all their grotesqueness, had never seemed to him quite as repulsive as the other Aktinans found them. Not tall or monstrous by any means, they were only as intimidating as one allowed them to be. And one Skiarchos with preexisting injuries, now that it had revealed its presence, would be no match for a fully armed Elite Leader.

There was another reason why he had no fear, but he was not ready to acknowledge it just yet.

"What are you doing here?" he heard himself saying. His voice echoed in the Hall's profound stillness, and he mentally chastised himself for speaking; but then he reasoned that he deserved some gratification and it would be amusing to taunt the creature before attacking it, to watch it squirm. "Are you so cowardly that you feel the need to come after me when I am alone, without my soldiers to come to my aid? I am aware that you and your people have started singling me out for attack."

You are astute.

"But you, apparently, are not. Why bother attacking someone who you just said is not a true warrior?"

The Skiarchos straightened up a bit, and though it was trembling from its wounds and still very much at a height disadvantage, it somehow managed to look him in the eye.

You know why.

"No, I do not," he objected testily. "If I knew, why would I be asking you?" Even so, he could not keep his uneasiness out of his voice. At that moment, *he* was the one who was squirming.

Instead of replying, the Skiarchos came toward him. It squelched and glided across the floor on its tentacles, leaving a trail of purplish slime and darker blood behind it. Stopping when it was no more than a foot from him, it reached up toward him with one tentacle.

The touch of a Skia was known to be dangerous, or even deadly. The Light-bringers thought it was something in the slime that caused the distinctive "Skiai burns," but no one knew why prolonged exposure to the slime could cause convulsions, fits of screaming, and even spontaneous death. To be this close to a Skia without having a Light-bringer immediately at hand to offer healing was a perilous proposition... but Psephos did not even flinch as the Skiarchos' tentacle approached him. This would not be the first time it had happened. Indeed, something similar had occurred only that morning, during the battle with the two Skiai in front of him....

The slimy tentacle wrapped around the bare skin of his forearm.

Just as before, nothing happened.

The Skiarchos showed its grinning fangs and looked almost triumphant. *Now you see.*

"See what?" he asked: calmly, but his mind was in turmoil once again. This very development had provided the impetus for his seeking a second bodyguard. He had wanted to ignore the issue, keep the Skiai away from him; but they had found him anyway, as soon as he left himself unprotected.

You see that what you have suspected is true, said the Skiarchos. *We cannot harm you.*

"And why not?"

You know why not, or you are beginning to suspect. We can sense your doubt. Look at this place. All these magnificent things, statues and runes, and none of them have anything to do with you. You begin to see that you have more in common with us than with those people.

"*More in common*"? The thought was unsettling, but it had its own strange logic. Looking once more at the Skiarchos that stood in a slimy puddle right in front of him, he observed that it was still holding on to his forearm. He went to rip the tentacle away, to sever it if necessary... but then he stopped. The tentacle could not harm him, and it did not seem hostile. Perhaps it was nothing more than a bizarre Skiai handshake....

We know what you want.

His eyes narrowed, and now he did rip his arm free of the tentacle's grip. He went to massage his forearm before he realized that it did not hurt at all. "How can you know what I want when *I* don't even know what I want??" he demanded.

How can we not know? We know everything about you. For, in a sense, we are *you. Bound to you, now and always.*

He frowned. These beings truly would say anything in order to obtain what they wanted.

We have the answers that you desire.

The voice was quiet, but insistent. Even as he berated himself and called himself a fool, he could not help listening to it. "Then do you know why I am weak—always fatigued and ill?"

That is due to your own foolishness; you are on the wrong side in this war. Every time you or your underlings kill one of us, you wound your soul even more. If you cease to exist, then so do we; that is one reason why we cannot hurt you. However, the reverse may also be true.

"If that's the case," he shot back, "then it is quite strange that you are approaching me openly in this manner. If you definitely cannot harm me, and all you have to go on is a supposition that I will be hurt if I harm you, how can your actions be called anything other than suicide?"

You will not harm us once you know the truth. To do so would be suicide on your part. Instead, you will work together with us, as should have been done from the beginning. We desire to go to the place that you call the Lightning-Struck Mountain, to ascend it... and, as it happens, so do you.

"I do desire to go there," he said, "but my intentions are quite different from yours. Is that mountain your base?"

The Skiarchos shook with what might have been laughter. *No, of course not. We have no base in this world. However, we could have one, and it could be that mountain. All we need is your help. Search your true motives, and you will find them not very different from ours. Think about it, and then seek us out. You know where to find us.*

With that said, the Skiarchos vanished, leaving behind it a small cloud of purple darkness that soon dissipated. Only the slime and blood on the floor remained as evidence of the creature's having been there.

Psephos took a deep breath, then let it out slowly. Never before had he been so much on the defensive during a conversation. And it had happened while he was talking to a monster! He truly was going mad. It was this place, this Hall of Warriors; it was stripping him of his courage, his confidence.

He definitely needed fresh air now. Trying to ignore a

rapidly developing headache, he strode out of the Hall, and then out of the Palace with its stuffy, dank stone corridors. The grounds, however, brought irritations of their own, as Ambushers and a few Finishers were milling about in the night, Light-bringers casting spells on injured warriors who lay near one of the Palace's walls. Not in the mood to hear about what had happened, he quickly distanced himself so that no one would see him.

The Field of Victory was mercifully quiet, the night air cool, the sky dark—except for the area around the Lightning-Struck Mountain. As always, a yellowish light emanated, beaconlike, from within the thick clouds that surrounded the peak. For the light to be visible at this distance, whatever was creating it must be very bright indeed. Not for the first time, he wondered what was up there.

"Don't do this, Psephos," said a voice behind him.

Turning, he caught sight of a human figure, cloaked and hooded, that was approaching him through the gloom.

"Eudrakes," he said dryly. "How *wonderful* it is to see you."

"We can dispense with the small talk, Psephos," Eudrakes said sharply. "I know what you are thinking of doing, and you must not do it."

"Is that so?" Psephos shot back. "I thought your '*eyes could not see everything.*'" As he spoke, he could feel his own eyes narrowing. For some reason, the sight of Eudrakes irritated him much like the activity on the Palace grounds had.

"I have seen this, just as I have seen that during this night, three young warriors—including one of your bodyguards—will approach me and ask about an age-old secret. You may not be able to rely on Khalkeonos anymore."

"Thank you for the warning," Psephos said shortly. "Now, leave me alone."

Eudrakes shook his hooded head. "I will not—until I have

said what I came to say. I cannot impress upon you enough the magnitude of the deed that you are considering. Do not betray your people."

"But *are* they my people?" Psephos asked.

"Ah, that's what it is," Eudrakes said, nodding sagely. "You are insecure, and you want answers. Well, I am now at liberty to give you those answers. I can tell you what you want to know."

"Can you? On whose authority?"

"On the authority of my rulers and the rulers of this world," said Eudrakes.

"The Ouranothen, then."

"No; I speak rather of the elemental spirits. The spirits of earth, the spirits of '*Water, Wind, and Fire*' as the old oath says. They are this world's only divine power, and though absent, they are very much aware of what is going on. Observe."

Reaching up, he pulled his hood down and took a step closer to Psephos. The bright light source atop the Lightning-Struck Mountain provided faint illumination, enough for Psephos to see that Eudrakes had a normal human face, if pale for lack of exposure to the sun... but his eyes were anything but normal. In the place of round irises and pupils, he had what looked like twin runes. As Psephos watched, those runes changed hue, cycled slowly among four colors: green, blue, white, red.

Psephos recoiled in shock and revulsion, but Eudrakes appeared unfazed as he kept talking. "I am their vessel. They see what I see, and in return, they tell me some of what they see."

"Hence, your prophetic powers."

"Yes," said Eudrakes, stepping backward and putting his hood up once more. "They come from the elemental spirits. Ironic, isn't it—Aktinos depends on knowledge from a source which its leaders do not know exists."

"Then what of the Ouranothen?" Psephos inquired, and it was difficult to keep suspicion from creeping into his voice.

"Ah, yes, the Ouranothen. Fascinating figures. They did exist, but not in the way you think. Look—if you can bear to set your eyes on your wrathful deities..."

He fell silent, and a moment later, twin beams of bluish-white light shot out from beneath his hood and struck the ground. This happened twice, and based on the ghostlike figures that appeared where the beams struck, three facts became clear. First, that the Ouranothen were—or *had* been—real; second, that they were mortal; and third, that they were not at all terrifying.

Four women: three quite young and clad in robes, the fourth somewhat older and in a plain outfit that had an almost military flair.

For ordinary people to be built up as gods and feared by a warrior society of no little strength... The thought left Psephos feeling oddly sickened. He swayed on his feet and could not prevent his non-axe-holding hand from going to the area of his queasy stomach.

"Such is the way of myth, Psephos," Eudrakes said wisely, nodding toward the four semi-transparent figures that stood in a cluster, apparently talking and laughing silently with one another. "Always twisted and distorted, but always with a grain of truth at the core. If you knew these individuals and their history as I do, you would understand why later generations might have feared their retribution. But now is not the time to discuss them." He waved his hand, and the four figures vanished. "This conversation is about you."

"About me," Psephos echoed, disgusted, and turned away to study a portion of the distant mountain range. "To talk about me, you had to inform me that my entire belief system is based on a lie?"

"Not a lie," Eudrakes objected. "As I said, every legend contains some small basis in truth, and this particular one has several. Those who could rightfully be called 'Ouranothen' did exist, and in fact still *do* exist; however, in the passing down of legends, they were conflated and eventually confused with the four women I just showed you. I am not surprised that this occurred, for the four women were extremely important in determining what happened next. And those events will finally reveal to you what you most want to know—the origins of the warrior caste and your status within it."

He did very much want to know that, so he turned back around to face Eudrakes. "Very well. Proceed."

"I told you a moment ago," Eudrakes began, "that the elemental spirits are gone from the world. That is true, but it was not always the case. In the time that we are discussing, the spirits dwelled quite close by and watched actively over their magic. It was a time of peace, but not for long, as the spirits fought amongst themselves. There was a war, a reconciliation, and then another war. The second war came about despite the efforts of several disparate human factions to prevent it, and it was utterly devastating to all sides. Humans, it seemed, were simply incapable of living in peace even when they professed a wish to, and perhaps the spirits recognized that their own bad influence was partly to blame. In their disgust at what was happening, they sundered the world and then departed."

"'*Sundered the world and departed,*'" Psephos repeated.

"Yes. Sundered it, broke it, forced it to submit to a new order—use whatever word or phrase you wish. They were trying to put an end to conflict, and they mostly succeeded; as you know, current society does not see humans fighting and killing humans, though that has more to do with the early Aktinans' moral caliber than anything else. Before the spirits left, however, they gave the people something of their power as a sign of their continuing goodwill. If humans showed themselves worthy, then perhaps the spirits would return. They made this power, which you know as the Aktinan magic of light, to be self-sustaining, and its inner nature resembles that of the old magic, stripped of its elemental quality. The source, the essence, of that power is up there." He pointed toward the shining peak of the Lightning-Struck Mountain.

"Of course," he continued, "someone was needed to protect this power from evildoers. The people of this new world of Andikha could not be trusted to carry out this task, since they were not really warriors in any sense of the word; and were they not the same people who had gone to war twice in recent times? To solve this problem, the spirits turned to a military organization, a fleet, with which they had previously crossed paths. The name of this fleet lies beyond my powers of sight, but in its day it had immense influence and unbelievable technology, and its warriors lived and traveled among the stars. One day, when some of the highest-ranking pilots were flying their spacecraft near this world, the spirits possessed them and induced them to crash there." Again, he pointed toward the Lightning-Struck Mountain. "These people quite literally came '*from the firmament*,' as is said in the myth. The spirits wiped their memories clean so that they remembered nothing of their past save that they were warriors. They received the magical Essence from the spirits, built a temple to house it, and then set about protecting it."

"And they became our warrior caste," Psephos concluded. "'*Desire fame among the stars*,' as our ritual text says—*we* are the Ouranothen."

"Not quite," said Eudrakes, folding his arms placidly. "The others are—Eudianax and Enedra and Ateles and your Elites and the rest of the Aktinan warriors. I am not, and you are not. I already told you what I am, and as for you... not even the spirits are quite sure what you are."

That last remark was enough to send chills down Psephos' spine, but he let it go for the moment. They were closing in on what he most wanted to know. "So, I would have been rejected if I had taken the test in the Hall of Warriors."

"Oh, yes, certainly; that test has a secret that actually is quite simple. When a candidate kneels at the center of that rune, the spell checks the person's background. Native Andikhans, remember, cannot be trusted to fight a war. Accordingly, any person who is to be considered for a place among the warriors must be at least partially descended from those foreign pilots who crashed on the mountain. The more foreign blood flows through a candidate's veins, the higher he or she can rise in rank. There is probably not one of your Elites who has a drop of native blood."

"Then Khalkeonos...?"

"He passed his test because of his foreign heritage. By contrast, the girl called Keraunia—despite her demonstrated skill in wielding weapons—failed because she is full-blood Andikhan. Great warriors are not made, Psephos. They are *born.*"

"Ingenious," said Psephos, twisting his wrist so that the blade of his axe moved and sparkled in the distant light. "That is a foolproof way of ensuring the purity of the bloodline."

Eudrakes nodded. "Exactly. At its core, it is a reflection of an old prejudice concerning who could and could not fight, but it plays the additional role of keeping the castes separate, preserving the current division of labor, and so forth."

"Then why grant loopholes to certain people?" Psephos demanded suddenly, and there was something dangerous in his voice. "I am under no illusions; I am quite aware that I should not be filling the post of Elite Leader. Am I being manipulated?"

"I wouldn't call it '*manipulated*,'" said Eudrakes. "As you are no doubt aware, I arranged for you to receive the promotion that elevated you to your present position. The job, by all rights, should have gone to your rival there—the Finisher, Ateles. He was next in line for it, and his heritage is immaculate. If he hates you for superseding him, he is more than justified in doing so."

"I rather think he should hate *you*," retorted Psephos. "After all, are you not the one who arbitrarily gave me the job without saying why I was the better choice?"

"Not '*arbitrarily*,'" Eudrakes answered calmly. "There is a reason for all of my actions, and for this one most of all. I bypassed the usual warrior screening system and installed you as Elite Leader because, quite simply, it had to be done. Whether you realize it or not, Psephos, you are extremely important in this war. You have it in your power to stop it; perhaps you are the only one who *can* stop it. Hence, I gave you this job in order that you might have the opportunity to act on that potential."

"So, someone who lacks the true 'warrior's spirit' has the ability to do what the real warriors have been trying and failing to do for years," Psephos said skeptically.

"Yes, you might say that," Eudrakes agreed. "But now you know that the concept of '*the warrior's spirit*' is a historical artifact that has its roots in prejudice. It should by no means be interpreted as maligning your fighting skill or potential."

Psephos paused a moment to consider this information, but before he could speak, Eudrakes went on: "Perhaps you don't believe it; I myself probably would not believe it were I in your place. But I have seen it, and I am as confident in it as I have been in any of my predictions. It is your fate, your destiny. Somehow, you can put an end to this war."

"And if I choose not to?"

"That is a very real possibility," Eudrakes conceded. "And it is why I have come and told you of these things—things which have been kept secret from the other Aktinans, and with good reason. It was my hope that, once you had learned the truth, you would use the information to come to the right decision. Please, Psephos. Do not turn your back on your loyalties. Do not deny your destiny."

Without waiting for a reply, he turned around and walked away, his cloaked figure seeming to melt into the darkness of the barren Field and the mountains above.

Now left alone, Psephos stood where he was and pondered Eudrakes' words. His destiny. Could he really be *"important"* to the war effort? Apparently so, for in the early part of this night, he had been approached by both sides—the people of light and the people of darkness. Each side wanted him to help its cause, but did he truly belong with either one?

And behind these confused thoughts lurked the dream that had awakened him and brought him out of the Elite barracks in the first place. It haunted him, and he could not help thinking that it was a significant piece of the puzzle.

After a time, he began to pace back and forth as he thought, his hand gripping his axe's haft more tightly than ever. Even as he walked, however, his gaze lingered on the peak of the Lightning-Struck Mountain—the place that was central to the war, that perhaps was the cause of it all. He stared at it for a long while, and then abruptly looked away.

The light hurt his eyes.

CHAPTER SEVEN
MIDNIGHT

KHRUSAOROS WAS IN the middle of a very pleasant dream when he found his shoulder being shaken roughly. "Wake up!" snapped a voice somewhere above him.

Thoughts of promotions and war-winning tactics and a new order of warriors flew out of his mind, and he blearily opened his eyes to see the familiar, if dark, backdrop of the barracks' common area. Night still ruled the sky outside, as the basement room's few small, high-up windows revealed; it could be no later than midnight. Far too early for the Elites to begin their daily duties. "What... is it?"

"Awaken the rest of the squad, then report to me outside the Palace," the voice commanded—its stern, yet not overly harsh quality revealing it to be Psephos'.

"Skiai... attack, sir?"

"No, and there is no cause for alarm. I will explain when I see you and the others. Make haste."

Still fighting against drowsiness, Khrusaoros sat up and cast his eyes around the barracks. Psephos stood over him, battle-axe in hand; this could mean that combat was imminent—or not, since he carried the axe with him wherever he went. In all other areas of the room, Elites lay deep in slumber. They all seemed to be present...

No. One was missing.

"Where... is Khalkeonos?" he asked dimly, fumbling around for his sword and scabbard and strapping the arrangement into place on his back.

Psephos had been heading for the exit to the Palace's hallways, but now he stopped and turned around. "...Not here. Don't worry about him."

"Don't *worry*??" Khrusaoros repeated, indignant and now fully awake. "Sir, if something's happened—"

"Your brother is fine," Psephos interrupted. "I sent him away to run an errand for me, and he will meet up with us afterward. *Now*, Khrusaoros. I expect to see you and the others outside the Palace grounds within minutes."

"Right away, sir," Khrusaoros muttered, but Psephos was already gone. And he was not of the patient sort. It would not be a good idea to keep him waiting.

Rising to his feet, Khrusaoros went around the room and woke up the other Elites one by one. A few of them grumbled about having their sleep interrupted at such an early hour, but most were excited by the prospect of another battle. Fighting truly was in their blood, it seemed.

Well, it would have to be, he reasoned, *or they would not have risen so high in rank.*

Thanks to the unusual time of night, there was no one around as the Elites headed through the Palace's torchlit corridors. It did not take long for them to reach the huge golden double doors at the entrance, and then they had trooped past the outer wall and onto the Field of Victory.

Within moments, a tall figure emerged from the darkness and came up to meet them. "Excellent," said Psephos' voice. "I see that you are all here."

"What are your orders, sir?" asked one of the lower-ranking Elites.

When the squad members' eyes had adjusted to the nighttime gloom, they could see that their commander was smiling eerily. "To put an end to this war," he said. "Tonight."

At this, there was a great deal of muttering among the Elites as they tried to figure out what he meant. Glances were exchanged, eyebrows were raised, but no one dared raise an objection.

"I have lately received intelligence," Psephos went on, "that concerns the Lightning-Struck Mountain: the very place that the Light-bringers were too cowardly to investigate. It seems, however, that their cowardice was *not* misguided—for the peak of that mountain is, in fact, the base and the headquarters of the Skiai."

More muttering ensued at this pronouncement, but Khrusaoros did not take part in it. He frowned at the relevant mountain's peak, with its swirling cloud and brilliant yellowish glow. "Are you certain, Lord Psephos? The light emanating from there is extremely bright. Surely it would blind the Skiai?"

"That is what they want you to think," Psephos replied. "Although they prefer darkness, they can tolerate light if necessary; that is why they have been able to attack us during the daytime. They assumed we would never think to check out the place that is most antithetical to what they stand for, and until today, they were right.

"What we are going to do, Elites, is scale the mountain. Then, once we have arrived at the peak, we will launch a surprise assault on the Skiai base. The path to our destination will be difficult but not impossible, for we will have guidance."

So saying, he took a few steps to one side, and his soldiers saw—behind the spot where he had been standing, arrayed in perfect battle formation—an entire troop of Skiai.

"Sir!" gasped an unknown Elite, but the others merely gaped in silence. The shadow creatures stood placidly enough, each one festering in its own puddle of slime, yet every Aktinan—including Khrusaoros, who had been wounded only the previous morning—knew all too well the destruction their kind could wreak. Some members of this slimy squad even held in their front tentacles what looked like small bows, miniature mockeries of the larger weapons used by the Ambushers.

"These brave Skiai have graciously agreed to assist us in this task," Psephos said, answering everyone's unspoken question. "In so doing, they will be betraying their own cause. They want this war to end no less than we do; indeed, their need for peace is even more urgent than ours, for we have been slaughtering their people by the hundreds. They have sworn that, when the battle is over, they and any others who choose to surrender will return where they came from and leave Aktinos alone."

Khrusaoros watched the diminutive monsters twitch and fidget in their formation that was so similar to Aktinan Elite formations, and he felt repulsed... even nauseated. "An alliance with some of the Skiai," he mused. "This is a major decision that could have far-reaching effects; has it been cleared with Lord Eudianax?"

"There will be no need for that, Khrusaoros," Psephos replied in a flat, but threatening voice. "Eudianax will find out soon enough... and won't he be surprised to learn who saved this realm."

Khrusaoros sighed; Psephos' tone was a warning not to argue further, much stronger than any stated threat could ever be. "Yes, sir," he said sullenly. "Do you plan to accompany us up the mountain?"

Psephos blinked, momentarily startled out of his resolve. "Why would I not?"

"Once or twice in the past," said Khrusaoros, "you have put me in charge and stayed behind when our squad was assigned extensive or exhausting reconnaiss—" But one glare from his leader silenced him.

"I wish to be there when the war reaches its end," Psephos said coolly. "Now, no more delays. We march."

Except for soft clinking and squelching sounds, a deep quiet reigned as the Elites set out for the Lightning-Struck Mountain, the Skiai archers—for so Khrusaoros supposed they were—in the lead. The shadowy shapes of civilians' homes and solitary dead trees crept by in the distance, all as still as the night itself; the only real hazard was the rising ground at the back of the plain. Then, when a trail emerged from the shadows at the base of one of the lesser, nearer members of the mountain range, Psephos called a halt.

"From this point on, the Skiai will occupy the middle of the formation," he commanded. "I want the tallest of you Elites in front of or beside them. The rest of you, form a protective half-circle at the rear."

Khrusaoros frowned. "I don't understand—we're concealing the Skiai from *their own people* at the top of the mountain? And I thought they were our guides, to go in front and help us scale the slope."

Psephos rounded on him in what was, for the Elite Leader, a rare display of outright anger. "*Silence!*" he snapped. "It is not for you to question your orders or your commander."

But Khrusaoros would not be deterred. Some of the things that Khalkeonos had said to him the previous afternoon were replaying in his mind, and he began to wonder, perhaps belatedly, if his brother had been right. "Khalkeonos isn't coming, is he," he stated; it was not a question. "There was no '*errand.*'"

Psephos said nothing.

"Please, sir!" Khrusaoros persisted, crossing his arms and standing his ground near the base of the trail. "I will follow your every command—as I have from the beginning of my time as an Elite—if you just tell me: *is my brother dead?*"

"I don't know," Psephos said flatly. "And, frankly, I don't

care. You had best not question me further, or *you* will be the one dead." As he spoke, the hand that held his battle-axe twitched: a tiny motion, but a clear indication that he meant what he said.

Khrusaoros reluctantly subsided and uncrossed his arms, but he could not shake a sudden feeling of foreboding. Something was very, very wrong.

"Now," the Elite Leader continued, turning around again to face the rest of the squad, "form up like I told you to and follow me up the trail."

His warriors obeyed with hardly a word, and slowly they began the treacherous climb.

✳✳✳

THE PALACE OF LIGHT

Far from the Mountains of Air, Makheteon had no idea that his brother was concerned for him, and if he had known, that knowledge would not have meant much—at least on this night, at this hour. For whenever he started to reflect on something, he found that it paled in comparison to his current task.

He darted through the Palace's halls at near-top speed, pausing only long enough to regain his bearings or look out for human figures. Anyone who saw where he was headed would have to be killed; he accepted that fact calmly. But no one was in sight as he rounded a corner and...

What felt like a wall of chill air hit him, and he skidded to a halt, looked around in confusion. The nearly empty hallway in front of him—bare of tapestries, sporting only a few actively burning torch-flames—did not match his expectations. Nor did the single, dilapidated door that stood between two inactive torch-holders near the corridor's end, closed and silent and half in shadow as always.

He shook himself, though the motion resembled a shiver more than anything else. If he had ended up in the Cold Corridor—this passage that Aktinans had shunned for generations—then he must have taken several wrong turns after leaving the large, common-access library where he had spent the last few hours. Fighting to calm his mind, his eyes fixed on the distant door, he backpedaled a few steps before turning and stumbling back the way he had come.

Thereafter, he exerted a conscious effort to slow his pace; he stopped at every intersection of hallways to reevaluate his position. And soon the brightly lit, heavily tapestry-laden walls announced that he had entered the one wing of the Palace which was unequivocally forbidden to people of his rank: the living quarters of the ruling family, squad of Protectors, and high-ranking advisers.

Much of his evening had been spent conducting unsuccessful research on what Keraunia had said, and he had eventually decided to take the Essence of Fire from Eudrakes' rooms without his knowledge. The secrecy surrounding the four Essences—which included their omission from every Aktinan book—meant that there was someone very powerful who wanted to keep the elemental magic under wraps. Eudrakes would probably not take kindly to a warrior's asking him outright; hence, the need for stealth.

Even if this approach was highly risky and not very promising.

The High Adviser's quarters were just ahead; Makheteon shifted his gait to a near-tiptoe as he examined the shining golden door. No torchlight was emanating from around or under it; the room beyond was dark and, hopefully, unoccupied. Just to be sure, he knelt down to peer through the crack between the door and the floor, pressed his ear against the latter to listen for sounds of movement—

Footsteps assaulted his hearing—not from beyond the

door, but farther up this rulers-only hall. He froze, his heart hammering in his chest, then stood up and dove for the nearest tapestry. The cloth's long yellowy fringe reached down to the floor: barely enough to conceal his feet as he tried to stand perfectly still.

No sooner had he hidden himself, sandwiched between the tapestry and the wall, than a vague shadow appeared on the other side of the thinnish cloth: the outline of a tall, armor-clad person. The figure appeared to be in something of a pensive mood, as it walked slowly with its head down, and sometimes it would stop altogether and stand motionless, looking at the floor. One of these pauses came when the figure was right in front of Makheteon's hiding place, and he did not dare to twitch or even breathe. He could not tell who it was, nor did he care at all, but one fact struck him as odd: the figure did not seem to be carrying a weapon.

At last, the figure passed out of sight, and its ponderous footsteps soon receded into silence. Immediately, Makheteon pushed the tapestry aside and made a dash for the door. Wrenching it open, he darted inside and then slammed it shut behind himself. The next few moments saw him leaning against it, trying to catch his breath and calm his racing heart.

That had been close—too close. Perhaps he could have ambushed the unknown figure as it passed; however, a light spell cast in self-defense could have struck him dead before he had taken two steps, and he needed to be alive to finish Keraunia's mission. It was better this way... risk of detection or no risk of detection.

Once he felt calm enough, he stepped away from the door and took his first look around the small, dark antechamber in which he found himself. The darkness being too deep for him to see much, he drew a quick rune to create a light source, which projected a faint yellow-white beam out of one of his gauntleted hands. Not much, but it and the equally faint rune were enough to serve their purpose.

There was no time to lose. Swiftly he went around the antechamber, examining every corner and every nook for the Elemental Essence. Though small, the room contained a great deal of furniture, which looked like it had not been moved or used in quite some time. As he turned cushions over with one hand and opened up desks, clouds of dust flew into the air, causing him to sneeze.

Quite likely, Eudrakes had never spent significant amounts of time here. This was not surprising, as there was always something going on that required his attention and input. How could the all-seeing eyes see all that they saw if they were not there to see it? The result, however, was that Makheteon had to wade through not only dust, but also grime and cobwebs as he conducted his search. The experience was enough to make him appreciate the servants who were under standing orders to clean his own living space, the Elites' barracks... but perhaps Eudrakes himself valued secrecy over cleanliness.

One corner of an inner chamber was covered in thick cobwebs that ran about two and a half feet up the wall, their dark hue indicating that something was concealed behind them. At once, Makheteon sank the fingers of his free hand into them to tear them apart, even as an unexpected breeze swept through the room and ruffled his hair—

"You are late."

He just about jumped out of his skin at that. Whirling around, he peered through the doorway behind him and saw the brown-cloaked figure of Eudrakes, standing in the middle of the antechamber. When and how had he come in? No sound of the outer door's opening had signaled his arrival—but there he was.

In one hand, he held the red-gleaming Essence of Fire.

"What took you so long?" he asked, his tone so calm and

casual that he might have been discussing the large bricks on the walls. "Your two friends came here hours ago. Are you experiencing doubt, Makheteon?"

"That... isn't... my name," he stammered without thinking. The sight of the Essence had rooted him to the spot so that he would not have considered running for it, even if Eudrakes had not been blocking his only escape route. "Y-You know I... w-was... promot—"

Eudrakes gave a slight shrug. "I am using the name that you prefer. I know that you prefer it, just as I know why you have invaded my quarters tonight. You want this." He lifted the Essence of Fire, held it in Makheteon's direct line of sight.

Nodding in what he hoped was brave defiance, the young Elite stepped through the doorway back into the antechamber. "Yes, I want it. Am I going to have to fight you for it?"

Eudrakes chuckled, and his heavy hood trembled. "Don't be crude; this world has moved far beyond such primitive means of resolving conflict. Was that not the gods' goal all along?"

"I don't know what the gods have to do with anything," Makheteon shot back, "but I *do* know that I need the Essence of Fire. If we are not going to fight, then please just give the artifact to me."

"I could," Eudrakes conceded, "but are you sure you need it? Is this the right thing to do? My eyes see much, and they recognize your primary motives in these events. You are doing this not because you truly believe it will save your realm, but because of the girl, Keraunia."

Makheteon gave a start, but quickly gathered himself again. "Maybe so," he said defensively, "but there's something in what she says. Why do you think the other three agreed to the plan?"

"It is just what you thought at first," Eudrakes answered. "They think Keraunia is mad, and they hope that by playing along with her scheme, they will prove her wrong. You have good instincts. Perhaps you should listen to them more often."

"But—you defended her in the council!" Makheteon exclaimed. "Why are you speaking against her now?"

"Of course I defended her," Eudrakes said easily. "I am obliged to defend a fellow servant of the elemental spirits."

"Then, by all logic, you should be cheering for her now."

Eudrakes shrugged again. "I do not take sides in these struggles. I have been around longer than you can imagine, and in that time I have seen a great many changes of leadership; one more, if it comes to that, would not make much of a difference to me. Rather, my task is to advise *all* sides to the best of my ability—in the name of my masters, the elemental spirits, who desire to see and influence the events taking place in this world. If I give people information, I receive information, which in its turn is passed on to the spirits. In this case, I am charged with making sure you know exactly what you are getting yourself into with this quest."

"I already know that," Makheteon said, clenching his non-spell-holding hand into an impatient fist. "I am to retrieve the Essence of Fire and then travel to the Hall of Warriors, where I will join my three allies in casting a spell to summon the elemental spirits and revive their power and magic. Then, we will use the elemental magic as a sort of secret weapon against the Skiai."

"Yes, but that is only the half of it," said Eudrakes. "As the one who holds the Essence of Fire, you will be most instrumental in the endeavor—the leader, if you will. Without you, the others cannot hope to succeed."

Makheteon frowned, and his fist unclenched itself. Keraunia had never mentioned anything about that.

"Far away," Eudrakes continued, in the distant tone of a man talking to himself, "in a place whose technology would be impossibly foreign to you, there once was a warrior society that was not unlike your own. A great space fleet. It was divided into four squadrons, each with its own distinctive color, and red was the color of highest rank. For generations now, that society's fate has been intertwined with that of this one, and its influence can be seen everywhere.

"Take, for instance, this spell that the Keraunia girl wants you to cast. There is no connection between the fire magic and authority; rather, the link is with this ancient fleet's most elite squadron—the very same group from whose members you are descended, Makheteon. Before the elemental spirits departed the world, they reorganized it on the model of that faraway society to better protect that which must be protected, or to ensure that someone outside the elite caste and unfamiliar with the old structures would not be able to cause real harm. If all four magics were to be combined in a massive, large-scale spell, they would need direction from some source; therefore, the spirits arranged things so that the power would be channeled through the 'red' magic, the fire magic. If you go through with this mission, Makheteon, you will direct everything. The spell will be yours, and the responsibility for any ensuing death and destruction will likewise be yours."

Makheteon's head was spinning. What was with these elemental spirits—did they worship this other society and loathe their own people? But there was no time to think deeply about that.

"Whatever," he snapped, his frown now a full-fledged scowl. "Are you going to give me the Essence, or not?" This was taking too long; perhaps he should simply blast Eudrakes with a light spell and be done with it...

But Eudrakes appeared to chuckle again. "I don't recommend attacking me, for I possess more power than you can comprehend. However, I have fulfilled my duty in these events; I have passed along all necessary information and will give you your Essence of Fire—with a warning. Not even the spirits can predict what will happen next. Your decision, your actions, may have unforeseen consequences."

This said, he walked forward and placed the sphere onto a nearby table. Then, retreating into an area that Makheteon's light source could not reach, he appeared to become one with the shadows.

Shaking off a sudden chill, Makheteon turned away and attempted to collect himself. That man, if man he was and not one of those spirit things, was more than creepy. But he was inconsequential, as were whatever machinations he was devising. All that mattered now was Keraunia's mission... and Keraunia herself, of course. She had shown great faith in him by assigning him the most important role in the task. Why had she not mentioned anything about it?

Finally, when his thoughts had settled down somewhat, he turned back around and walked to the table on which the Essence of Fire sat. Exactly like the Essence of Water except for the fact that the light swirling within the sphere was in countless shades of red, it looked almost meek there on the table—yet when he picked it up, he saw that it was anything but. The red light swirled manically, like the heart of a raging inferno.

This magic was not like the serene water magic; it was chaotic, unpredictable, and powerful. It was the perfect magic for the one who would lead the spellcasting. And its power was already filling him, imbuing his spells with the qualities of fire. As this happened, his magical light source flickered and faded and was replaced by a floating object that looked like a torch. The corresponding rune quickly changed from weak yellow-white to a strong, fiery red, and the magical torch with its brilliant red flames beat back the shadows in all corners of the room.

This was the magic that would turn darkness into light.

On this night, Aktinos would be saved.

***

AKTINOS, REALM OF LIGHT
HOUSE OF KERAUNIA

Just in front of the simple stone structure whose basement contained the remnants of a sacred Elemental Shrine, Keraunia paced and fretted. While her helpers had been away retrieving the remaining Essences, she had been reduced to waiting in a state of dependence, and she did not like it one bit. They should have been in position by now.

Aglaë was there—the Ambusher's night-shrouded form had walked right past her, the Essence of Water held proudly in both hands, and had even asked permission to enter the house—but there was no sign of the others. Had they found their Essences, their runes? She needed to see them and make sure, but most urgent was her need to speak to Makheteon; the mission would be lost without him.

If only she had told him the truth about the fire magic right away, instead of worrying about how the other warriors would react. If only she had not been so arrogant as to assume that he would return to see her that evening.

Making matters even worse for her was the fact that she still was not certain that what she was doing was right. Was it what they would want? She did not know, for she had not been able to commune with them. The elemental spirits did not speak in language as humans did; their communication would be rather indirect even if they were not impossibly far away, beyond the range of all but the strongest magic. But surely they would appreciate it, this thing that she was doing for them. This world had gone astray—its old structures turned upside-down, its rulers replaced by those who lacked the true magic—and it was time to put things right again. The elemental spirits would be enthroned again, the Aktinan impostors and their warrior culture and their newcomer gods cast down. *"Runes ruin the rulers."* The leading Aktinans had yet to learn the true meaning of that sentence.

And of course, when it came to the Aktinans, there was another factor that only added to her unease now: namely, the strange conversation she had had with that *other* Ambusher woman shortly before Makheteon had appeared at this very spot. No doubt motivated to come by the story of the failed warrior test earlier in the day, the woman had walked up to her where she sat on the top step, looked down at her with a piercing gaze, and asked: *"You have a great secret, don't you?"*

Even as tight-lipped as Keraunia had learned to be when discussing her family's task and legacy, she had ended up making some remark that disparaged the Ouranothen: not the safest move to make, but her mood had been exceedingly bad, and at least her interlocutor had appeared to share her skepticism. The woman had closed the conversation with a comment along the lines of *"whatever you're planning, it's a good idea"*—though Keraunia had not believed it for a second, as the Ambusher's eyes had carried an insincere gleam and her mouth had twisted into a tiny sardonic grin before she finally walked away.

Whatever the woman's feelings and motivations, however, Keraunia had found it highly unnerving to hear her ideas praised by an Aktinan warrior. Perhaps Eudianax had sent the woman to scout her out as a possible threat to the realm and/or mislead her about Aktinos' stance on the issues at hand—an idea that could receive support from the fact that the woman had not asked her what she was planning, so much as what *stage* her plans were at.

Now was not a time to take chances, and any possibility of awareness or interference on the Aktinan side was a strong temptation to abort the mission altogether. Could she wait until all the scrutiny had died down?

No—she shook herself as she continued pacing—this was pressing and necessary. It was for the spirits, those all-important, all-powerful entities, and no one else mattered... yet even so, it was regrettable that she had to do this to Makheteon. Rather handsome and exceptionally kind for an Aktinan, he had obviously been quite charmed by her, despite the lack of an evening visit—but his allegiance to Eudianax and the realm made him her enemy. And betraying him would prove to be worth it in the end.

Although her attempts to communicate directly with her divinities had failed, she had recently come to feel a faint presence akin to the spirits' auras that were told of in the old stories. The presence, though elemental in nature and half-hidden in the mists of time and space, was slightly stronger when the Skiai were attacking Aktinos, and she knew it was encouraging her and all other enemies of the "warriors." The spirits could see what was going on—of that she was certain— and they wanted to witness the end of the Aktinans and their usurper Ouranothen. She would help them with that goal by paving the way for their return from exile, and they would reward her for it. There would be other young men for her: residents of the reborn Region of Air.

All things considered, then, it was not worth it to abort the mission for Makheteon or anyone else—and even if she wanted to find someone to take his place, she could not. She had allotted the fire magic to him for a reason: he was the only one she could trust...

Sudden movement caught her eye, and she paused in her pacing. Someone was passing by within a mile of this residential area. Could it be Selaä and Ganaï, moving into position at last?

Cautiously she crept closer, tried to peer between the intervening buildings to identify the shadowy figures. There was a line of armor-clad warriors—too numerous to be her helpers—with a very tall, somehow familiar man in the lead. And very soon, when the leader figure crossed into a more open area, the light from the tallest mountain's peak glinted off something metal that he was carrying. A huge battle-axe.

So... the Elites.

And they were heading straight for the mountain.

By Water, Wind, and Fire—by the old, vanished world order itself! Never in all her planning, all her devising, had she expected that the Aktinans would do something like this. They seemed to fear that mountain, even went so far as to connect it to their deities, their Ouranothen. But now their highest-ranking squad was marching toward that area of the range, seemingly with every intention of beginning the long trek up to the peak. Already the group was near the edge of the plain, and showing no signs of changing direction.

Her heart pounding, she pondered what to do. No one must tamper with the Essence of Light, especially in these circumstances, or disaster could result. Therefore, regardless of the Elites' knowledge or plans, they had to be stopped. But she was only one person, and she did not even have full use of her magic....

Even as she watched, they began to ascend the lesser mountain that marked the beginning of the trail. She could see them clearly, and was sure that they could see her; her white clothing would stand out sharply in the darkness.

So, her cover was blown. Her only recourse now—for she could not distract her helpers from their all-important task— would be to seek help from the other leading Aktinans; and she did vaguely remember that Eudianax had forbidden his underlings from embarking on a mission of just this kind. He had to be warned—or not warned, but *told*.

In desperation, she took off for the Palace of Light.

CHAPTER EIGHT
EARLY HOURS

THE PALACE OF LIGHT
THE GREAT HALL

Entering the Great Hall, Lord Eudianax paused a moment and looked around. The sight of the immense, hallowed room usually filled him with powerful senses of majesty and duty, but this time it only added to his disquiet. The long walk he had taken through the Palace—after word came of the evening's skirmish on the grounds outside—had done nothing to clear his head.

As he passed the division leaders' table, he found Photizousa already seated there amid the Hall's gloom. "Greetings, my lord," she said pleasantly when she saw him. "I see that I arrived before you."

"Yes," he replied. "Your response to the summons was very quick indeed."

"The messenger who brought it said the matter was urgent, my lord; I saw no reason to delay. No doubt the others will be here before long, and I'll have a great deal to report about the recent battle...."

Eudianax nodded and walked away without another word. In truth, he wished the other division leaders would delay a little longer before coming. How could he conduct a council when he had no idea what he was going to say, command, or ask—requests for post-battle updates notwithstanding?

Upon reaching the raised platform on the far side of the room, he sat down on his royal throne. Its golden luster seemed a bit diminished, possibly because it was late night and no sunlight was seeping through the windows... or because the light of Aktinos was about to be swallowed up by the void of oblivion.

"A late-night meeting of the leaders?" said a deep voice right beside him, jarring him from his unpleasant thoughts. "What are you going to discuss with them, my lord?"

He heaved a sigh, but did not turn toward the voice. "Do you ever sleep, Eudrakes?" he asked dryly.

"No," Eudrakes answered bluntly. "I must be in all places at all times. How else would I be able to advise you?"

"Then offer me guidance now. I am disturbed by recent events, recent attitudes—including my own. Ever since the council this afternoon and the Skiai attack soon thereafter, I have feared for the future of Aktinos. We are losing control of the war... and perhaps losing control of ourselves."

"You did overreact a bit during that council, if I may say so, my lord," Eudrakes commented.

"Yes, so it would seem. But I am willing to make amends for it. I have summoned the division leaders here so that we may discuss matters in an open and free manner. It is time to take the war in a new direction. What do you recommend that we do?"

Eudrakes did not answer for a long moment. "An admirable sentiment... my lord," he said at last, slowly. "But what if you are already too late?"

In the next heartbeat, there was a commotion at the Hall's distant entrance, and a white-clad figure burst into the room with thundering footsteps: the young civilian, Keraunia.

"Treason, my lord Eudianax!" she screeched, dashing past the table where Photizousa sat and going down on her knees in front of the throne and raised platform. "They are betraying you! Heading for the Lightning-Struck Mountain—to scale it! You must send forces stop them all—"

"Listen to the girl," Eudrakes intoned from beside Eudianax.

"Very well," Eudianax assented. Leaning forward, he studied the kneeling girl, who was looking down and now trembling with fear. "Who is betraying me? Who is responsible for this? Answer me!"

Keraunia straightened up a bit, looked Eudianax in the eye. Her own eyes widened, but she did not say a word.

"Well, young woman?" Eudianax demanded, gripping the arms of his golden throne as a sign of his agitation. "Speak!!"

Now she gasped a little and opened her mouth—yet what came out was not words, but a thin trickle of blood. It dripped downward like water from a melting icicle, staining the front of her white tunic, as her eyes glazed over alarmingly. An instant later, she toppled forward, collapsed to the floor.

From her back protruded two purple-feathered arrows, one in the area of each lung.

In a flash, Eudianax was on his feet. "Is this your prophecy, Eudrakes??" he bellowed. "Is this what you foresaw, what you intended? Protectors, to me! Defend your lord!"

But no footsteps, no slight breeze, signaled movements of the invisible warriors. And then, Eudianax saw what he had not during his outburst of a moment before: at regular intervals around the room, where each of the Protectors had been stationed, welled a large pool of blood. Their spells of invisibility had remained intact even in death, as their comrade whose turn it was to hold the rune for those spells would be secreted away in the squad's barracks as always.

And this silent end had also befallen the Protectors' leader, who had been standing in the corner to Eudianax's right.

Panic consuming him, the Aktinan ruler surveyed the carnage of the Great Hall. Photizousa was still alive, to his relief; she had already drawn a rune to protect herself, and four human-high walls of yellow-white light surrounded her, followed her wherever she went. Meanwhile, Eudrakes had vanished.

Photizousa's glowing shield came closer, stopped at the fallen figure of Keraunia, and then the mage's hands emerged from behind one of the walls to examine the girl and the weapons that had felled her.

"The fletchings on these arrows are unfamiliar, my lord," the Light-bringer said presently, her voice echoing in the huge, empty-seeming room. "The arrows themselves are also smaller than those our Ambushers typically use, and there may be traces of Skiai slime here near the tail end. I think they may have been designed specially for use by a Skia archer."

"Which means that some of our people have allied with the Skiai," Eudianax concluded grimly, sitting back down on his throne. "You must go, Photizousa. Find the other leaders and put a stop to this. I will remain here; report back to me when you have information."

Photizousa made a noise of assent, and her brilliant shield distanced itself for a few steps before stopping again. "...You are unarmed, my lord," said the mage's voice, "and it would be unseemly to abandon that long-respected tradition of ours when an alternative is available. I will not leave you without defense."

With that, a shield similar to hers sprang up around her seated ruler. He could see through it, for shields were translucent to the people they protected. When Photizousa was gone, the second yellow-white rune she had drawn—left behind when she departed—was the Great Hall's only remaining light source.

✱✱✱

AKTINOS, REALM OF LIGHT
FIELD OF VICTORY

Photizousa sped as fast as her long robes would allow over the Field of Victory—which, she thought wryly, would now be more appropriately called the "Field of Slaughter."

Now that she was outside, she could see a possible reason why the other leaders had not responded to Eudianax's late-night summons: their squads, and even some of her own Light-bringers, were already in the fray, no doubt drawn there by the sudden arrival of the Skiai. It was a battle on a much larger scale than the brief clash early in the evening... and the Aktinans were not faring well in the deep darkness. The Skiai had made it some distance up the slope of a minor mountain and were using that advantage of height to rain arrows down, while non-archers would periodically descend the slope to finish off their wounded or trapped opponents—an absurd mockery of the Finishers' tactics, she thought.

Her duty bound her to save and care for those same wounded Aktinans, and she tended to as many of them as she could, but knew she could not become distracted from her main task. Eudianax had told her to "*put a stop to this*," and that meant ascending the mountain and confronting whoever was up there. To her astonishment, there seemed to be human figures among other Skiai ranks, which could be seen moving through a higher portion of the trail....

A flash of movement on her own level catching her eye, she turned to see the Skia archer that had felled Keraunia and probably the Protectors as well, making its squelching, skittering escape back toward its fellows on the mountain. A small bow was still clutched in one slimy tentacle, a similarly-sized quiver in another. Photizousa drew a quick attack rune, and a thin beam of light burned the Skia to a crisp.

That done, she quickened her pace. Her shield would protect her from enemy attacks, but she could not hope to avoid the battle's chaos for long, since her shield was extremely bright and the rune that powered it was floating along conspicuously beside her. She needed to get as far as possible before the hordes of Skiai combatants noticed her presence.

Right now, at least, luck was with her: she managed to leave the Aktinan plain and start up the slope of a different mountain without incident. But as she picked her way across the smaller range on her way to the main peak, she saw something that gave her pause: Enedra, covered in Skiai burns, lying among the path's many boulders with her wide eyes staring blankly at the dark sky above.

Swiftly, Photizousa bent down to check her fellow division leader's condition—even though she already knew what she would find. As she stood up again, she felt a wave of anger rising from the pit of her stomach, almost in the same manner as nausea. Enedra was so young—*too* young to suffer this fate. Though recently promoted, she had not had a chance to contribute to the overall war effort.

"You will be avenged," the Light-bringer promised her fallen friend.

With renewed vigor, and the anger still burning inside her, she set off again for her destination. After a time, her path joined up with the same one she had taken the previous afternoon—really less than one day ago?—and she worked her way to the other side of the enemy forces without detection.

She had just concealed herself behind a massive boulder when a group of enemy fighters came into view: a hideous alliance of humans and Skiai, gingerly making its way along a particularly dangerous portion of the trail. On one side, the mountain face acted as a sort of wall against which the humans could stabilize themselves and regain their balance; on the other was a steep, nearly vertical cliff that tumbled all the way down to the Valley of the Gods, far below Aktinos itself.

As the small army of enemies slowly came closer along the edge of this cliff, Photizousa observed that the human warriors' formation encircled that of the shorter Skiai as if to shield them from something; she could not guess what. Far more interestingly, the light emanating from the Lightning-Struck Mountain's peak—which was much brighter here, closer to its source—revealed the humans to be Elites: nearly the whole squad. And they were led by—

"Psephos Anolethros."

Photizousa jumped in startlement, as did several of the Elites. A quick look around revealed who had spoken: Ateles, who had suddenly planted himself in the middle of the path about ten feet ahead. In one hand he held his sword, from which Skiai blood dripped onto the ground. Blood was also splattered over his armor, in his unruly, short-cropped blond hair, and painted several diagonal streaks across his face. He looked grim, even more so than usual. And he had called Psephos by his full name, unshortened, with the added title included.

That, Photizousa thought, was the best indicator of his mental state at the moment.

"Ah, there you are, Finisher," Psephos said calmly. "I was wondering where you were while your fellow warriors were fighting the battle. It reassures me to learn that you may not be such a coward after all."

"Cut it, Psephos," Ateles snapped. "The time is gone for trading insults. You and I both know why I am here."

"*You* may know," said Psephos, "but I don't. Please explain—and take your time, if you wish. I have nothing else to do, as you are blocking my only path up the mountain."

His voice was dripping with sarcasm, but Ateles' reply maintained a deadly seriousness.

"I have never liked you, Psephos; you know this. And it was not merely the issue of the promotion that you stole from me. Never mind that you came in as an outsider and usurped my position, or that you lacked the qualities traditionally expected of an Elite Leader, or that your methods were unorthodox. Quite simply, I never liked you, never trusted you. But not even I ever thought you would do something like this. Why turn your back on your people, your realm? You were a loyal servant of Aktinos once, and you profited from that service; why leave that behind and ally with the forces of evil? Why defy the gods themselves by ascending to their dwelling, to which they have denied mortals access? I cannot understand this, even from you."

"Is that all?" Psephos asked. "Such questioning is pointless, and you know it. If you come up the mountain with me, you can learn the answers directly from the gods... or whatever they are."

Ateles shook his head firmly. "Never. I intend to stop you, and I will do so until my last breath. If I should stand here a thousand times over, and be faced with a thousand of these decisions, I would resist you every time. It is *over*, Psephos."

His expression was frightening now, almost dangerous. This was the expression which he would reportedly use to terrify disobedient soldiers into submission, which had been many a Skia's last sight. His battle tactics were legendary for their savagery, even their brutality, and Photizousa, as she watched him from an awkward side angle, could believe every tale that had been told about him. Though she was not the target of his present wrath, and though he had never been anything other than amicable to her in the past, she found herself cowering a little... inching back behind her boulder as if it could protect her.

Psephos, however, merely laughed. "Over? I think not. *Can you stop me? Would you dare spill human blood?* No, for your 'Ouranothen' have forbidden such acts. I think, Finisher, that you can consider yourself *finished.*"

With a sudden lunge forward, he swung his battle-axe in a wicked horizontal slice. The huge blade cut through Ateles' thin armor and opened a gaping wound in his side, from which blood poured. This knocked him off-balance—but Psephos' second stroke knocked him off the path altogether. Falling headlong down the cliff, he soon disappeared from sight. Long moments passed, turned into long minutes; there was no sound to announce that he had hit the ground far below.

At this, nausea rose once more within Photizousa, and she could not suppress a gasp. Meanwhile, the Elites were muttering among themselves and reaching for their weapons, on the verge of a riot—and no wonder, given that they had just seen a division leader, a man they had all respected, knocked aside like he was nothing more than an obnoxious insect. Things like this should never happen in Aktinos.

In a flash, it came to Photizousa to end this madness, to finish what Ateles had started and follow Eudianax's orders, and she raised her hand for an attack spell aimed at Psephos—

A red-stained silver blade flashed into her field of vision, to collide with the yellow-white rune that hovered beside her. It disintegrated along with her shield, her only means of defense. Crouched behind the boulder, her spellcasting process interrupted by her distraction, she looked up fearfully—and beheld Psephos, who had come closer in a split second and was now standing over her. In the odd lighting of the mountainside, his eyes appeared to glow with an unholy light. He looked strange... even inhuman, nightmarish.

This was a nightmare, she thought. Only a nightmare. Any minute now, she would wake up....

"...Photizousa," Psephos drawled, as calmly as ever. "How convenient—all the leaders showing up here at once."

"We're '*showing up here*' because we have to stop you," she snapped. "This—this is insanity! Allying with the enemy, killing your fellow leaders! What do you hope to accomplish?!"

He hesitated for a brief moment before answering, and she thought she saw the eerie light in his eyes diminish in intensity. "I have... no quarrel with you, Photizousa," he said at last. "With you, or with the majority of your people. But this must be done. You are Aktinans, the people of light, the people of bright things and warm things. I do not belong among you; indeed, I never did. You could not possibly understand."

She was preparing to reply, but he turned away before she could speak. "I have no time for this; we must go on. Elites, we continue the ascent. Skiai... take care of her."

That last sentence was all the warning she received as the Skiai, having come closer during the brief dialogue, swarmed over the boulder like a flood, or an avalanche. She fell back in panic, hands raised to shield her head—but to no avail. One Skia seized them so that she could not draw any runes; she screamed as the Skiai burns blackened her fingers and traveled up her wrists and arms.

But still they did not relent. More of them came, and then more, to submerge her in a purple sea of fur and fangs and ooze and tentacles. They did no direct violence, but this was not out of any sense of mercy; the burns were as effective as any attack would have been. Within seconds she felt like one giant burn, and before long, she could feel nothing at all.

Her last sight was Psephos and the Elites, continuing their march up the mountain. Not even Khrusaoros had turned to look back.

THE PALACE OF LIGHT
HALL OF WARRIORS

Right as Makheteon reached the bottom of the stairs to the deepest basement, a tremor and low rumbling seized the entire Palace, and he stumbled. Something was going on outside; even on this level he could hear shouts and screams and the clash of arms, smell the stench of slaughter... feel the dread of impending doom.

Another Skiai attack, no doubt. And that meant it was even more imperative that he finish his work quickly.

Having regained his footing, he walked down the Hall of Warriors as rapidly as he dared, lest he drop the Essence of Fire. Although the sphere was clutched tightly in both of his hands, he still did not feel safe—for he had found that he could not even look at it. Its swirling red light enthralled him, called out to him. Begged him to tap into its power. Apparently the fire spirits, far away though they were, wanted to see their magic used once more in the world after such a long silence.

Their time would come, he thought firmly, but not until the right moment. A distraction right now could spell disaster.

But upon reaching the end of the Hall, he hesitated and wavered, staring at the immense, dormant runic symbol that covered the floor just in front of him. What was he supposed to do? He knew what a summoning spell entailed, or thought he did, but first he had to tap into the rune's power and connect to his three allies via the magical network, and Keraunia had never mentioned how to do that....

Something red moved at the bottom of his field of view, and he looked down to see the sphere's light swirling some more, rearranging itself. Within seconds, it had formed a complex runic symbol that stared at him from beneath the sphere's glassy surface.

Cautiously he shifted the sphere to the crook of one elbow, held against his body, then raised his other hand and began to draw the rune that the red light was showing him. Its strokes appeared in a deep, vivid red—his magic had been aligned under fire ever since he had picked up the sphere in Eudrakes' quarters and the red torch had appeared. That spell had used only a minuscule amount of power; this one would use much more. And the spirits knew this. The red light was swirling again, and now it seemed pleased.

One by one, his rune's strokes continued to come together. It was an exact replica of the symbol at his feet, he now realized, but somehow he knew what that meant. This was an ancient spell, an age-old trick that the spirits were teaching him even as he drew the rune. It would allow him to harness the power of the huge rune so that, when he cast a spell, it would use all the magical strength that the huge rune possessed. And sure enough, when his symbol was complete, the one on the floor began to glow the same exact shade of red—and the same shade it had glowed during his test. The two glows pulsated in perfect sync with each other. The runes were connected; when he channeled his power through one, he channeled it through both.

When this was done, he sought the other three magics, and in his mind's eye there appeared a sort of void, black as deepest night. It was mighty, overpowering all other thoughts and images, but contained nothing except three tiny pinpoints of light: one blue, one green, one white. They were already in position, and waiting for him; they gave off a reflected aura of agitation... impatience.

But now he had arrived. Though he could not see his own red light, he knew that it was growing stronger, making itself known to the other lights and their wielders. A moment later, the other lights strengthened in turn and appeared to grow larger as they rushed toward him, to be subsumed under him and the fire magic. As Eudrakes had said, the spellcasting would be his. He would be wielding all four magics at once.

The other three elements were rushing into his mind and soul. With a feeling of confidence, even exhilaration, he began the spell.

CHAPTER NINE
PRE-DAWN

AKTINOS, REALM OF LIGHT
SLOPES OF THE LIGHTNING-STRUCK MOUNTAIN

Khrusaoros was no longer sure what to think.

Throughout his career as an Elite, he had been secure in his beliefs, confident that the Elite way was the right way. Yet ever since Psephos had awakened him back in the barracks and this latest mission had begun, the number of dreadful deeds that he had seen committed had shaken him to the core.

An alliance with the enemy. Photizousa and the other non-Elite leaders, slaughtered one by one; he was not certain that Enedra had suffered the same fate, for none of the Elites had been around to see it happen, but he assumed that she had, since she had not turned up to try to stop them. His brother, lost somewhere in Aktinos, perhaps dead as well. And now, this trip up to the forbidden realm of the gods. The night was well advanced by this point—dawn was no more than a couple of hours away—and he could not shake his sense that this dawn would look upon a completely new Aktinos.

As he and the others continued their somber march up the mountain trail, he tried to occupy his mind with something else, but no matter where he looked, the same feelings of heartache and dread came back. Far below him, the other divisions' defenses had broken, and the Skiai appeared to be overrunning the realm. Beside him, more of the Skiai—they truly were disgusting monsters, he thought—seemed to be doing their best, squelching imitation of a human warrior's march. It might have been his imagination, but he thought they looked a little taller, almost as if the journey up the mountain was strengthening them somehow.

Just ahead, Psephos strode along at the front of the formation: his fatigue evidently gone for the moment, perhaps out of excitement about whatever it was he was planning to do. And farther in the distance, at the mountain's peak—which was visible now, since the group had just broken through the surrounding cloud cover—something had come into view. It was a building, or it seemed to be one, but it was metallic and like no building Khrusaoros had ever seen....

Right as he made this observation, the distant building emitted a blindingly bright light—even stronger than the brilliant yellowish glow that emanated from the structure's interior. The Elites immediately halted in their tracks, shielding their eyes as the light shot toward them. When it had faded, they looked back, only to find an opposing group. An opposing army.

Khrusaoros felt wonder stealing over him as he gazed—or tried to gaze—at the beings that now blocked the path to the odd-looking building. They were tall, brilliant yellow-white, and ethereal, seemingly made from light itself; their large white wings flapped gently in the soft breeze of the mountaintop. They looked just as Photizousa had described the being that had visited her, their glows too strong to allow for direct scrutiny. And they stood in a very military, V-shaped formation.

For a long moment, these ethereal beings stood motionless, studying the Elites as the Elites were attempting to study them. Then, suddenly, the one at the front of the formation walked—or rather glided—forward a step. It said nothing aloud, but Khrusaoros could hear its voice in his head:

We are angels of light. What business do you have in coming to this place that is forbidden to all who do not walk in the light?

Khrusaoros could feel himself trembling at that; in the darkness of pre-dawn, the beings shone even more brightly than Photizousa had described. Though he was a powerful warrior, he knew that they could annihilate him with merely a thought. "I... beg forgiveness, Great Ones," he murmured. "I did not intend to be insolent."

We do not speak to you, young one, the being answered softly. *For you walk in the light. We speak to the one who leads you.*

Speaking to Psephos? Why not to the Skiai?

But before Khrusaoros could ponder this question, Psephos spoke up. "I do not need to answer to you," he snapped. "Stand aside, and we will not harm you or your kind."

You are not like the others, the being went on—to Psephos only, but Khrusaoros could sense every word, and the looks of shock on the other Elites' faces revealed that they could as well. *Your power is not our power; your magic is not our magic. We know not who or what you are. And yet, your soul cries out in agony. We pity you. If you stand down now, we will allow you to return to the realm below.*

"I don't need your pity," said Psephos. "Elites, prepare for battle."

Was he serious? Even if these beings—"*angels,*" they had called themselves—were not the Ouranothen, they obviously possessed divine power of some kind, connected to the bright light in the strange building. But Psephos had meant every word; he was hefting his axe, swinging it to loosen the muscles in his arms. Reluctantly Khrusaoros drew his sword, and at his signal, the other Elites followed suit.

At once, the angel leader glided backward to rejoin its

formation. It raised a vaguely shaped hand, and bright light flared, which quickly resolved itself into what looked like a sword. Ethereal, shining yellow-white, the blade looked just as deadly, if not more so, than the real thing. Smokeless flames danced up and down along its length. It was a sword of light and fire all at once.

More lights flared, one in front of every angel warrior, and a similar fiery sword appeared in each one's hand as the entire formation glided forward to meet that of the Elites. Grimly, Khrusaoros readied himself for battle.

THE PALACE OF LIGHT
HALL OF WARRIORS

The night-black void grew larger, ever larger, until it consumed Makheteon's entire being. He explored it, probed its infinite boundaries, as he searched for the elemental spirits. For he knew they dwelled in there somewhere, hidden from sight, beyond some impossible veil. He was the diplomat, the emissary from the human world armed with all four of their powers, charged with finding them. And they sought him, too.

Somewhere on the fringes of his consciousness, he was aware of their invisible presences coming closer, slowly… almost hesitantly. There was no need to summon them directly, he now knew; they would come on their own before long. All he had to do was remain filled with the elemental magics, as those strains of power would act as a different kind of light, a beacon, and signal to the spirits where he was, where their world was….

But then there was a fluctuation, a brief flickering of the pale-white glow that was one of the four glows he possessed. The air magic. It winked out, then recovered, like a flame momentarily disturbed by a sudden breeze. Was one of the others losing concentration, or losing control? If so, it was hardly surprising; this was a huge spell, requiring immense amounts of power—both human and runic—to create a beacon bright enough for the spirits to see. He himself did not think he could hold it much longer.

Agonized, he waited for the spirits to arrive. Like the sun rising over the horizon, they came closer, and gradually he came to feel what might have distracted the one who was providing the air magic.

The presences that were slowly but surely approaching him, and now revealing their tinges of color, were... different.

They were not different in the same way that the light magic and the fire magic were different; this distinction was subtler, conveying both relatedness and unrelatedness. The only power he could sense outright, that of the reddish presence, felt somewhat like the power he was wielding, yet quite different from the power in the sphere he held. The sphere trembled against his body, and its red light swirled in frantic protest, almost as if it were being subdued against its will. This was absurd, of course—a light could not have a will—but it was the overwhelming impression he was receiving.

And all four presences carried with them a certain sense of destruction. Even now they were seizing upon the powers, the magics, with which he was providing them, and something was being... torn apart... to admit them into the human world....

As Makheteon stood there, just in front of the massive red-glowing rune, and weaved his magic, the realization hit him in a flash:

These were not the spirits he wanted to summon.

***

AKTINOS, REALM OF LIGHT
SLOPES OF THE LIGHTNING-STRUCK MOUNTAIN

Khrusaoros grunted in sorrow and desperation, sweat pouring down his face, as he moved his sword to parry an angel warrior's attack. The two blades collided, producing a shower of brilliant sparks and a sensation of unbearable heat.

Even with both hands on his sword's normally one-handed hilt, leaning into it with his entire weight, he could barely keep his adversary's flaming blade at bay. The weapon's yellow-white flames licked at his armor, scorching it, staining it, tainting it. If any of the flesh on his hands, arms, or chest had been exposed, it would have been burned to a crisp—and it did not help that both the blade and its wielder still glowed too brightly to look at. Elite or no, he had no chance against such an opponent.

And yet, something was strange: namely, the fact that he was still alive. The angel, he had no doubt, could have obliterated him in seconds, but the half-seen movements of its sword were slow, almost reluctant... or sad.

Sadness. The angel was sad. As soon as he had the thought, it made perfect sense, though he could not have said why. Perhaps the angel did not truly want to fight him because he was, in essence, one of its people. Its leader had implied as much, and hinted that the group's quarrel was with Psephos only—and even him they all pitied, because his soul was in agony, whatever that meant.

And sure enough, when Khrusaoros risked a quick peek over his shoulder to see how the other Elites were faring, he saw more half-hearted duels between human and angel. One Elite was down on his hands and knees, gasping and retching with his sword lying abandoned a few feet away, but none of the angel warriors moved to finish him off. Only the duel between Psephos and the angel leader was a serious one, with flaming sword and shining battle-axe coming together, separating, and coming together again, all faster than lightning itself—

The familiar fiery, yellow-white streak sailed at Khrusaoros once more, and he quickly backed up a step to give himself time to raise his own weapon. That movement took him away from the intense duel he had just been observing—and in that moment, the angels' tactics crystallized before him. They intended not to kill the Elites, but merely to exhaust them, incapacitate them, or herd them away so they could not go to the aid of their leader. Out of the corner of his eye, Khrusaoros even glimpsed a flash of bright motion that confirmed this theory: more angels, moving into position as the Skiai had the previous morning, preparing to converge on Psephos from behind once the field had been cleared of Elites....

But then it was Khrusaoros' opponent that was backing up, one step and then another; he followed briefly before he realized that the movement was one of retreat. All around the battlefield, other angels were doing the same; their wings beat agitatedly at the air, and their glows flickered erratically. Khrusaoros had only to turn around to see what had them so alarmed.

Somewhere in the distance, far from the mountain on which he stood, the sky was opening up—not metaphorically, as was the idiom on the occasion of torrential rainfall, but literally. It seemed to be a rift of sorts, covering an ever-wider patch of sky, as if a hole had been punctured in the very heavens. Swirling, purplish-black mist bled out from that hole, in whose heart a darkness could be seen: vague, roiling and rumbling, and even deeper than the slowly brightening, pre-dawn gloom around it.

As Khrusaoros stared in horror at this rift, this stain on the firmament, he had the sudden feeling that it was a door, or perhaps a window, into another world. A dark world. The hole quickly enlarged, more dark mist polluted Aktinan air—and the Skiai warriors, who had cowered in fear as soon as the angels of light had appeared, seemed to stand even taller, stronger, more confident....

A blinding flash off to one side caught his eye, and he turned to see all of the angel warriors vanish, or rather burst, each in its own miniature explosion. As their light's final remnants dissolved into nothing, a few white bird's feathers drifted downward to settle on the ground before they, too, vanished. Even the angels' swords were gone.

Amazed but apprehensive, Khrusaoros turned again—and found himself looking directly at Psephos. The Elite Leader looked even taller than before, if that were possible, and his eyes—despite the general, rift-induced darkening of the sky—had a distinctly eerie, even sinister gleam. One hand held his battle-axe, as usual, but the other was raised in front of his chest in the classic "rune-drawing" position.

Rune-drawing. No one had ever seen him draw a rune or do anything connected to magic. Most Aktinans, including the Elites, had concluded that he either had no magic or preferred not to use it.

"You...?" Khrusaoros began, but his voice failed him. The hand that held his sword trembled uncontrollably.

"Yes," Psephos answered; "my magic is of the dark. What is filling this world now"—he raised his axe-holding hand and pointed with the weapon at the ever-widening dark rift overhead—"fills me with life, with vitality. And the best part is"—he grinned unexpectedly, the expression almost grotesque in the circumstances—"that you have your brother to thank for this. So the dark divines tell me."

Your brother"? "*Dark divines*"? But Khrusaoros could not speak. Behind him, the other Elites stood dumbstruck as well:

stunned by this betrayal, if that was what it was. A few of them were raising their swords valiantly, to prepare for a last stand, but Khrusaoros knew it was hopeless. With a single spell, Psephos had gotten rid of the divine angels; who knew what else he could do, aided by this new *"vitality"*?

Accordingly, when the first purplish-black stroke of the attack rune appeared in front of his leader-turned-enemy, the young Elite merely closed his eyes so he would not have to see.

AKTINOS, REALM OF LIGHT
VALLEY OF THE GODS

Ateles opened his eyes to near-total darkness. Straight ahead, a huge, hulking shape registered vaguely on his vision: probably a mountainside like the one against which his back now rested. Similar structures loomed in other directions; only a narrow gap to the southwest, some ten feet across, offered access to clear air.

This would be the Valley of the Gods, he thought dimly: the deepest valley in the realm, and possibly in the entire world. Boulders dotted the barren, narrow floor, including a few quite close to him that must have become dislodged from the cliff face above when he had...

When he had fallen.

With a swift, frightening clarity, the memories came back. His encountering Psephos on the mountain path; the sudden attack of the battle-axe, followed by searing pain as the blade cut through his thin Finisher's armor. The beginning of his terrifying fall from the mountain, past Aktinos, and into death and damnation. The knowledge that his life was over.

The light in the valley had grown a bit stronger as—still confused—he turned his gaze downward. On his right side, as expected, a long cut in his battered armor announced where

Psephos' axe had struck, and the area between the cut and his hip was completely stained with dried human blood. Some of it had even dripped partway down his leg... but...

He picked frantically at the stained areas, pulled the two sides of the cut apart like a man insane: no new blood was flowing, and the flesh beneath the armor had closed up. And then there was the fact that he could move his arms, legs, back—no broken bones. How could he come out of a fatal fall with nothing to show for it but a few stains and scratches on his armor?

There was a rustling nearby, followed by the soft *creak* of leather, and he became aware of the warm presence of his girlfriend, slowly coming closer. Her long brown hair was down now, no longer braided, and it brushed against his face and shoulder as she settled down next to him at the foot of the mountain. "...Seems you've finally come around."

Abandoning a new, futile attempt to see anything up above—just sheer mountainside, no trace of the trail or any Aktinan buildings—he turned his head to look at her. The valley's faint light came from a brilliant, pure-yellow rune hovering beside her, which she had no doubt drawn for this purpose. Her face was no more than a foot from his, mouth showing the barest hint of a smile, eyes shining with a strange warmth. She was beautiful.

"How... am I...?" he rasped.

She shifted her sitting position slightly, looked at him with an unwavering gaze. "Magic."

"Magic?! But..." One spell to break his fall, one to heal his wound; just the first would have taxed the energies of Photizousa herself, Aktinos' most talented mage, to an unmanageable degree. And here was still a third spell, the rune-light. "The magic is weak. Limited. How could you have...?"

"Quite simply," she returned in a cool, unmoved voice. "I

reached into the past."

"Reached into—"

With another *creak* of leather, she leaned forward, pulled his head toward herself, and brought her lips down on his. He returned her kiss, his arms encircling her thin form, and pulled her as close as he could. As the two of them eventually drifted apart, he played with a few strands of her hair, looked down at her hand that was even now moving across his shoulder blade, and thought of the enjoyment that they had shared only the previous afternoon. Everything else was, for the moment, forgotten.

"Why did you choose me over Psephos?" he asked, almost without being aware of it.

Her eyebrow rose sharply, signaling her indecision about whether to answer. "...Three reasons," she said finally. "Two of them I'm not telling you. But as for the third..." She paused again, gave him a considering look. "You seem to be on the right side in this war."

War.

That single word snapped him out of his trancelike state, and—after rising to his feet—he stumbled across the valley floor in search of his sword. No sign of the weapon anywhere. He stood as tall as he could, craned his neck once more to try to see the mountain peak... to no avail. *Something* was going on up there—that much was certain, given his memories—but it was so distant that he could not see or even hear it. Only a slight, ominous darkening of the patch of sky that was visible between the rows of mountains pointed at something unusual, and probably magical as well.

That the Ouranothen, even the malevolent Avengers, would allow such things to happen in their own realm was unthinkable.

Then, without warning, a hand fell on his arm and turned him around forcibly. "Listen to me. Forget your sword; forget the events up there. Right now, I need you to get out of here. Leave the realm."

He uttered a contemptuous snort and found himself glaring at her. Her yellow rune-light had followed her to the place where she now stood, and its glow illuminated her tan Ambusher's armor, spotless and looking brand-new—no Skiai blood anywhere. The valley floor held no trace of spears or any of the other weapons that Ambushers typically used.

Gradually, the realization began to dawn.

"I mean it," she went on with a surprising urgency, stepping forward to grab his other arm as well. "What you know up there—the realm of Aktinos—it's all coming down tonight. There will be explosions, all manner of disasters, and there is nothing you can do to prevent them. Take that path"— she nodded toward the trail to the southwest—"out of the mountains, and don't stop until you reach the world's lower regions. Do you understand?"

As if on cue, a rumbling tremor rocked the ground. In the sky, the odd darkness had deepened.

When the tremor had passed, Ateles stood motionless and considered. There was no doubt that she meant, and believed, what she had said; and yet her words had been matter-of-fact. Her eyes showed no trace of fear, only a slight concern for him.

The idea of leaving when the realm was at war was distasteful... dishonorable. Yet even as his spirit rebelled against the thought, his mind knew that he would go—and simply because she had asked him to. It was ironic, he thought: he was one of Aktinos' most feared fighters, with an insatiable thirst for battle, and this one woman rendered his warrior side powerless.

"Very well," he said shortly. "But only"—he reached out and seized her arm as she made to walk away—"if you tell me one thing. Your name."

Her eyebrow rose again, farther than before. Her entire

face displayed blank incredulity.

Seized by a sudden annoyance, he growled deep in his throat. "I *do* know a few things besides war and battle," he snapped. "*Erroguia*—it means 'broken one.' An obvious pseudonym. You and Psephos both—"

"Your point?" she interrupted brusquely.

"*Answers*," he shot back with equal force. "I will do as you say, leave and wait out whatever disasters are coming, but *only* if you tell me the truth. What is your *real* name??"

A few frozen, interminably long seconds crept by. That impasse was first broken by a very slight narrowing of her eyes, which did not at all match what he had previously gleaned of her character—and then she pulled free of his grasp, crossed her arms over her chest, and took on a facial expression that might have made all of Aktinos quake. "...Aichme."

At that moment, the rune-light winked out. Ateles cast about in the sudden darkness, looked up at the sky in the hope that the action would allow his eyes to adjust faster.

When he looked back, eyes adjusted, she was gone.

✸✸✸

AKTINOS, REALM OF LIGHT
PEAK OF THE LIGHTNING-STRUCK MOUNTAIN

No more than fifty yards from the mountain peak, Psephos stood contentedly—his axe's shaft leaning against one shoulder, the double blade hovering near his head—and breathed in the cool early-morning air. A light breeze soon came up and ruffled his cape, and for some reason, even that small action pleased him. He could not remember ever feeling so strong. So alive.

While his mind wandered, his gaze went to the still-widening dark rift overhead and then descended to the trail behind him, where the bloody remains of his Elite squad lay in various states of burning and/or dismemberment. A few feet away, his troop of Skiai stood in an uneven line, each creature showing long yellow fangs in what was apparently an approving grin.

Perhaps discerning his ultimate intentions, the group now began squelching toward the light-emitting building that stood at the end of the trail—but he stayed them all with a raised hand and turned away again. He would investigate the temple in due time, but for now, he preferred to reflect on what had been given to him this night. On how it could be that he had fought so many successful years of war *without* the great, dark power that now burned in his veins.

A sudden fluctuation in the dark rift catching his attention, he looked up even as a violent tremor made the mountain shudder. The tense, crackling energy in the air was palpable.

Edging to the side, off the trail, he peered through a hole in the cloud cover at the realm below, but detected nothing— just a vague, indescribable sense that a massive amount of magic was being expended down there. What kind of spell it was, he could not have said, but he did not need to look back at the dark rift to know that it was growing ever larger in response. The entire region, from the tiny, distant Aktinan buildings to the silent mountains and plain, seemed to be holding its breath.

There could be no doubt about it: this was his cue.

With that, he returned to the trail, pointed his axe-blade at the Skiai to tell them to stay put, and then set off for the strange temple at the slope's highest point. Five feet from the arching entrance, he stopped and looked up at the irregularly shaped, silvery-gray structure before him: similar to those he had seen in his recurring dream, only duller in hue and much larger.

Jagged gray spires, presumably made of the same metal as

the rest of the building, extended upward from seemingly random locations, their bottoms melded inextricably to the other pieces. The walls, though far from even, containing numerous gaps, and obviously constructed from many components, worked together to form a lightly curving shape around a single, nearly round room: the temple's center and the origin of the light that was visible from everywhere in Aktinos.

Many areas along the walls also sported chipped red paint in a design that looked just as jagged as the spires above. It reminded him of the traditional Aktinan myths, but also of what Eudrakes had told him about a foreign warrior society with unbelievable technology....

Shaking the thought off—there was no time for distractions or idle theories—he laid his hand on the cool metal beside the doorway and glanced inside. Contrary to his expectations, however, the single room that made up the temple's interior was nearly empty. It contained only a thick, medium-tall pedestal, standing in the center and likewise made of uneven gray metal with remnants of red paint; and atop this pedestal rested a large, whitish-yellow sphere.

This sphere was the source of the bright, ambient light, but its appearance struck him as—for lack of a better analogy—sickly. Perhaps as much as half of its surface area was covered with large gray blotches that drifted to and fro like leaves floating on water. The blotches were similar in hue to the metal of the immediate surroundings, almost as if the sphere wanted to adopt the primary color of the building and pedestal—but, of course, Psephos knew that this could not be the case.

What had created the blotches was not clear, but it was obvious what they represented. They were a kind of disease... and the reason why the Aktinans' magic had been so weak. For this was the very magical source that Eudrakes had told him about: the object that the warrior caste had been charged with protecting.

He laughed. This was going to be easier than he had anticipated.

Earlier that night in the Hall of Warriors, the Skiarchos had told him to "*search his true motives*"—and he had. His meditations had revealed much, and now that he could see the interior of this so-called sacred place, everything was starting to come together. His questions, problems, fears, objectives: they all related to this sphere, and this sphere related to them. It was the reason why he had been driven to ascend this mountain, even if the true facts of the matter had initially been concealed under a false premise.

Looking for the Skiai's base. He wondered how he could ever have harbored such a nonsensical idea, based as it was on numerous faulty assumptions. But that was in the past now.

Behind him, the dark rift still crackled in anticipation. Waiting to be harnessed. He nodded in acknowledgment of its request.

It was finally time—to take action, and to make good on the title that formed part of his name. Psephos Anolethros, the Indestructible. For the first time that he could remember, he was about to help himself.

The sphere's glow, and the room's light, seemed to have dimmed an infinitesimal amount. Smiling to himself, he stepped toward that light—only to stop again, the smile fading, as his peripheral vision caught movement. He turned around.

The motion he had seen was the army of ethereal, yellow-white angels, which was rematerializing and reassuming its formation on the gentle slope that led to the temple. Behind and to the right of the brightly shining group, the Skiai cowered in terror—useless creatures, he thought with a snort.

And dead ahead, coming ever closer and just barely visible

in the space between two of the angels, was a distinctly human figure.

Psephos raised an eyebrow.

He thought he had gotten rid of everyone.

CHAPTER TEN
DAWN

AKTINOS, REALM OF LIGHT
ABOVE THE VALLEY OF THE GODS

HIGH ON A trail that snaked between and across members of the surrounding mountain range before joining with the path up to the highest peak, Aichme walked at a pace that was brisk enough to show haste, without also hinting at a panic that she did not feel. Everything was under control.

As she approached a point where the trail took a sharp turn to correspond to the current mountain's curvature, she paused and looked down one final time at the Valley of the Gods. From this height, and in the lingering darkness of early morning, the figure of Ateles looked like little more than a pale speck, trudging toward the gap in the mountains that she had pointed out to him. She stood still for a moment, watched his slow movements, and was surprised to find the muscles of her mouth curving into a smile.

She was perfectly willing to admit that she had entered into that relationship on a whim, seizing an opportunity that had been presented to her. Yet, now—however strange the thought would have seemed at the time when she had made that initial decision—her views had progressed to a point that she could genuinely wish him well. He was attractive, with a fierce yet intelligent spirit, and had proven to be an agreeable companion and lover. These had been a pleasant past few months, more than enough to justify the spells and her other efforts to aid in his survival—as well as her carving out time to spend one final afternoon with him the day before.

And those factors were almost enough to make her forget the pain, if not the repercussions, of her long-ago failure....

Shutting the thought out, she continued on her way.

Before long, she had climbed to a level that was a few dozen feet above the plain of Aktinos, and her nose caught a distinctly decay-like scent rising on the breeze. Below her, hordes of Skiai had stormed every corner of the small realm; above her, an electric crackling announced an intensifying of the temporal fluctuations.

She glanced upward: the huge, dark-purple rift gaped in the sky like the open maw of some giant monster, its edges swirling and dancing, its power bubbling in the nearby air. Her proximity to it was sufficient to send chills down her spine, but even as she shivered, a second smile split her face— this one wider than the first. After so much time spent waiting, observing, adjusting her plans, and speaking to inconsequential civilian women about *their* plans, the moment was finally here.

With that, she drew a rune, stepped forward, and put much of the remaining distance behind her in less than a second.

Ascending the last quarter-mile of the trail, she took in the scene that was playing out just in front of the metal temple. A squad of angel warriors had just begun to converge on the tall, yellow-and-white-clad man who stood by the temple en- trance... but at her approach the group turned, seemed to study her, and stepped aside deferentially. She ignored them all.

Her gaze fixed on the tall man, she came to a halt. "*Psephos*," she began, with emphasis. "See how far you've fallen—very far indeed, even for one who had never attained a great height in the first place."

"If you've come here to taunt me, save your time and your breath," he shot back harshly, hefting his axe. "I—"

She took a step closer to him, and he fell silent.

"Do you know what this says to me?" she asked, making a hand gesture that encompassed the corpses of the Elites on one side, the twitching and scowling group of Skiai on the other. "Messy. It tells me of a man who has no idea what he is about."

He snorted. "What does an *Ambusher underling* know about..."

His voice faded as tall, brilliant yellow flames erupted on both sides of the trail. The Skiai jumped in terror and tried to flee, but were incinerated without a sound. Far below, the scent of burnt matter—mingling with the decay-like smell as it wafted upward—announced that the same fate had befallen the Skiai on the Aktinan plain. Psephos staggered briefly, one hand clutching his chest, and then whirled toward the temple entrance: more flames blocked the doorway.

Slowly, he turned back to face his interlocutor; his legs still wobbled somewhat, and his entire face was a mask of shock. Aichme considered. It was obvious that he did not recognize her, given his brief, ill-fated bid for her attention immediately after her arrival. Perhaps she should...

Yes. Even a woman on a mission deserved some gratification.

She took a step toward him amid the flames' heat, watched their bright reflections play on the blade of the massive battle-axe and in his wide eyes, and drew another rune. *Light of understanding. Light of memory. Let that light take root and shine in this one.*

Instantly, his eyes grew even wider; he blinked once, and his jaw dropped before he took a step backward, his facial expression twisting into something like revulsion. "Ai... Aichme."

"That's right." After walking the final few feet to him, she placed her hands on his chest and gave him a shove that sent him stumbling backward. "And now, you're going to answer to me about your betrayal. Speak!"

Having regained his balance, he turned his axe upside-down and shoved the blade against the ground for extra support. "Is that what you call it?"

"What else??" The wrath was bubbling up inside her; she let it spill over, listened as her voice rose ever higher in pitch. "I refrained from putting you out of your misery when I had the chance, thinking your situation would make you useful, and *this* is how you repay me—you and that other failure of a man who created the mess with his attempt at heroism? I should have let you both die with the whole forsaken lot of them."

He blinked again, but showed no sign of emotion. "Have you considered, *Aichme*, that you might be going about this the wrong way?"

She raised an eyebrow. "No."

"Well, *I* have, and I'm done. In fact, I wouldn't be surprised if the whole damn thing blows up in your face. Does the opposite of what you intend. Trust me—I may not know much about this particular case, but I'm more of an expert on people than you are."

Closing her eyes, she inhaled once, let the breath out, and then decided to ignore the greater part of what he had said. Instead, she fixated on his first statement, and her anger soon obliged her first by returning, and then by burning hotter than ever.

"*Done*?? I can't imagine what better..."

His eyes cut to a point behind her, and she broke off, turned to follow his gaze; it appeared that he was looking at the dark rift overhead.

"Ah. The Skiai." She nodded knowingly and turned back to

face him. "You won't figure that one out—unless the *rest* of your memory has more retentive and associative power than the one portion I just corrected. And even then, your small mind would never recognize your own complicity, your own blame and fault. So it always is, isn't it?"

There was a long pause; his eyes drifted to the sky directly above him and then grew wide again. Finally gathering himself, he shook his head sharply and spun toward the temple entrance once more: the yellow flames were still blocking the doorway, growing taller by the second.

"You will never get in my way again," Aichme said with a quiet dangerousness.

He growled under his breath, whirled back around, and charged at her, his axe held high. Calmly stepping to one side, she ducked under the flashing blade and drew a rune. In seconds, a miniature explosion flared an inch from the spot where his hand gripped the handle, knocking the weapon away, even as a second spell filled the blade with the light and heat of the sun—

His gauntleted fist came into contact with her stomach; she staggered, gasped in brief pain, then swung her leg around in a kick that collided with his upper calf and knocked it out from under him. The mountain path trembled as he fell flailing to the ground.

"...Nice one," he panted, an inexplicable smile on his face.

But in the next moment, the smile had given way to an openmouthed stare as he caught sight of the glowing, semitransparent yellow bubble that now surrounded his opponent. That bubble retracted in on itself for the briefest of instants, before exploding outward in a circular wave that sent him flying backward in a cloud of dirt and small debris. Unable to stop his flight, he passed through the wall of yellow flame in front of the temple; there was a dull *thud* from the other side; and then all was still.

Aichme let the flames dissipate, then looked up and down the mountain trail: nothing was moving for miles around. Nodding in satisfaction, she gave the watching angel warriors a sign to retreat, massaged her stomach area absentmindedly, and set out toward the temple entrance.

THE PALACE OF LIGHT
HALL OF WARRIORS

Somewhere within the dark void of his consciousness, Makheteon fought. To free himself. To free the world.

But no matter what he did, how he tried to pull back or break his concentration, he could not. It was as if the dark presence—so far from the benevolent spirits he had intended to contact—had gained a foothold into the world and was slowly, inexorably worming its way into it. The presence was stronger now. He could hear it laughing in his head with many voices, telling him how this was all thanks to him. Gloating about how easily it had duped him, and duped that girl as well: that ignorant girl who had not remembered as much history as she thought and should never have meddled in what she did not fully understand. It was too late, far too late, to do anything....

A sudden idea hit him, and he tried to tune out the voices as he fumbled over his shoulder—it was strange to realize that, even here in the void, he had corporeal substance—for his sword. If he could only kill himself, drive the blade into his own heart, then the summoning spell would be broken, irrevocably aborted—

But the voices only laughed all the louder.

Something hit him then, and he recoiled—snapped forcibly out of the void. The familiar Hall of Warriors re-formed itself before his eyes; the spell was over.

Over... but *complete.*

The entire Hall shook as an apparition appeared: the huge ghost of a monster, right on top of the giant rune that was still glowing red, but a darker red than before. The creature was the color of fire, or it was on fire, or it *was* fire. With a huge, amorphous body, several eyes jutting out from the top of its head atop thin stalks, it reminded him of a slug. And, though it was fiery, it also struck him as slimy somehow—slimy like the Skiai, but slimier than any Skia he had ever seen. Two immense, flaming, crablike claws, one on each side of the creature's shapeless body, completed its horrifying aspect.

It was not actually one of the dark presences; it was but a phantom, or so he thought; but terror filled him nevertheless. He knew he should fight, but for some reason, all he wanted to do was run for his life.

Yet as soon as he took a step backward, the phantom monster began to grow taller, and larger, as if imbibing energy from the very air. Before long, the tops of its eyeballs nearly brushed the high ceiling, even as it raised one massive claw high into the air—and Makheteon froze again. He could not tell whether the claw was aimed at him, to crush him, or at the giant rune beneath the monster's slimy underside. If it was the latter, the collision between the creature's dark magic and the light magic that had been coerced into performing this task could... could...

The claw came down, and it was aimed at the rune. The blow produced a shower of sparks and a massive, red shockwave; Makheteon was knocked off his feet and flew backward, partway down the Hall. A sickening *crack* announced his collision with one of the warrior statues, and as he slid to the ground, the Essence of Fire rolled away from his limp arm to take shelter in a forgotten alcove.

His world went dark mere seconds before the Hall of Warriors exploded.

✱✱✱

AKTINOS, REALM OF LIGHT
TEMPLE OF THE OURANOTHEN

Psephos awoke to pain. Gasping softly, he opened one eye a crack, just enough to see that he was collapsed in front of the temple's curving gray wall. His armor, coated with a thin layer of dust, showed heavy singe marks from the yellow flames that he had passed through. The flesh beneath the singe marks ached, seemed alive with the memory of the flames: like the heat of the suns in his recurring dream, but palpable, corporeal, and all too real. The dream itself was real, an echo of an actual event—of this he was certain—but what kind of event it was, he could not say.

A searing pain at the back of his head announced a wound, obtained when he had struck the wall, and it had taken with it any prior awareness of the distant past or who that Aichme woman was. Why she had spoken to him as she had, he had not the faintest idea; why he had reacted as *he* had, he could not imagine. Only one piece of knowledge remained: she was his enemy.

Movement at a corner of his vision announced her presence, though the angle was awkward and she looked like little more than a pair of tan-clad legs, walking toward the center of the room. He moved first his hand, then his lower arm; they still obeyed him. Putting both hands on the floor, he pushed his torso upward a couple of inches and looked around for his axe...

Too late, the memory crashed down on him. His axe was gone.

Both hands scraped against the floor, straining under the weight, as he pushed himself up a few more inches, so that he could get his feet under him—and suddenly his view of the temple was torn away, replaced by an image that played out before his eyes in plodding slow motion.

Himself, kneeling at the center of the great rune in the Hall of Warriors—the yellow-white light flickering—the color changing to a deep, reproachful, maroon-like red.

He gasped—the brief vision was gone—and he thudded back to the floor as his arms gave way, his entire body racked with burning pain.

The tan-clad legs had reached the room's center and now stood just to the left of the silvery-gray pedestal. Slowly, exerting an immense effort, Psephos stretched one hand in that direction—

At that moment, the room and mountain shook violently. The walls vibrated, creaked, threatened to give way under some great, invisible force that tore from side to side like an angry hand swatting at an insect. From far below, the sound of explosions was audible; a tall plume of blue light shone through one of the gaps in the wall, green light through another, and still more colors behind him. For one split second, the room was filled with multicolored light, reflecting off every surface and contributing to the rising, electric tension in the air. And in that same heartbeat, a slight dimming of the yellowish light announced that Aichme had put her hands on the yellow-and-gray sphere.

The tension increased fivefold, tenfold, until its crackling produced tiny sparks in the air, and then resolved itself into a kind of strange wind that whipped in circles around the pedestal. Psephos lay where he was, too weak even to guard his face against the rushing air, and looked up at the tan-clad woman who stood, shoulders hunched, over the sphere.

One second passed—two—and then she straightened up in a flash of motion, threw her head back, and let loose with a raw, full-throated roar: far louder, deeper, and possessing more visceral power than anything else he had ever heard coming from a female vocal tract. It was enough to make the ground vibrate again—and yet, it was not a roar of wrath. It was a cry of anguish.

A piece of the ceiling came loose and clattered to the ground; another followed it, then another; everything else was shaking; the whirlwind around the pedestal had intensified. In the middle of that maelstrom of energy, Aichme stood motionless, both hands placed firmly on the sphere, and roared. Tears, mingled with tiny droplets of blood, glistened on her cheeks. The sphere's light flickered, dimmed, and was obscured by the purplish darkness now rushing in through the temple entrance. The air that brought the darkness also carried a faint scent, like smoke but having a magical aura: the obvious remnant of the explosions from Aktinos. And from one explosion, another usually follows.

At last the roaring ceased, but the winds continued to swirl. Psephos gathered his remaining strength, ignored the bits of ceiling and wall that had started to come down on all sides, and found his footing in the darkness. It seemed as though he were moving in slow motion again.

Once he was half-upright, he lunged at his enemy—but the deafening thunderclap-like sound that filled his ears, and the sensation that his stomach was sinking down to his toes, soon made him aware of the terrible truth:

Whatever she had been doing with that sphere... it was done.

CHAPTER ELEVEN
MORNING

AKTINOS, REALM OF LIGHT

When the sun rose that morning, it was nothing but a pale-yellow speck, half-concealed behind a shroud of purple and black. The dark rift now covered the entire expanse of sky, swallowing into itself all vestiges of the life that had existed below. What clouds there were appeared as thin, unhealthy white streaks, drifting to and fro in the stagnant air; and after a while, even these gave up the struggle and ceased all visible movement.

Atop the Lightning-Struck Mountain, a gray sphere sat on a gray pedestal amid the ruins of the metal temple. Less than half of the immense structure remained upright, the rest having collapsed in on itself or tumbled partway down the mountainside; some of the beams, panels, and spires showed heavy scorch marks, signs of a battle that had taken place inside the temple.

Of the two combatants, Psephos and Aichme, there was no trace. No footprints led back down the mountain trail: neither there, nor on the slope where most of the Elites had met their end, nor farther down, where the two female division leaders lay dead.

On the Aktinan plain, silence and emptiness reigned supreme. Many buildings still stood but gaped like great cave openings, their doors and windows having been shattered in the earth tremors and the powerful aftershocks that had followed. Around those buildings, the remains of hundreds of Aktinan warriors dotted the plain and stained the dry soil red with their blood. All motionless, lifeless; only smoke moved as it rose from the Palace of Light, the former Shrine of the Air Magic, and two more far-flung locations. In the dim light of the half-hidden sun, those vapors were every bit as dark as the black splotches on the ground that announced where members of the Skiai horde had been incinerated.

In and around the Palace, entire corridors had caved in, as had the wall that enclosed the grounds and one wall of the Great Hall. Here there were no black splotches, only red ones: some scattered at regular intervals around the Hall, beside the now-visible bodies of the fallen Protectors, and a small one lying next to the arrow-pierced corpse of Keraunia. The golden throne held the seated form of Eudianax: leaning against the huge chair's back but his head bowed forward, his eyes closed, their light extinguished. Photizousa's shield, and the corresponding rune, were long gone. As if to replace them, the purplish darkness was beginning to reach its gaseous tendrils through the shattered windows high up the still-intact side wall.

Movement, behind and to the left of the throne.

Slowly, the cloaked figure of Eudrakes steps out of the shadows and walks across the raised platform. A few inches from the edge, he stops, the hem of his long robe whispering as it settles around his feet. He raises one pale hand, pulls his hood back so that the cycling runes in his eyes are exposed to the air, and looks around at the bodies of his lord and the young servant of the elemental spirits, then at the windows' fallen shards and the dark tendrils that are wafting into the room, swirling and expanding in midair.

Ten, twenty seconds he looks upon these scenes before shifting his gaze to the Hall's arching entrance opposite the throne, and all three of the intact walls reverberate as he speaks with the full force of his powerful voice:

"All is not lost. All is not lost. What is gone may yet be regained; what has died may yet live again. For the realm lost in time, time is the only answer. The one who finds the angel finds all."

Before the echoes have died away, he disappears from the platform—leaving the Hall empty and silent as the dark tendrils arrive at the farthest corners, the tapestries on the walls fluttering in the cold and foul wind that has arisen.

EPILOGUE
ENLIGHTENED

VILSE, THE LOST REALM
SECRET LIBRARY

THE SMALL PARTY of three reached the end of the huge tome and then sat back in their seats. Much of the text on the last two pages was smeared, suggesting that the words were freshly written—so freshly that Ljuset, after picking the book up to show it to her two companions, had closed it on wet ink.

Suppressing a yawn, filled with a mix of boredom and apprehension, Brinna poked the writing end of the quill that lay nearby and examined the tiny dot of half-dried ink it had left behind on her fingertip. "Well, we've finally gotten through this massive thing. I don't know what we thought we'd learn. Even before we started it, we knew how it would end."

"Not quite," Ljuset chided her. Reaching over, the robed woman dragged the heavy book closer to herself and began flipping through pages. "There were a number of things that I didn't expect."

Brinna snorted. "Like what? The names of the poor wretches who were in power when the realm met its demise? And a totally unnecessary, confusing history lesson in the middle of the narrative??"

"Exactly—the history. I've never heard about any types of magic besides light and dark, but somehow, they all must be relevant...." Ljuset shook her head, an obvious attempt to bring unruly thoughts into line. "And then there were the events at the end. If this account is correct, then the person who actually 'destroyed' Aktinos, who dealt it the deathblow, was a wielder of my own magic of light. I find that... disturbing."

"As opposed to dark? The idea that not all light mages are good?"

"The idea that light was destroyed by light. So much infighting.... This realm need not have fallen, if it had only focused on the task at hand instead of battling itself."

Brinna shrugged—Aktinos had deserved its fate—but then she fell to thinking about the winged beings the text had described, the ones on the Lightning-Struck Mountain. "Angels," they were called—and so similar to the chalk drawing on the Palace's door. The final words of the Eudrakes character played over and over in her head. *The one who finds the angel finds all....*

At length, she became aware of Salainen, who was still sitting at the table but not acknowledging the two women at all. His back was as straight as a spear, his eyes wide, his face deathly pale.

Picking the quill up, she threw it in his direction. "You still alive over there?"

He shuddered, blinked once, and appeared to awaken. His dark eyes focused on her for a brief moment, moved to Ljuset and then back. "...Yes," he said quietly. "And Ljuset is right. This conflict isn't about light against dark—not exclusively. There are many factors in play."

Ljuset raised an eyebrow, evidently surprised to find support from this quarter. "What makes you say that?"

Salainen leaned forward ever so slightly, looked again from one woman to the other. His face had lost even more color, if that were possible. "I've heard stories of some of the people mentioned in that text. And some of the organizations as well."

"And?" Brinna pushed out with considerable effort, just barely able to keep her rising dread out of her voice. People? Organizations?

"And what I've heard would be enough to make you wish them far away," he replied. "If they were here, and took an interest in Aktinos, then..."

He paused, and his eyes were lit from within by a gleam of plain, unfettered terror.

"Then this world is in very serious trouble."

RUINS OF THE PALACE OF LIGHT

Except for the *tap, tap* of slow footsteps, there was hardly a sound to be heard as the three explorers picked their way through the Palace's half-destroyed stone hallways. Before their departure from the secret library, Salainen had recounted what he knew about the various factions referenced in the story of Aktinos' fall, and his long and complicated tale had effectively struck his two companions dumb. Brinna's head spun; connections, relevancies, and implications danced hither and thither in her mind and filled her with an ever-increasing sense of stomach-twisting anxiety. And beside her, she had only to look at Ljuset's frown and slightly pursed lips to know what the magic-user was thinking: she was wishing that she had the text to hand.

It had been a disagreement that bordered on a shouting match. Ljuset had wanted to take the ancient book with her to allow for easier fact-checking as new ideas or evidence came to light, and it had taken the united front of Brinna and Salainen to dissuade her from this plan on the grounds that the massive tome would make running—or fighting—near-impossible. They needed her at full capacity during this exploration, they had said; and it was not as if the book was going to run away or be stolen by some scholarly Skia. Their arguments had been long, wearisome, and seemingly without purpose, but eventually Ljuset had given way. And now, Brinna thought as she reflected on the group's time in the library, the loud arguing was showing a cruel side—for the memory of it only made the currently prevailing silence all the deeper, all the more isolating.

In that silence, she also had to consider what her next move would be, given all that she had *learned* in the library. Would she have to act sooner than originally planned—before ascertaining whether Salainen would side with her on more than just the question of taking the book along?

Through one more dark-tinged hallway the three went, and then another, and near the end of the second one, a tapestry appeared to them out of the gloom: it was tattered and torn, had frayed a bit at the edges, and reached from the wall's upper third almost all the way down to the floor. Ljuset leaned toward it to take a closer look at the images it depicted, but this was unnecessary, as it was not the tapestry's subject matter that would tell them where in the Palace they were.

Picking her way around a few dark bricks that had fallen into the middle of the corridor, Brinna gazed warily at the massive, ornate door that stood beside the tapestry: the door that, according to the descriptions in the ancient text, led to the royal adviser's quarters. The door sparkled in the corridor's sparse torchlight; it was made of metal, likely some variety of gold, but had since been tainted with a purplish-black hue, as almost everything else in the building had. "Tell me again *why* we have to explore this room?"

Ljuset rolled her eyes. "Oh, for the great light's sake, Brinna. The text we read *must* have been written by the adviser, Eudrakes: because only he could have seen or known everything that went on among the warriors, first of all, and secondly, because he obviously lived through the realm's fall. It sounds like his extended lifespan allowed him to live indefinitely, and if he's still in the area, he must be up to *something*. Maybe we can even enlist his help with lifting the cloud of darkness from this region."

"Seems like a dangerous idea to me," Brinna shot back, "because we don't know if he'd be friendly to us. Not to mention... didn't the book's cover say that the authors were '*renowned scribes*'?"

"That was merely the last volume in the history of the Skiai wars, not the *only* one; the earlier ones were arranged on a shelf in a corner, as you would have seen if you had been paying attention. I opened a few of them before we left the library, and they were written in other handwriting, sometimes multiple handwritings in a single volume. Also, an adviser *can* surely double as a scribe, right? Especially if the 'official' scribes perished with the realm and are in no position to write about what happened to it?"

Brinna made a noncommittal noise, but knew she was defeated: Salainen was already at the gleaming purplish door, trying to pull it open, and now Ljuset moved forward in a flurry of robes to help him. Uttering a little sigh, Brinna tried to steel herself for what was coming, even if she did not know precisely why. Her overall situation might be growing more dire by the moment, but she had no fear of abandoned rooms... or of ghosts.

Under the combined effort of the magic-user and young swordsman, the large single door slowly creaked open, and the three found themselves met with a decayed, dilapidated variant of the small antechamber they had read about in the text. A single yellow-white torch flickered feebly on one of the dark-tainted stone walls: illuminating shelves, a blown-out window on the opposite wall with glass shards scattered on the rug beneath, as well as many items of furniture that looked like they were too large for the room.

Brinna stared at one overturned cushion and then another, imagining the young warrior Makheteon, who had searched this room for the Essence of Fire. Even back then, the room had been described as dusty. And that small table there, just to the left of center, must have been the one on which Eudrakes had finally put the Essence down....

"The dust over here looks like it's been disturbed recently!" Salainen announced from the right side of the room, near the broken window. Shocked out of her reverie, Brinna gave a start; but she blinked a few times, recovered, and watched the young man investigate first the curtains around the window, then the glass shards on the floor. Before long, she found herself reaching out to tug on Ljuset's sleeve.

"What do you think of him?" she whispered, jerking her head in Salainen's direction.

"Him?" Ljuset echoed absently. "Odd, and came a long way to indulge simple curiosity, but not a bad young man. No, what interests me is"—she stuck out a hand to block Brinna's path as the latter made to advance farther into the room—"the first line from the text: '*the war had gone on before and would have again.*' I can't get it out of my head. Do you think these wars occurred in some kind of cyclical fashion, and the cycle was broken when the darkness took control?"

Brinna shrugged. "To me, that line just means that there were other wars in the past: if not against the Skiai, then against something else. Those belligerent warrior types would never have stopped looking for *some* enemy to fight."

Ljuset looked at her for a long moment, one eyebrow raised, then gave a brief nod and swept away toward the back right corner of the room. Shaking her head in mild annoyance, Brinna crossed over to the largest couch, whose original brown was also tainted purplish-black in places, and began looking under the remaining cushions for any artifact that might be of interest.

"Look at this!"

Again, it was Salainen's voice that shattered the silence. He had been on the left side of the room, at a spot that had not been visible from the entrance due to an inner door that stood open just in front of it, and now he emerged from behind that inner door—with a sphere of swirling blue light in his hands.

"The Essence of Water!" gasped Ljuset.

"Yes," Salainen agreed. "It was just sitting on this shelf here."

He kicked out and pushed the inner door closed, and Brinna caught her first glimpse of the single shelf—now empty—that ran across the wall to the right of the door, just below eye level.

"So, Eudrakes *has* been somewhat active since the realm fell," said Ljuset, "enough to retrieve one of the Essences that was closest to this location. I wonder if he plans to... *by the sun and all other powers of light, I don't believe it!!*"

Brinna, who had been on her way to touch the blue-glowing sphere and see if she could sense the water magic's power, whirled around. Ljuset was standing in front of a small, dark-stained desk near the room's back right corner, one trembling index finger pointed at something on the surface.

Her fellow explorers looked at each other, and in a flash, they had joined her. That turned out to be a dangerous proposition, as both of them almost tripped over a nearby chair, but eventually the three stood clustered around the rickety writing table. The blue sphere, still held in Salainen's hands, threw light onto a dust-covered parchment that lay on the desk's surface beside a nearly threadbare quill.

"Is *this* all?" Brinna demanded in disappointed tones.

"Don't be like that, Brinna," said Ljuset. "No, don't touch it!" she added to Salainen, who had shifted the Essence of Water to his left hand and was reaching down toward the parchment with his right. "It may fall apart if you do that. Just look."

The magic-user held her finger just above the parchment, then moved it slowly down what looked to be a list of people's names, most of them preceded by the first letter in the name of one of the Aktinan military divisions. To the right of each name/abbreviation was a row of checkmarks, some of which terminated in a large "X." Brinna saw the names of three of the old division leaders, each accompanied by a row of checkmarks that ran all the way across the page.

"Eudrakes... was tracking the warriors' ranks," she said tonelessly.

"And their bloodlines," Ljuset added. "Remember what the text said? And look—some of them didn't make it very far at all." She pointed to a name near the top of the list. "This man barely made it farther than the Keraunia girl the text talked about, which means he must have had quite a bit of non-foreign blood in him."

Brinna frowned; this possibility had not occurred to her. "How could any of the warriors have had non-foreign blood, if the text's account is accurate? Relationships with Aktinan civilians at some point in the family tree?"

"Not likely in that elitist and separatist culture," Ljuset objected, "but you never know. What do you think, Salainen? It sounds like your people know a bit about the history of this place."

Salainen hesitated for a moment. "We do know something of worlds and history which other peoples have forgotten," he said at last, slowly, "but our knowledge ends well before the founding of this realm. I believe that, even in years past, there was some question as to who the five main founders actually were and why they started a new and complicated society in this remote corner of the world."

"If there are more of these parchments, going further and further back in time, they might give us some clue," Brinna suggested. "Or, maybe there's some record of the first Eudianax's real name?"

"Both good ideas, Brinna," Ljuset said, impressed. "I suggest that we search these rooms thoroughly and then go back to the..."

She trailed off, leaned backward in apparent surprise, then hunched over the parchment again and made a hand motion toward the Essence of Water. "Can you bring the light a little closer, Salainen? Right about here...."

The sphere's blue light beat back the shadows that had previously obscured the long, scroll-like parchment's top right corner, and now the group could see the word "Aichme?", written in the same handwriting as the other names and enclosed in a circle. Next to it, a single word had been scrawled messily, underlined several times for emphasis.

"What does that word say?" Ljuset asked, squinting and leaning closer. "The underlined one?"

"It looks like the word 'remember,'" said Brinna. "If we interpret that scribble there as a—"

Sudden motion interrupted her: Ljuset had straightened up and spun on her heel, away from the desk. "That seals it," she snarled with uncharacteristic savageness. "Whatever we needed to know about this Eudrakes' character, it's all here in this one word. He won't help us lift the darkness. After all, he *knew about Aichme* and still didn't do anything to stop her??"

A silence fell as Ljuset and Brinna reflected on what Salainen had told them about this most feared woman. How much had Eudrakes known?

"Maybe... his *'eyes couldn't see everything,'* as he always said," Brinna finally offered with a shrug; this was a minor issue in the grand scheme of things.

"It's clear that he could see *her*, at least," Ljuset shot back. "Enough to know her name?"

"I don't know..." Brinna said dubiously. "It looks to me like he was uncertain. And maybe, at the end when she shed her disguise, it was already too late."

"Or, maybe the elemental spirits wouldn't allow him to stop her," Salainen said quietly.

Ljuset scowled. "Which, to me, would be even more damning than deliberate inaction on his part. Even if absent, those elemental spirits were supposed to be forces for good. Why *wouldn't* they come back, why wouldn't they intervene through Eudrakes or otherwise, if such an intervention would save their realm?"

But Salainen shook his head. "Forces for good or not, it doesn't mean much. Some scholars would say that bad outcomes are more common than good ones, even when intentions are good."

There was a pause. Ljuset stared openmouthed at the young man, perhaps surprised to hear such a scholarly comment from a person who had openly professed a lack of interest in reading. Salainen stared right back, with a look on his face that could only be called "defiant," and so the scene remained until Brinna called the pair back to task by suggesting that they all search the list of names for everyone they had read about in the text.

Sure enough, the names were there—except that of Psephos, who had never taken the warrior test—and the records matched the accounts that the book had provided. Even the name "Keraunia" had been entered in at the bottom, her row ending right at the beginning, with a large "X" in the first slot and no abbreviation of a military division to the left of her name.

A brief search of the desk's compartments revealed no

additional parchments or clues, and as Ljuset was no longer keen on the idea of asking Eudrakes for help, Salainen simply put the Essence of Water back where he had found it and then followed the two women as they hurried out of the room. Back through the deserted corridors they all went, past the secret library—even Ljuset admitted that she could use a change of scene after the long hours indoors—and headed for the Palace's main entrance.

Brinna already had several ideas about where they might take their search next, and she struggled to hold them in her mind while she helped Ljuset and Salainen open one of the massive double doors. First the locations of the other Essences, to check the veracity of the stories the book had told, and then any other structures that looked like this Palace, where some of the warriors might have been hiding out *or* might have hidden more documents. Anything that could verify or contradict the complication implied by the parchment in Eudrakes' room....

But just as the group had filed out onto the plain and she had turned her back on the burned, blackened wasteland to assist in closing the door, her peripheral vision caught a flicker of motion—scant seconds before there was a dull *thud* somewhere nearby.

Spinning around, she saw that a figure had just walked backwards into Salainen, who was still struggling to regain his balance; but her hand was less than halfway to her bow and supply of arrows before Ljuset's hand on her lower arm arrested the motion. Looking up, she saw the older woman shake her head and point with her other hand toward the scene of the collision.

There, having just now become disentangled from Salainen, was a young woman with very long, reddish-brown hair, clad in a set of wrinkled robes that was covered in soot over almost its entire length but also looked reddish. The soot even formed several streaks down her face, which was pale, the green eyes wild and horrified. Those eyes blinked once, twice; looked at the three explorers without seeming to see them at all. And then, suddenly, she started spinning in place, face toward the shining purple-and-black sky, both hands raised to shoulder level in an obvious gesture of desperation.

It could not have been clearer to Brinna: this was no person the group had read about in the text. But then, why did she seem almost familiar?

Slowly, arms extended to both sides to hold her companions back, Ljuset approached the spinning figure; and perhaps the sight of another robed person was comforting to the young woman, for she made only two more rotations before stopping. Swaying slightly on her feet, she studied Ljuset for a few seconds—and then she dashed forward, extending her hands in supplication, and the words poured out of her like a landslide. "Please, can you help me? I'm a fire mage from Tetrachtha, and I think I was sent here by accident.... This devastation, it's... it's terrible... but I can't stay. My friends are waiting for me, they have no idea I'm here.... Please, help me get back...."

Ljuset frowned briefly, but then saw the young woman's wide, panicked eyes and arranged her priorities accordingly. "Calm down, please; we'll help you if we can. Who did you say you were?"

"I'm Pyr... a fire mage from Tetrachtha...."

Pyr. Tetrachtha.

Ljuset turned and looked at Brinna, and both raised their eyebrows—their minds again full of the tale Salainen had told them in the secret library.

–END OF PART 0–

INTERLUDE

EUDRAKES, WATCHING FROM AFAR:

HAVING WITNESSED ALL that went on among the three known as Brinna, Ljuset, and Salainen, I sense the unspoken questions that remain. What makes Aktinos/Vilse, this realm with hidden magical and technological histories, "the realm lost in time" as I designated it? Can it be saved? What connections lurk behind the interactions of Psephos, Aichme, and the Skiai? And, more urgently, what does Brinna want? Like many facts relating to the realm itself, the answers lie in the past.

Therefore—to put it in your world's terms—we shall hit the "reset" button for this one time only. We shall cast our eyes back in time and preview our main narrative: the same backstory that was alluded to by Salainen, Keraunia, and myself. There, a cast led by the young fire mage, Pyr, will chronicle the early clashes among the various worlds and factions. And in this grand cycle, the loops of time and tale may begin to close....

THE JOURNEY CONTINUES IN

PART 1
BEYOND THE HOSTILE SKY

One who inquires as to the nature of darkness will derive only confusion from the attempt—for the forms of darkness are as undefinable as they are many. Indeed, there are instances in which light itself can become a darkness.

In such instances, it is as if time has stopped, and one is left standing on the edge of the abyss, staring with an empty heart into the nothingness beyond.

-fragment from a text by a famous soldier-philosopher known to later generations only as "X." His writings, largely pessimistic in nature, contributed to the decline and fall of several civilizations throughout the galaxy.

PROLOGUE
AGE-OLD

TETRACHTHA
SHRINE OF THE EARTH MAGIC

He approached the Shrine cautiously, pausing for a moment beneath the arching entrance to see if some young mage-in-training was inside practicing spells or studying. Many mages felt drawn to this place; that had applied to him once, and in some ways it still did. But no one was in there now. The gloom beyond the arch, interrupted only by a faint green glow, seemed to invite him to enter.

The earth spirits welcomed him, then. A small, carefully controlled part of his mind wondered if they would regret that decision when he had done what he had come to do.

Once inside the rectangular, single-room Shrine, he moved rapidly to the immense runic symbol that was carved into the stone floor's center. Now, in the darkness of night, the rune's green glow seemed even brighter than usual. Other, smaller runes glowed green around the large one, but only the large one's light pulsed at regular intervals.

Great power flowed through that huge, complex symbol: the power of the earth spirits themselves. It was said to be the source of the earth magic, which every Tetrachthan earth mage tapped into unconsciously, but none knew its secret. *He* did, now, after many years of intense magical study. To the others, the rune was unique, foreign, incomprehensible. Only he knew that it was, in fact, accessible—as was the root of the power that the symbol represented.

His green robes brushed against the magical carving as he slowly headed for its center. Sparks flew and crackled, shattering the silence, and he sent a panic-stricken glance toward the shadowy stone alcoves dead ahead, where the light cast by the side walls' torches of green flame did not quite reach. The earth spirits sometimes dwelled in those alcoves, it was whispered. But no hostile beings materialized to do battle, and he chastised himself for his paranoia as he began his spell.

Raising his hand, he began to trace the rune in the air. Little by little it appeared, seemingly etched in green fire in front of him. Though it was the most complex rune he had ever drawn, it was soon complete—a miniature duplicate of the huge symbol on the floor. And, just as he had expected, it began pulsating in perfect sync with its twin. The two were linked; no, they were the same.

Cast a spell through one rune, and he would tap into the other and access the power of the earth spirits. No longer would he be merely Gethen, earth mage of Tetrachtha; with such might at his disposal, he could rule the world, travel to the legendary realm of the elemental spirits, and inaugurate a new world order. And the power was already his; he could feel it filling him even before he tapped into it. The glow emitted by the carvings at his feet intensified until he was completely surrounded by bright green light.

The earth magic had a new master; he was about to take the first step toward fulfilling his duty. Smiling to himself, he began to speak the sequence of sounds that the rune represented.

All at once, the Shrine's torches flared up. The green flames shot almost to the ceiling, their shadows dancing menacingly on the walls behind them. At the same time, the rest of the room darkened even more, as if the green fire were devouring all other light.

Startled, Gethen broke off in mid-speech... but it was too late. A sense of external anger came crashing down on him, an incredible wrath that filled the room, surrounding him, cutting off all air. So palpable was the divine fury that it could almost be put into words: *You know too much.*

Gasping for breath, he attempted to maintain his balance. The green flames were climbing even higher.

"I am not afraid of you!" he bellowed as soon as he felt able to. "I know your secrets. I *will* defeat you!" Again, he began to speak the rune that hovered in front of him.

As soon as the first syllable passed his lips, green lightning lanced forth from the massive torch-flames to strike the hovering rune, which exploded dangerously. Nevertheless, he stood his ground with a determined stubbornness and began to redraw the symbol when the explosion had cleared.

On the room's far side, in the shadow-shrouded alcoves, creatures were now appearing—perhaps rising out of the ground, or simply materializing out of nothing. The deep darkness prevented Gethen from getting a good look at them, but he could see that they were tall and advancing rapidly— right at him.

Swiftly, he converted his half-finished rune into an attack spell. One, and the ground rippled violently under the advancing beings, knocking them down and throwing them into confusion. Another, and a wall of thorny bushes sprang up between him and his foes to slow their charge. Yet another, and a section of the floor split open into a chasm that, in its few seconds of existence, swallowed dozens of creatures. He drew rune after rune, cast spell after spell, faster and faster, but it was never enough; for every creature he destroyed, at least three more were spawned.

Finally, fatigue demanded its tribute and he could do no more, but the army of the earth spirits—if that was what the monsters were—was still charging toward him. Cursing loudly, he whirled around and sprinted back toward the Shrine's entrance.

More lightning flashed behind him—this time aimed at his destination—and where it struck, a mound of earth sprang up to block the exit. Now, at last, terror filled him; but he turned around calmly to face his doom.

To his great surprise, the host from which he had fled was gone, with small, scattered mounds of dirt the only evidence of its having ever existed. But for those and the still-oversized torch-flames, the Shrine's interior would have looked almost normal.

A phantom army, then. Perhaps the earth spirits were going to pardon him after all?

No. The aura of wrath had intensified still more; it was crushing him, smothering him. *We will destroy you utterly,* it seemed to be saying. *You will regret what you have done this day. The whole world shall regret it.*

And then, the ground began to shake. Chunks of stone from the ceiling plummeted to the floor mere feet from where he stood frozen. A violent, localized tremor then seized that same floor, which gaped open, splitting the huge runic symbol in half; its green glow began to fade as the power slowly seeped out of it.

Now the earth spirits' plan was clear: they intended to destroy not only the one who had offended them, but also the Shrine itself, the center of the earth magic on Tetrachtha. Surely there must be some escape... but what?

The earthquake raged on, the Shrine continued to collapse in on itself with falling blocks and shattering torch-holders. In panic, losing his balance and surrounded by deadly destruction, Gethen cast about him for a rune, *any rune....* His eyes fell on one, a small carved symbol just below the now-sundered large one, and without even pausing to think, he drew it with faint and fading green lines.

There; it was complete. He shouted something—just what, he was not sure—and shoved with all his might and waning magical power; *something* opened up before him; and then the ground heaved beneath his feet and he fell forward. When he landed, there was brief pain, and then the darkness consumed him at last.

✦✦✦

THE GALAXY, TETARTON SECTOR

"Now approaching the enemy's position. Reduce your pursuit speeds for now, but be ready to assume attack formation on my command."

At once, acknowledgments of the order came over the comm, their sounds seemingly filling the space inside the single-pilot ship. They varied widely, with nearly as many types as there were members of Erythron Squadron. "Yes, Squadron Leader." "Acknowledged." "I copy, Squadron Leader Aïdelos." "Awaiting further orders, sir." Then they were gone, silence reigned, and Aïdelos was again alone with his thoughts. They were many, and none of them pleasant.

Some kilometers in front of the twelve silver-and-red spaceships of Erythron Squadron, a second squadron moved through the star-spotted vacuum of space. Those ships, grayish and clunky in appearance, belonged to the enemy—the opposing force against which Aïdelos and the rest of the Nautikon Ouranothi were fighting in this already interminable war.

They were strange, these enemies. They had come out of nowhere some months before, just barely detected by the long-range sensors in the fleet's base as they zoomed with guns blazing toward an inhabited region of a different sector; luckily, one of the lower squadrons had coincidentally been in the area and intervened to prevent the assault. After that, the war had begun with a vengeance. Never had the Nautikon Ouranothi found out what the enemy had wanted in that region of space; nothing was known about the foes themselves, much less their motives. All Aïdelos knew was that they were like no other opponent he had faced in his nearly twenty years as a galactic fighter pilot.

He watched the enemy vessels carefully, looked for signs that one of them had detected Erythron Squadron. Nothing. The ships flew on, and there was nothing to do but maintain a pursuit course until their destination became clear.

Not for the first time, the actions of the enemies baffled him. It was strange enough that they maintained total comm silence; they had never once contacted the Nautikon Ouranothi, not even for purposes of demand-making or intimidation, and not a single transmission or bit of chatter had ever been picked up from their side. But to fly obsolete, generations-old spacecraft was an entirely different level of "odd." The enemy fighters were old enough to be recognized only by patrons of museums dedicated to the history of space warfare... and yet, they did not fly and fight as if they were ancient.

No, they were dangerous. And deadly. Many fighters had already been lost in the war—in one way or another—and many more would follow, unless there was a tactical or technological breakthrough.

"It seems they're headed for an inhabited part of this sector, sir," one of the pilots said suddenly over the comm. "Maybe we should strike before they get there?"

His reverie broken, Aïdelos tore his gaze away from the fleeing vessels and looked down at his gleaming, silvery console with its lights and screens. A few calculations and a glance at the star chart in his ship's database quickly verified what the other pilot had said and then some: the enemy was on a direct line with a system that was startlingly close to the location of the war's first skirmish. These foes, whoever they were, could not be allowed to visit their aggression on innocent inhabitants of other worlds.

"Thank you, Ischuron-6," he said presently. "Erythron Squadron, form up into flights. Engage the enemy, and fire at will." The comm again buzzed with acknowledgments of the order, and within moments, the squadron had assumed the traditional "triple-V" attack formation.

Accelerating to intercept velocity, Erythron Squadron swooped down on its adversary, and bright-red lasers lit up the blackness of space as the assault began. The old-looking enemy ships seemed to absorb much of the laser fire without sustaining significant damage, but the same could not be said for the onslaught of missiles and photon torpedoes. Within moments, one particularly well-placed torpedo had torn into an enemy fighter, consuming first its engine and then the rest of it in a spectacular fireball.

One down, Aïdelos thought to himself—but he knew that the battle would cease to be so one-sided as soon as the enemy started fighting back. And that did indeed prove to be the case.

"That's another hit on my hull! By the stars—I can't get rid of him!!"

The voice, coming in over the usual mid-battle squadron chatter, was loud enough to catch Aïdelos' attention, and although the pilot had not named himself or his ship's designation, his voice was recognizable as that of the Ischuron pilot who had spoken earlier. A quick look through the battle's regulated chaos at the squadron's Ischuron contingent revealed one ship that was flying erratically, trying to shake off the relentless pursuit of an enemy fighter. The escape attempt's success would depend on Ischuron-6's speed and agility, and bombers were not known for either.

Swiftly, Aïdelos scanned the field, his trained eye cutting

through the confusion of spaceship motion and weapons fire to recognize the formations and tactics that the other flights were using while his mind computed how many more direct hits a bomber's armored hull might be able to absorb. Once he had a satisfactory plan of action, he opened up a limited comm channel to his own Synethon Flight and issued a few quick commands.

"Are you sure, Squadron Leader, sir?" asked another familiar voice in tones of consternation. "It's risky. One of us could easily—"

"Trust me on this, Lieutenant," Aïdelos cut in smoothly. "I have a plan. Just keep them busy while I execute the maneuver."

Breaking away from the formation, the Squadron Leader punched a sequence of buttons to send his ship into a slight dive, waited a few seconds, and then moved from the dive into a steep climb. The second maneuver, precisely timed, brought him into the heart of the enemy's formations without disrupting what his own squadron was doing. Weaving this way and that to avoid collisions, sending the occasional laser or missile after enemy vessels to add to their confusion, he had no trouble locating and eliminating the small, if swift, craft that had been pursuing Ischuron-6.

"Wow, sir! Thank you! I haven't seen flying like that in a—"

"Concentrate on the battle," Aïdelos said sharply. He spoke over the general comm channel, so as to bring an end to the enthusiastic effusions of his other squadronmates—but the word '*battle*' was not yet out before a fireball engulfed a different Ischuron ship, which had likewise been under enemy pursuit for the last several seconds. The unlucky pilot's scream drowned out the final few "*Well done, sir!*"s and "*I can't believe it!*"s, and it seemed to resonate in Aïdelos' mind long after the light of the explosion had faded from existence.

He sighed. This was, by far, his least favorite part of being a fighter pilot: the need to face the knowledge that one could not do everything. And it would never do to underestimate these enemies. Their ships might be old, and they were sometimes slow to react to mid-battle changes, but now—as often—Aïdelos came away with the impression that the two sides were, on the whole, evenly matched.

While he was on his way back to his place at the front of the Synethon formation, his console beeped warningly, and he realized just in time that a seeker missile had his ship targeted. Veering away from his fellow fighters, he quickly began a sequence of evasive maneuvers.

Up and down he flew, in circles and spirals; yet the missile remained behind him, untiring, unyielding. He knew he could not ask the others in the squadron for aid; they were occupied with their own battles, and a decade had passed since the fleet had seen someone who could shoot small projectiles down in mid-flight.

Only one course of action seemed doable in any way, though it was a good one—satisfying in more than one respect.

With that, he increased his ship's speed to maximum and entered into a wide, downward arc toward the enemy formation. As he flew down past the enemy ships, they were between him and the missile, and as the missile continued to home in on his position, it slammed into one.

Heaving a sigh of relief, feeling like he had avenged the fallen Ischuron pilot to some extent, he rejoined his own formation, surveyed the field again, and—finding it to his satisfaction—began to encourage his fighters to take out what enemy ships remained...

But found himself cut off by another voice. "Squadron Leader Aïdelos?" The scout.

"Yes, what is it?"

"I'm detecting some strange energy readings, sir. Sensors picked them up just a few minutes ago. Transmitting data now."

Irritated, Aïdelos started to tell the scout that he was in the middle of a battle and could not waste time on something so insignificant... but he fell silent as the sensor readings appeared on one of his instrument panel's largest screens. They were indeed odd, the data lines green and jagged and illogical—like no form of energy he had ever seen or learned about. "You picked these up a few minutes ago?"

"Yes, sir."

"Where did they come from?"

The scout paused for a moment. "W-Well, Squadron Leader, they appeared to be coming from a nearby planet, s-so I... I flew over there...."

"And you are there now," Aïdelos said flatly.

"Y-Yes, s-sir," the scout stammered. "I-In orbit."

A grayish enemy ship flew past Aïdelos' fighter just then, and he fired savagely at it with red lasers as he reprimanded the scout. "You were not assigned to go chasing after energy signals. Your area of expertise is military tactics, and we need you behind enemy lines, analyzing movements and coming up with strategies! What do you have to say for yourself?"

"Nothing," the scout said timidly. "The signals were very faint, and I thought they might be of importance to our war, so I decided to check them out...."

The enemy fighter exploded, overcome by Aïdelos' concentrated laser fire, and with the imminent threat gone, he took another look at the data the scout had transmitted. "What do you mean? How might they be of importance?"

"First of all, they came from a planet near the system where we first encountered the enemy, where it first displayed its aggression. Maybe it's a coincidence, but there's very little space traffic in this part of Tetarton, and why else would we be all the way out here if not to protect..."

"Point taken," Aïdelos told the scout sharply. He really had to stop the man's rambling if he was going to bring himself and the squadron safely through the battle. "Proceed."

"Well, sir, I wondered if that's what the enemy is interested in—"

Aïdelos, who had been wheeling his fighter around to engage another enemy ship, stopped abruptly, his attention seized by what the scout had said. "You think it might be a weapon?"

"I'm not sure, sir. I've never seen anything like these readings before. But whatever made the signals, it's certainly powerful. It seems to have leveled an entire stone building on the planet's surface...."

Aïdelos' ship shook from an enemy attack, and he rebuked himself for his lapse in concentration. Turning his fighter around to engage his foe, he said to the scout: "I will inform the Commander. But have the planet's inhabitants detected you in orbit?"

"I don't think so, Squadron Leader. This seems to be a pre-space-travel civilization. Scans indicate little to no technology—certainly nothing that could see through a cloak."

"Good. Transmit the planet's coordinates to me, and then return to base. I will take care of the investigation from here."

"Acknowledged. Sending coordinates now."

When the conversation had ended, Aïdelos saw in surprise that the battle was also over. Had the enemy squadron been defeated? No—it was withdrawing in the direction it had come from, some Erythron fighters following in eager pursuit before Aïdelos stopped them. Both sides had suffered losses in the brief skirmish, as proven by the weakly shining space debris that littered the immediate area, and neither had won outright—another stalemate.

This entire war was turning into a stalemate, with little to no progress made by either side. If it continued in this way, both combatants would be obliterated, Nautikon Ouranothi and mysterious foes alike. At this point, *anything* that might turn the tide in the fleet's favor would be quite welcome, and Aïdelos very much hoped that the Commander would decide to pursue these odd energy signatures.

After all, he reflected as the other members of Erythron Squadron gave casualty and damage reports, there was only one thing more frightening than the prospect of such a mutually destructive war: namely, the fear that the enemy would reach the source of the strange and powerful energy, whatever it was, first.

CHAPTER ONE
LIGHTNING-STRUCK

THE RUNE HOVERED amid the dry desert air, its color a blue so dark that it was almost black. It glowed menacingly, but instead of countering it right away, Pyr looked at it, scrutinized it, tried to read it. An attack spell, even if she could not know more; water mages had their secrets that those who wielded the fire magic, however far they progressed in their magical studies, could never find out. Still, she tried to glean *something* meaningful from that foreign symbol floating before her.

Seconds later, the young man who had drawn the rune cast his spell through it, and a thick stream of steaming water shot from it in Pyr's direction. She hastened to draw a rune of her own, this one glowing a blazing red, and summoned a wall of fire between herself and the water. The liquid sizzled and evaporated as it struck the protective barrier. She grinned triumphantly—

But then the dark-blue rune moved of its own accord, higher and higher, and aimed its liquid stream over the fiery wall. In response, she added strokes to her red symbol, which still hovered near her hand, and fed it more power. The wall grew to greater and greater heights, raging but under complete control. As the blue rune flew to her right, she made the fire expand sideways, wrap around her with hardly a foot to spare, until it formed a circle. There; she had won.

Suddenly, the sand just beyond the wall erupted as something shot up out of it: a massive serpentine head and neck, eyeless and scaleless, made entirely from bluish water. She jumped in fright, and her protective flames diminished as she started to lose concentration.

The watery serpent opened its mouth and spat from above the weakening wall, drenching her with ice-cold water from head to toe. Her focus shattered, she had no choice but to watch the flames fade.

Swinging its giant head, the water-serpent struck the now-exposed red rune, which fell apart, its glow dying like the fire. The duel was over.

Pyr shivered as she glared at the triumphant young water mage. "You didn't have to *soak* me!" she snapped.

"Well, you didn't have to let me," the young man shot back with a very small smile.

"What do you mean? How could I have anticipated *that*??" Filled with indignation and bafflement, she pointed to the round hole in the sand where the serpent had come from. The serpent itself was gone; only a small puddle of water remained. "You have too much faith in me, Aneuthen."

"No, you couldn't have anticipated the serpent. But you could have broken my spell long before then."

She looked at him incredulously.

"You spent all your effort just now on defense," he continued. "Why shield yourself from the water attacks when you could have struck out with fire and destroyed the rune? You know that fire, unlike water, is highly destructive in all its forms, and you saw that I had left the rune unprotected. One single attack spell, and you would have won."

With that, he began lecturing her on the advantages of offensive magic over defensive magic, and she stood silently under the hot sun of her home Region, wondering—not for the first time—how he could know all that he was telling her. After all, he could not be more than twenty or so years old. *She* was eighteen, not all that much younger than he was, and still in training to be a fire mage, while *his* blue robes and immense magical knowledge revealed him to be a full water mage. But then again, she reflected, there was a lot about him that she did not know.

She had not the faintest idea, for example, what had led him to offer to help her train. Some weeks before, he had come upon her practicing spells here in the desert-bound and volcanic Region of Fire and, after introducing himself, wasted no time before making the offer. From that moment on, he had had her training and practicing for most of her waking hours. Yes, it was decidedly odd.

Not that she felt no gratitude toward him for his assistance. In fact—she told herself for about the hundredth time since she had met him—she had never seen anyone so *handsome*. Tall and looking quite thin even in his rippling water-mage robes, he had short dark-brown hair, a well-proportioned face that offered just the right blend of masculinity and friendliness, and the most beautifully profound brown eyes in the world. Even his name, "Aneuthen," had a pleasing sound to it, in her opinion at least. Best of all, however, was his slight accent: a low and soft drawl that rolled off his tongue and served to emphasize the fact that he hailed from another part of the world. His voice was never very loud, which often forced her to stand quite close to him to hear him—though that, of course, was no more a burden than having a close-up view of those serious brown eyes was.

So, she liked him—more than she had expected to and much more than she had liked any of her fellow trainees back home—but, without a doubt, he remained a very mysterious figure. Among the mysteries being... why would someone from the Region of Water want to help train a fire mage?

"This is what I've been trying all along to teach you," he droned on, and she relieved her boredom by attempting to dry herself off *without* a rune to focus and direct the magical power, the presence of which would alert him to her inattentiveness. If this handsome young man had a fault, she decided, it was that he was so all-business all the time. He always wanted to talk about the magic and her training—that and nothing else....

"...You should focus on attack magic first and foremost. Defensive magic can shield you, but if you're quick and precise with your attack, you won't need to think about defense at all: foes will be defeated with less effort and even less time. Let's practice again, with this in mind."

Now completely dry, though more because of the desert air than her "no-rune" experiment, she just barely caught the end of his lecture. "Yes, Aneuthen," she replied tonelessly as she waited for him to make the first move in another mock magical duel—at least the fortieth such duel today, and the day was young yet....

In a flash, he was tracing another dark-blue rune in the air. Remembering what he had told her about offensive magic, she did not let him finish before drawing a symbol of her own: one of the simplest and quickest ones. It immediately sent a thin stream of fire toward the partially complete water rune, which started to melt and cave in when the fire touched it. At last it fell apart, and the water spell was broken before it could even be cast.

But Aneuthen was not done. After flashing her another small half-smile as a sign of his approval, he began drawing the same rune again, this time more rapidly. As she struggled to catch up with her own spell, he added a stroke to one side of the complex figure, and the rune vanished. An instant later, he cast his spell through the now-invisible symbol, and jets of water erupted from the sand all around Pyr, surrounding her with their tall fountains.

Quickly, she modified her half-finished red rune, and multiple streams of fire issued from it, each aimed at the base of one of the fountains that obstructed her view of her opponent. Those fountains died down in small explosions of steam, but more sprang up elsewhere as if to mock her with the knowledge that Aneuthen's spell was still active—that the invisible rune, wherever it was, remained intact.

At one time, she would have considered experimenting with the runic language to see if she could break the spell of invisibility... but not now. Attack magic was indeed working as Aneuthen had said it would, and she determined to keep using it. And so, while maintaining her first spell to keep the fountains in check, she drew up a new rune and sent all her available magical strength into it.

Instantly, fire exploded from it in all directions to form an expanding circle, like rippling water or a shockwave, at the height where Aneuthen had originally drawn his rune before making it invisible. The fiery circle was not meant to hurt him, of course; she had been careful to limit its radius so that it would not reach him. But it *did* apparently reach, strike, and obliterate the invisible water rune, because the fountains of water vanished and no new ones sprang up.

"Very good," said Aneuthen as Pyr ended the spells she had cast and dispelled the runes. "You're really starting to make progress, and I suspect you'll be a powerful fire mage one day. What do you think: should we take a short break?"

A break. Never had such a simple phrase sounded so good to her.

Instead of replying verbally, she let herself fall into the warm sand and took slow, deep breaths as she tried to recover from the strain of holding two spells active at the same time. Even as she did so, however, she was under no illusions that the lesson would stop altogether; and sure enough, Aneuthen soon began to pace back and forth in front of her while he continued speaking.

"As you know, elemental magic works with substances. Fire, water, earth, air: each is a natural substance, and magical theory holds that these substances stand in a hierarchical relationship to one another."

Pyr rubbed her forehead absentmindedly while she tried to remember what she had been taught during the first stage of her training. "Well, it's a circular hierarchy. Each element has its own set of characteristics, and they're all different so that no element is strong against everything *or* weak against everything."

"Right. This is a useful concept where the theory is concerned, but when we look at the practical side of things, there is one major drawback: ideas such as this one imply that the four substances are entirely separate when we intuitively know this to be untrue. Water can turn into ice, in which form it's solid like earth and rock, or it can resemble air when it turns into steam. Similarly, volcanic lava burns like fire but is liquid like water—and since it's really molten rock, we can look at it as also falling under the category of 'earth.' In that sense, it's just another of the materials the world's core is made out of."

"But even so, no one would ever confuse the categories. No one would mistake a block of ice for a rock, and no one would look at a pool of lava and decide to go for a swim in it. Regardless of specific forms, water is water and fire is fire."

"True," Aneuthen conceded with a nod. His blue robes rippled and kicked up sand as he continued his pacing. "And that's my point. The magic actually respects the categorical distinctions you just mentioned, even as it also allows some flexibility. That last spell you cast, the fiery circle, doesn't resemble any naturally-occurring form of fire, and yet you were still able to create it. If used responsibly, this freedom can be helpful, but if taken to the extreme, it can be dangerous."

She raised an eyebrow. "...Dangerous?"

"Yes." He backed up a few steps. "Create a standard fire between the two of us, as close to the midpoint as you can."

Obediently she raised her hand, though she remained seated to protest how short this "break" had been. A few rune-strokes later, a small fire had sprung up at the indicated spot: a bright but contained blaze, rather like a campfire but without a pile of wood beneath it.

"Good," said Aneuthen. "Now, modify your spell to change the fire into liquid form, like lava."

She moved her hand to the side to draw a new rune, but stopped when she saw him shaking his head. "No, don't cast a new spell," he told her. "Whatever the rune for 'liquid fire' looks like, change the rune you already have to look like it."

Biting her lip despite her best efforts not to, she stared at her red-glowing rune; this was a highly unusual exercise. Eventually, however, an idea came to her and she went to work, adding and removing strokes as best as she could without tampering with the original rune's root.

Aneuthen clapped his hands once, loudly, and she looked up to see that her standard fire had shrunk and seemed to be halfway between its original form and a liquid form. The remaining flames danced; what liquid there was bubbled; both areas flickered before giving way to a bright, if small, explosion.

Pyr, skidding backward in fright, saw Aneuthen waving one hand as if to dispel the rune. Swiftly, she imitated the motion, and the symbol vanished together with the exploding, fiery mass.

Stepping closer, the water mage looked down at the charred area that the spell had left behind. "There are substances in nature that just can't coexist. Like the previously-mentioned lava and water: the former would burn away the latter. And the magic knows this; it knows that fire and liquid are, on some abstract level, separate."

"That's why I couldn't modify my spell?"

"Yes, and this is very important. You can cast a 'liquid fire' spell with the proper runic root, but you should never add it as a characteristic to a normal fire spell because that would create a contradiction. It's best to treat the magic with care and respect its boundaries, because if you don't, you might trigger a reaction that will blow up in your face like that one did."

"Point taken," she murmured, likewise staring at the charred area. "I wonder why the mages at the School never mentioned anything about this."

He shrugged. "Most mages just cast the spells that were taught to *them*; they don't have your innate creativity and imagination. That's why I knew I had to emphasize this point in one of our lessons."

She was silent at that, remembering her course in Beginners' Spell Modification. The teacher of that class had seemed creative enough and had assigned his students more than a few challenging exercises. Memory after memory flooded her mind, and the flow did not stop until she became aware that Aneuthen was looking at her expectantly.

"Hmm? Did you say something?" she inquired.

"I asked if you felt rested enough to resume the mock battling. I have something a little more challenging in mind this time, to further test your abilities...."

Those words were ominous, and as it turned out, his spell was formidable indeed. The rune he drew, breathtakingly complex, pulsated with power as it hovered, but nothing happened while Pyr was pushing herself to her feet or for several seconds thereafter. Then the sky darkened as clouds materialized directly above the two young people, a few moments before torrential rain came pouring down. Thunder roared in the distance.

Once again being soaked in the middle of a desert, Pyr tried several spells to destroy the dark-blue rune that hovered, glittering among the raindrops, but her fire was extinguished by the watery downpour every time. Aneuthen seemed to be preparing another spell, perhaps an attack spell, and she saw nothing that she could do about it. The "holding-two-spells" episode, as well as the other events of this lesson, had drained her, and she could not think for the weariness.

It seemed certain: she had failed, and Aneuthen was going to win again. Lightning flashed and thunder crashed somewhere nearby, mirroring the chaos of disappointment and failure and exhaustion all swirling around in her mind.

Then, suddenly, a loud *roar* came from overhead.

Their concentration shattered, both combatants looked up into the sky to see… *something*. Silver and red in color, shining metallically in the light of the distant sun, it appeared to be struggling as it tried to escape the storm. Its path was erratic, it was slowly losing altitude, and smoke was issuing from it in several places.

"…Standard fighter," Aneuthen muttered.

Pyr turned to him in surprise. "What did you say? Do you know what it is?" But he said nothing and continued watching the sky, his blue rune floating forgotten in front of him.

As the two of them watched, another bolt of lightning shot out from the localized clump of dark clouds and struck the strange flying metal object. The roaring sound grew in intensity until it was almost deafening, and flames broke out in many places on the object's surface as it plummeted downward and landed with a *crash* somewhere in the distance.

Her fatigue and the storm's soaking rain forgotten, Pyr

turned to Aneuthen, who was now staring moodily in the direction the flying object had gone. "Let's go see what that was!"

"No," he said shortly, without turning around.

"No?" she repeated, taken aback. "We can continue practicing later—and you said earlier that I'm making significant progress. So why can't we take a *longer* break this time and do something else?"

"What's happened isn't our concern," he replied. "You saw the foreign technology. Whoever was flying that... that *thing* isn't of this world. Come on; let's go somewhere else."

She stared at him, appalled. "But—someone may be hurt!"

"Or, someone may be hostile. Our magic wouldn't stand a chance against foreign weapons—we'd be destroyed! Forget about it. It's too dangerous, Pyr."

Finally he turned to face her, and she thought she saw a glimmer of real fear in his eyes. He must truly be concerned about danger, then. Never before had she witnessed a manifestation of fear from him; he had always been calm, collected, and confident.

But mere apprehension would not stop her from investigating the recent occurrence and satisfying her curiosity. How was she to get away?

The cessation of rainfall and a sudden brightening of the sky interrupted her thoughts: Aneuthen had let his storm spell dissipate and was walking away, apparently expecting her to follow. She grinned to herself. *Now* she could escape.

As quickly as she could, she drew up another fire rune, and a circle of flames surrounded the walking water mage, who immediately stopped and whirled around to see what was going on. Unfazed, she added a few more strokes to the fiery symbol in front of her, as she had done earlier, and the flames rose taller and taller until Aneuthen was completely obscured from view. *There.* The fire would not harm him—unless he touched it, of course—but only distract him for a time.

Whipping around, she took off at a rapid sprint toward the spot where the foreign metal object—*what* had Aneuthen called it?—had vanished from her sight. The sandy terrain with its dunes and cacti, dotted with boulders cast long ago from the line of volcanoes that loomed on the southern horizon, was not conducive to running, nor were her brown robes of a mage-in-training; several times she tripped and fell face-first into the sand, only to scramble to her feet and sprint onward. On one occasion, she glanced back while running at full speed to see if her fire spell was still intact—it was, the circle of flames towering toward the sky—and fell over a large rock in the process. Again, however, she pushed herself back up and resumed her flight.

If Aneuthen were to catch up to her now, all would be lost. Enough was probably lost as it was, she realized: she had most likely earned his ire and lost his help in the training process. It would be unbearable to lose that *and* the opportunity to see the crashed object.

Finally, after what seemed like forever, she caught sight of the wreck, which was still giving off smoke in places, and moments later, she had arrived. Stopping to catch her breath, she gazed intently at the winged object.

It was quite large—larger than it had seemed when it was in the air—and mostly the odd, metallic silver she had glimpsed from a distance, with red designs in the shape of lightning bolts running down the sides. As impressive as the painted bolts were, however, it had been a bolt of real lightning that brought this thing down.

Black structures, most long and thin but still massive, protruded from beneath both wings, all intimidating in appearance and all pointing in the direction that she assumed was "front." Were these the weapons Aneuthen had spoken of? Either way, it was clear that this object had not been designed with any peaceful purpose in mind.

After completing one half-circuit around the huge, silvery shape, she discovered what appeared to be a door of some kind built into one side. It took a few moments of alternately yanking and pushing, but eventually she managed to tug it open—at which point it fell off into the sand. Only darkness was visible within. Taking a deep breath, the young would-be fire mage climbed up into another world.

That was what it seemed like, at least. After the bright sunshine outside, the inside seemed pitch-black at first, despite the meager light let in by a severely curved window at the other end of this... room, or whatever it was. Pyr blinked several times to help her eyes adjust to the new lighting, and when she could see again, she noticed with surprise that the object's interior was a lot smaller than it had seemed from the outside: only a group of two or three might have been able to stand comfortably in the narrow, cramped space.

But then again, she recalled, the exterior *had* been dominated by the object's wings and other bits of foreign technology, the latter of which was omnipresent here also. Rows of small, raised lights were everywhere: some brightly lit or blinking, but most dark and damaged. Even as she watched, some of the still-glowing lights gave off sparks, flickered, and went dark; other areas had apparently been scorched, judging by the dark markings that covered them and—in a couple of places—the tiny tendrils of smoke that were still rising into the air. The whole place exuded a foreign and ominous aura.

And then, the silence was shattered by a faint sound resembling a groan.

Startled, she followed the brief disturbance to its source: a person lying on the floor near the oddly-shaped window and some kind of chair at what—as she had correctly guessed—was the flying object's front. The person was dressed strangely, in a non-robe-like garment whose basic black was mottled with a small quantity of chaotic red markings, and appeared to be seriously hurt.

Pyr wasted no time. Within seconds she had knelt beside the injured person, who turned out to be a young man, perhaps two or three years older than Aneuthen, with dark hair that was currently encrusted with dried blood. He was also handsome, though not quite at Aneuthen's level, she decided; and despite the one groan, he was so still that she deemed him to be on the brink of unconsciousness.

Despite Aneuthen's warnings about danger, she found herself feeling fascinated by, and drawn to, this foreigner. What could have injured him so badly? The crash, obviously, but what about it? His clothing was torn in places, bloody in others, and scorched in still others, but there was no trace of a major wound that had left him in this state. Perhaps it was the head wound. She stretched out a hand to touch the back of his head, to see if she could locate the injury—

Without warning, he came to life, opening his eyes and attempting to move away from her—only to collapse with a pain-filled groan. Nevertheless, he still shrank from her and fixed her with a nervous gaze.

"It's all right—I'm not going to hurt you," she told him reassuringly, hoping at the same time that he could understand her language. "My name is Pyr, and I'm in training to be a fire mage. Who are you?"

After several tries, the young man managed to speak—in a voice so hoarse and faint as to be nearly unintelligible. "You... inhabitant of this... planet?"

She gave a start. "Of course!" she exclaimed, but then remembered that *he* was not. Although he looked human enough, he was not from Tetrachtha. "What are you doing here?"

"S-Sent here," he gasped. "Recon... mission. To watch...

for... enemy activity."

"Enemy activity? Are you fighting a war?"

He nodded slightly.

"Where?" she asked, her eyes widening. "In the... sky?" Perhaps that was why he had been flying this odd machine.

"Beyond... the sky. Beyond... this world. In many sectors of... the galaxy."

If Pyr had been fascinated before, now she was enthralled. This wounded man was not just a non-Tetrachthan; he was a fighter! "But... why were you sent *here*? We don't have any... technology... like yours in our world."

Though paler now than he had been, and exhausted from talking, the young man tried very hard to continue; his nearly bloodless lips moved and trembled, attempting to form sounds, before he was finally able to push a few whispered words out. "This... planet... This planet is in..."

Before he could finish, his face turned several shades whiter, and he fell back to the floor—still alive, but barely. Blood continued to ooze from his various wounds.

The stranger's half-finished statement forgotten, Pyr cast about frantically for some way to help him, to prevent him from dying of his injuries. There was one possibility: a healing spell that she had read about during the earliest stages of her training, but had never actually tried. Not the best of options, to be sure, but her only one at the moment.

As slowly as she dared with the young man bleeding his life out before her, she drew a rune from the spellbook that all mages-in-training studied and memorized. As it was one of the more complex symbols, she drew it carefully—she would not have done so with a rune for an attack spell, studied diligently and practiced with Aneuthen until drawing it was second nature—and examined it when it was complete. It *looked* correct, but there was no way to verify that without consulting the spellbook, which she had left behind in the

School for the Training of Fire Mages and the Study of the Fire Magic upon beginning this second, "magic-in-practice" stage of her training. She had no choice but to cast the spell and hope for the best.

And so, before she could convince herself not to, she fed the rune magical power. *Fire as purifier. Fire as preserver. Fire as life-giver!* The glowing red rune began to lose color as its power seeped into the wounded young man. So far, so good....

Sudden footsteps behind her announced Aneuthen's arrival. Fearfully she turned around, the remnants of the pale-red symbol collapsing in on themselves as her concentration was shattered, and waited for the wrathful lecture that was sure to come.

But Aneuthen now stood frozen, his face draining of all color as he fixed a terrified gaze on a point just beyond her. Exactly what he was looking at, she was unsure, but his dread was obvious.

"Aneuthen?" she asked gently. "Are you all right?"

Still apparently oblivious to her presence, Aneuthen stood silently and began to tremble. His eyes never moved from whatever he was looking at, but the rest of him shook as his face finished its transformation from a healthy tannish color to sheet-white. He looked like he was about to be sick.

Seeing this, she stood up and went to him. "Aneuthen," she repeated, laying a steadying hand on his arm. "Look at me. Are you all right?"

His strange, trancelike state broken, he jerked his head around and glared at her. "Don't touch me," he snapped in a low but dangerous tone, yanking his arm roughly from her grasp. Despite the fierce glare, however, his eyes still gleamed with terror, and his voice shook slightly as he continued: "You shouldn't have come here. You have placed both of us in grave danger."

"*Grave danger*"? This strange crashed object represented

many things, but Pyr could see no potential peril in it. "What are you so afraid of?" she countered. "*Him?*" She gestured at the injured young man, still lying unconscious on the floor where she had found him. "He isn't dangerous. He was very nice, and he's severely hurt anyway!"

In a sudden—and unusual—flash of caution, she decided to leave out her attempted healing spell. Had it lasted long enough to work? At the moment, she did not dare check. "There was no hostility whatsoever; in fact, *he* was afraid of *me* at first! And..." Her voice took on an awed tone. "He was telling me about a war in the sky."

Aneuthen ignored her. "It's time to go," he announced, and with that, he herded her toward the doorway. Once they were both outside, he led her away from the wreck, this time looking back every few seconds to make sure she followed and did not cast any spells.

Surprisingly, he manifested no more anger toward her and gave no indication that he would stop helping her with the training. Indeed, everything seemed to be back to normal— almost. During the long walk back to the pair's unofficial dueling ground, the young water mage seemed to exude fear, and he clearly was still flustered, more than Pyr would ever have thought possible for him. What was more, every so often he would pause to glance back in the direction of the wreck, even long after it had passed out of his range of sight, with an agitated and apprehensive expression.

Pyr, who had found the incident and the discovery of a non-Tetrachthan stranger thoroughly fascinating, could understand neither Aneuthen's fear nor his silence. What could it be that had so upset him?

CHAPTER TWO
FOURFOLD

A TERRIBLE SILENCE descended on the Chamber of the Hypsothi, from one wall of plain gray stone to the next, as the four mages seated around the room's large square table attempted to absorb what had just been said. As the joint leaders of Tetrachtha, all four were accustomed to grim news and difficult decisions, but none of their years of experience could have prepared them for *this*.

"Are you certain that what you have said is correct?" asked one of the seated mages, dressed in white robes, of the green-clad earth mage who had brought the report. The man had stated his position as some high-ranking teacher or researcher, but that, along with his name, had been forgotten as soon as he delivered his news. "That there isn't some mistake?"

The earth mage's eyes flashed with indignation, but he recovered quickly and said humbly: "I am certain, High One. It is as I told you."

"Perhaps this is an isolated occurrence," suggested the red-robed fire mage who was seated on the table's south side. "Fluctuations in the magic. It isn't always stable, after all." Even as he spoke, he knew the improbability of his theory; but he felt a need to propose an alternative explanation. *Anything* other than what had already been said.

The messenger shook his head. "The problem is universal, and it started just after that strange earthquake last night. Usually we can detect quakes through the magic, but this one started suddenly, without warning. After the tremors ceased, every single earth mage lost the spellcasting ability. Including myself." He lowered his gaze in apparent shame.

At this, three other heads turned to look at the earth mage who sat at the table: the Hypsothi member who represented the Region of Earth, the earth magic, and those who wielded the latter. She was sitting silently, head bowed and eyes closed as she attempted to commune with the earth spirits using a nonmagical skill that was taught to newly-chosen leaders, but that common mages were not aware of.

Seeing this, the lead water mage said to the messenger: "Thank you. You are dismissed." The messenger, after a bow and a quick "As you wish, High Ones," shuffled dejectedly out of the Chamber.

Next, the water mage turned to the young mages who stood at the room's four exits, called "attendants" but mostly functioning as ceremonial guards, and dismissed them as well. They protested, of course; for if they departed, how could they protect the High Ones from whatever enemy had destroyed the earth magic?

"You may protect us some other time," the water mage snapped. "This matter is for us to discuss in private. And tell no one what you have already heard. In fact, it would be best if you forgot what has been said here today. Begone!"

At his peremptory tone, the young attendant-guards quickly scurried away. Within seconds, the four Hypsothi members were alone.

"What do you think, Fire?" the white-robed mage, the youngest of the four leaders, asked her red-robed colleague while they waited for the earth mage to come out of her trance.

"Is it serious? Will it spread to the other magics?"

"I don't know, Air," the fire mage replied. Fire and Air. Those were their names now, the names of the elements they represented and were supposed to embody. All who were elected to the Hypsothi shed their former names and remained "Fire," "Earth," "Air," and "Water" for the rest of their lives. It was impossible to resign from the Hypsothi, though some of the four would have liked to just then.

Following that brief exchange, Air, Fire, and Water sat in tense silence and watched Earth as she attempted to learn what was wrong. She was frowning, which did not bode well.

At last, she opened her eyes and raised her head. Her three colleagues looked at her expectantly.

"The earth spirits wouldn't communicate directly with me," she reported in a tone that was disappointed, but somehow matter-of-fact as well. "All I sensed was wrath. Implacable wrath. It seems they're very angry at something— or some*one*."

"That anger must be the reason behind the earthquake," Air mused.

Earth frowned at her. "Absolutely not! The earth spirits are benevolent. They would *never—*"

Water, the oldest and widely held to be the wisest of the four, raised his hand, and Earth fell silent. "Until we learn the truth," Water said firmly, "we can't rule out any possibilities."

"I agree with Air," Fire put in unexpectedly. "The quake *must* have been divinely directed! If it weren't, why would the mages have been unable to sense it before it struck? Combined with the wrath that Earth sensed just now, it makes perfect sense."

Earth nodded reluctantly. "If the mages couldn't anticipate it, it couldn't have been natural."

"Then we are agreed on that point?" Water asked. "We must also consider what the messenger told us about where the earthquake struck."

"He said it hit the primary Shrine of the Earth Magic," said Air.

"But there was no mention of any other damage," Fire pointed out. "Why, for instance, was this building not hit? We are so close to the primary Shrines that this building should have been destroyed, yet we felt only a small tremor."

Earth nodded again, slowly. "...All right. The quake was the work of the earth spirits." Though her tone was still calm, she looked a little sick as she spoke the words.

"I propose that we go to the Earth Shrine," said Air. "There, we can see the damage for ourselves and ask around to see if there was any suspicious activity in the area last night. That information might help us figure out what angered the earth spirits."

Water nodded approvingly. "Very good idea. Any objections?"

There were none, and soon all four mages had risen from their seats and were on their way outside.

Normally, when a formal meeting was adjourned, the four leaders exited the square-shaped room through separate arching doorways, one built into the center of each wall. Each arch, representing one of the four elements by its color and the carvings it bore, led up to the spacious quarters of that element's Hypsothi member, while the lower levels housed high-ranking advisers and scholars, the young attendant-guards, and others who were summoned to serve the Hypsothi for a few months after completing their training. On the lowest level of all was one of four libraries filled with books on history and magic, and then study and research rooms connected to a hallway that led outside. In its turn, the exit to the outside world pointed toward that element's most important Shrine, from which the mages drew their power, and, far in the distance, toward the major region of Tetrachtha , that was associated with that element. In all four directions from the Chamber of the Hypsothi, the layout was the same, one area dedicated to each element and mages of the other three elements forbidden there by longstanding custom.

Now, however, this part of the elaborate ceremony and practices surrounding the Hypsothi's headquarters was abruptly discarded. All four leaders left the Chamber through the green arch to the east, the one dedicated to earth, and hurried through the halls, ignoring the inquiring—and sometimes horror-stricken—stares of the earth mages who saw them. Before long, they were outside, on the featureless pale-brown plain of Tetrachtha's Central Region.

Hurrying toward the Shrine of the Earth Magic, they immediately saw the destruction the earthquake had wrought. Where there had once been a large and magnificent building, there was now a pile of rubble; not one gray stone brick still stood in its former place. Some bricks had even split apart from the force of their collisions with one another, and tiny dust particles lurked in and around the scene: awful reminders of the decay and disintegration that had set in over a single night.

As Earth gazed at what was left of the Shrine and—by extension—the magic she wielded, she began to sweat as her face grew paler to match Air's robes. Undoubtedly, she was wondering what she and Tetrachtha's other earth mages had done to deserve such misfortune. The other three Hypsothi members might have tried to reassure her on that point, but Air and Fire, whose corresponding Shrines were in visual range, had turned toward them. Water, meanwhile, was now looking back at the gray, palace-like façade of the council's headquarters, his brow creased in concern and his eyes searching here and there for signs of structural damage.

Silence reigned for a long time until Water turned back and spoke up: ostensibly to point out that no other building appeared to have been touched by the earthquake, but really to bring the others' attention back to the task at hand. The others immediately snapped out of their respective reveries, and Earth's face began to regain its color as she slowly recovered, but when the four continued their discussion, they talked in low, subdued tones full of unease.

They asked several passersby, whose reactions at seeing their leaders mingling freely in public ranged from surprise to all-out terror, if they knew what had happened in the Shrine on the previous night, both before and during the quake. As it turned out, not many people had been out at all, let alone anywhere near the Shrine, but a few reported having seen an earth mage heading in that direction a short time before the quake had struck. Numerous people offered this information, with their descriptions of the man's physical appearance confirming that they were all talking about the same person, but only one could provide a name: "*Gethen.*"

Earth frowned as her colleagues thanked the mage who had given the name, and as soon as the four council members were alone again, she spoke. "Gethen... Gethen..." She shook her head in frustration. "I don't know anyone by that name!"

"Then we'll just have to search until we find someone who does," Fire said with a shrug.

"Don't be upset, Earth," Water added. "We cannot know the name of every single person in our realms. It will take a little while, but we *will* find out who this Gethen is and why he entered the Shrine last night."

"But no one actually saw him go *in* the Shrine," Air pointed out. "He was just walking *toward* it."

"*Directly* toward it, as if he intended to go in," Fire countered. "But you're right, Air. We shouldn't assume that he went in, or that he was in any way associated with what happened."

"It almost doesn't matter," Earth said. "If he didn't go in, then he had nothing to do with any of this. And if he did go in... well, he's not coming out." She gestured at the huge pile of rubble. "No one who was in there when it collapsed could have survived."

Water nodded thoughtfully. "You make a good point. Still, we should pursue this investigation as far as we can. Even if it doesn't lead to this Gethen himself, it may lead to the reasons behind the earth spirits' anger. Then, once we understand the problem, we can try to find a solution. Agreed?"

The other three nodded in assent, Earth most vigorously, and then they all left the area to begin their investigation. When they were gone, the Shrine's ruins lay abandoned on the plain once again, concealing the mystery of the earth spirits' wrath beneath heaps of huge stone bricks so heavy that only the earth magic would be able to move them.

LOCATION UNKNOWN

The darkness receded, and Gethen opened his eyes—then wished he had not, for waves of pain crashed down on him in the form of a crushing headache. The room swam and spun before his eyes, but the stone floor a few feet away showed a small amount of blood, suggesting that he had hit his head there before sliding to a halt where he now lay...

He stopped; something did not make sense. Struggling to rise to a sitting position, he shook his head slightly to clear it. The searing pain intensified at the movement, but the fog of confusion lifted a little, and soon the room no longer spun in dizzying circles.

The room. That was it: the thought that made no sense. The last thing he recalled, before he had blacked out, was the Shrine of the Earth Magic collapsing around him in the midst of an earthquake. The Shrine should have been obliterated, reduced to nothing more than a pile of rocks and dust, and *he* should have been crushed. Yet here he was, dazed but alive, in a Shrine that had apparently suffered no damage?

However, he would not obtain the answers he needed by sitting there and doing nothing. Ever so slowly, he stood up; but as soon as he was on his feet, he had to grab hold of a nearby wall for support as the dizziness from his head wound returned with a vengeance. When the sensation had passed, he drew in a deep, ragged breath, took his first close look at his surroundings... and what he saw astonished him.

For the place in which he had woken up was the Shrine of the Earth Magic—and yet it was not. It had the same general appearance of a single room, rectangular in shape, with an arching doorway on one end and shadowy alcoves on the other. The size was the same, from the room's length and width to the height of the ceiling, all the way down to the individual stone bricks that made up the walls. The overall atmosphere was also nearly identical, with the same mysterious and sacred aura of a shrine or temple and a similar sense of divine wrath. The latter, though in no way reduced in ferocity, seemed a bit fainter and lacked the crushing quality it had had before, like a roar that is heard from a great distance away. And *that*, Gethen realized in increasing amazement, was only the beginning of the differences between the Earth Shrine and the place in which he now stood.

First of all, the walls, ceiling, and floor were the wrong color. Like the other Elemental Shrines, the Earth Shrine had been constructed with dark-gray stone; here, however, the bricks were a rich dark *green* in hue. It appeared to be the same material—the stone was equally cool to the touch and had the same texture—but the difference in color had Gethen doubting that fact. In addition, the lighting differed: whereas in the Shrine—the *other* Shrine—torches of green fire placed along the side walls had provided light, this eerily similar room had no such light sources. Much darker than the familiar Earth Shrine, it was lit only by a green glow emanating from the center of the room, which was empty except for a medium-tall pedestal of the same dark-green stone that made up the walls and floor. Hovering only inches above the pedestal was a large sphere of bright green light. Slowly, the sphere pulsated with power, its colors—seemingly infinite shades of green—swirling on it and within it.

Gethen stared at the pedestal and sphere with interest. That spot in the other Shrine had held the giant runic carving, the symbol from which all earth mages drew their power—and it had pulsated just like this sphere. His eyes widened. Could it be...?

Yes. The word, uttered by some external source other than the wrath-filled earth spirits, had not been spoken aloud, yet it filled his mind like a chorus of echoes. *You are correct, Gethen.*

The earth mage spared not a moment's thought on wondering how this strange mental voice, or collection of voices, knew his name. Instead, he stared openmouthed at the pulsating green sphere, which he now knew to be the source of the power for the huge rune in the other Shrine.

Centuries of magical lore and tradition had been wrong. That rune was not the source of the earth magic; this sphere was. Entranced, he stared at it until the brightness of its glow made his eyes water and forced him to turn away.

It does not shine as brightly as it once did, as it did only a short time ago, said the mental voices. *Once, you would have gone blind after looking upon it for only a few seconds. But already, the earth magic has been weakened—by you.* The last two words sounded pleased.

"Who are you?" Gethen burst out. "Where am I? What is this place?"

The voices laughed. *You know where you are, or else you*

could not have come.

He frowned. How *had* he come here? His headache still raged, but the fuzziness and confusion in his head had lifted, and soon he remembered fragments of what had happened. Needing to escape before the Shrine collapsed on him, he had glimpsed a small rune carved into the floor beneath the large one and had drawn it, used it.... Something had opened up before him, and...

All at once, the truth crashed down on him. The rune he had used for the spell, long thought to be merely a decoration or an untranslatable nonmagical inscription, had actually represented this place, a kind of parallel world. In his eagerness to get away from the collapsing Shrine, he had unconsciously called out a spell of transportation—seldom used in modern times, long distrusted and even considered a myth by many because no one knew what the specific rune was that activated the spell—and had opened up a pathway to this world.

But what *was* this world? Where had he unknowingly brought himself?

Cautiously, he moved toward one of the alcoves and tried to peer inside. Nothing; the darkness was too deep. Uttering a frustrated curse, he began to walk into those shadows—

He had not taken two steps before a divine presence sprang up out of nowhere, stopping him in his tracks as an intense dread consumed him. The presence was invisible, and it did nothing to harm him, but its warning was clear.

Gasping, he staggered backward. There could be no doubt: he had just encountered one—or perhaps more than one—of the earth spirits. He had felt their presence before, but never so close. And now, at last, he knew where he was.

This was more than a parallel world.

It was the legendary domain of the spirits, the plane on which they dwelled.

As this realization slowly sank in, he looked at the Shrine with new eyes. But it was more than a shrine, he now understood. It was a *temple*: holding not only some of the earth divinities, but also the true source of the magic that was derived from them. The familiar Shrine of the Earth Magic, however magnificent it might have been, had been dedicated to this place, not the other way around.

Another thought occurred to him. The earth spirits had tried to kill him back in the Shrine on Tetrachtha. Their wrath had not abated in the least; why, then, had they not attempted to finish the job here? Now that he was on their plane of existence, the task should be easier for them.

But even as his questions arose, the mysterious entities that had addressed him earlier laughed again in his head. *Therein lies their folly,* the voices explained. *In their wrath, they destroyed the Shrine and broke the link to the other world, thus rendering their magic unusable by all. They intended to punish you, and punish you they did—but, in so doing, they forgot that the link works both ways. Just as they give power to the human mages, so do the humans give them power; the more mages use their magic, the more powerful they become in turn. When they broke the link, therefore, they struck a crippling blow to themselves. Now they can be as wrathful as they wish, but they are too weak to act on that anger. You may think of it as if, in denying the magic to you, they have also lost it.*

Gethen tried to absorb all that he was hearing, but his mind was reeling. The earth magic, gone! He cared nothing for the situation of the earth spirits—it was irrelevant to his immediate objective—but the loss of the magic to which he had devoted his whole life was dire indeed. He had intended only to access the earth magic's root, not to destroy it, and if the power was dead, then all was lost.

All is not lost.

He stopped, now completely captivated by the quiet voices. He would have spoken, to ask for clarification, but he could not. The possible implications of the statement danced in his head until he could do nothing but stand there, silent and breathless.

The earth magic may be inaccessible, continued the voices, *but there are other forms of magic, better forms, that will be granted to you freely—for, by weakening our enemies, you have contributed greatly to our cause. With* our *magic, you will be able to cast spells you had never thought possible. You will gain immense power... power you have always wanted.*

It was too much for Gethen. His head was spinning again, his thoughts racing at a frantic pace, as he slumped against the dark-green wall once more. Absently, he held his hands against the wall for support and could feel them shaking as he attempted to evaluate his situation.

The spell he had intended to cast in the Shrine, the summoning spell, would have been powerful, but there was no guarantee that it would have worked even with all the power of the huge rune behind it. Making a second attempt was out of the question now, but if his theory about those mental voices and their power, which he was only now beginning to formulate, was even close to the truth...

He had to remind himself to keep breathing as his future course of action laid itself out before him. It seemed he had unwittingly made things easier for himself. *Much* easier. In his mind's eye, he could already see the incredulous faces of the others who had thought him ill-suited for this task.

Well, Gethen?

The two words resounded in his head: a different, and much more direct, mode of communication than the wordless auras he had encountered both here and in the Shrine—which was, in itself, more evidence for his theory. It took an immense effort to calm his breathing and bring his thoughts back under control, but—fortunately—it appeared that the brief lapse had gone unnoticed by his unseen interlocutors.

He cleared his throat. "Yes. You know me too well, and I will do whatever you ask of me in order to obtain this new power. Where are you?"

We are far away, in a place that is foreign to you, but you can come to us in an instant. Go over to the green sphere, touch it, and tap into its power. Use it to open a path. No rune is required, only that you think of us. Thus the path will open, and we will bring you to us.

"It will be as you command," he replied with a deep bow. Walking to the green-glowing sphere that hovered above the stone pedestal, he laid his hands on it and found it smooth and solid to the touch.

As soon as contact was made, he felt the power of the earth magic filling up his entire being, but he did not cast a spell. Instead, as he had been ordered, he thought of the mental voices, of the power they had promised him. Those thoughts, combined with the fact that he was the only person in the world—the *worlds*, he corrected himself—filled with the earth magic, must have acted as a beacon of sorts to help his new masters find him. For though he drew no rune, he soon heard behind him a noise as of cloth ripping.

Turning, he beheld a raggedly-shaped hole in the air, forming a wide tunnel with walls of seemingly infinite colors, as if the same hole had been cut through all the intervening space between where he was and where *they* were. Deep inside the hole, on the tunnel's far side, he caught his first glimpse of his destination. It was indeed foreign, like no place he had ever been before, all sharp lines and metal and bright many-colored lights....

The hole's edges fluctuated and began to shrink, a split second before... *something*... reached through from the other side. It had the appearance of a giant, dark-green arm tipped with claws, but its true nature was indeterminate. In a flash, it grasped him—painfully, the claws digging into his flesh—and then, before he could protest, pulled him forcibly into the collapsing hole between worlds.

TO BE CONTINUED...

GLOSSARY OF NAMES
& PRONUNCIATION GUIDE

(N.B. "Greek" refers to Classical Greek. Pronunciations are presented via an International Phonetic Alphabet transcription, followed by an informal approximation.)

-Aglaë [ˈagləˌeɪ] – *AHG-luh-ay*
Greek ἀγλαή, f. of ἀγλαός, "splendid, shining, beautiful"

-Aichme [ˈaɪkmeɪ] – *IKE-may*
Greek ἡ αἰχμή, "spearpoint, spear; battle, warlike spirit"

-Aïdelos [aɪˈidəlos] – *eye-EE-duh-los*
Greek ἀΐδηλος, "(making) unseen; destroying; obscure"

-Aktinos [ˈæktɪnos] – *ACK-tin-os*
Greek ἀκτῖνος, gen. sg. of ἡ ἀκτίς, "[sun]light; splendor"

-Andikha [ˈandikə] – *AHN-dee-kuh*
Greek ἄνδιχα, "asunder, in twain"

-Aneuthen [ˈanəθən] – *AH-nuh-thun*
Greek ἄνευθεν, "far away; distant"

-Anolethros [aˈnoʊlɛθɹos] – *ah-NO-leth-ros*
Greek ἀνώλεθρος, "indestructible"

-Ateles [əˈtiliz]/[əˈtɛliz] – *uh-TEE-leez / uh-TELL-eez*
Greek ἀτελής, "unfinished, endless"

-**Brinna** [ˈbɹɪnə] – *BRIN-nuh*
Swedish for "to burn"

-**Enedra** [əˈnɛdɹə] – *uh-NED-ruh*
Greek ἡ ἐνέδρα, "a lying in wait, ambush"

-**Erroguia** [ˌɛɹoʊˈɡiə] – *eh-roh-GHEE-uh*
Greek ἐρρωγυῖα, "she who is broken," f. perf. act. pple. of
ῥήγνυμι, "break"

-**Erythron** [əˈɹɪθɹɔn] – *uh-RITH-ron*
Greek ἐρυθρόν, n. of ἐρυθρός, "red"

-**Eudianassa** [ˌɛʊdiəˈnɑsə]/[ˌjudiəˈnæsə] – *EHW-dee-uh-
NAW-suh / YOO-dee-uh-NA-suh*
using Greek ἡ ἄνασσα, "queen, lady," by analogy with
εὐδιάναξ

-**Eudianax** [ˈɛʊdiəˌnaks]/[ˈjudiəˌnæks] – *EHW-dee-uh-
NAWKS / YOO-dee-uh-NACKS*
Greek ὁ εὐδιάναξ, "ruler of the calm"

-**Eudrakes** [juˈdɹeɪkiz] – *yoo-DRAKE-eez*
Greek εὐδρακής, "sharp-sighted, far-seeing"

-**Ganaï** [ˈɡɑnəˌi] – *GAH-nuh-ee*
Greek γανᾷ, "she shines," 3rd sg. pres. of γανάω, "shine,
glitter, gleam"

-**Gethen** [ˈɡɛθən] – *GEH-thun*
Greek γῆθεν, "from the earth"

-**Hypsothi** [hɪpˈsoʊθi] – *hip-SO-thi*
Greek ὑψόθι, "aloft, on high"

-Ikipimeä [ˌɪkiˈpɪmeɪæ] – *ick-ee-PIM-ay-aah*
Finnish for "eternal dark" or "ancient/primeval dark"

-Ikuisuudentorni [ˌɪkuiˈsudənˌtouɹni] – *ick-oo-ee-SOO-duhn-TOR-nee*
Finnish for "tower of eternity"

-Ischuron [ˈɪskəˌɹɔn] – *ISS-kuh-ron*
Greek ἰσχυρῶν, n. gen. pl. of ἰσχυρός, "strong, mighty"

-Keraunia [kəˈɹɔniə] – *kuh-RAW-nee-uh*
Greek κεραυνία, f. of κεραύνιος, "thunder-struck"

-Kevättären Valtakunta [ˌkɛvəˈteɹən #ˈvaltəˌkʊntə] – *keh-vuh-TEAR-uhn VALL-tuh-kun-tuh*
Finnish for "realm of the goddess of spring"

-Khalkeonos [ˌkælˈkeɪənos] – *kal-KAY-uh-nos*
Greek χαλκεῶνος, gen. sg. of ὁ χαλκεών, "forge, smithy"
(the underlying root is ὁ χαλκός, "bronze; bronze weapon")

-Khrusaoros [ˈkɹusaʊɹos] – *KROO-sour-os*
Greek χρυσάορος, "with sword of gold"

-Ljuset [ˈjusɛt]/[ˈljusɛt] – *YOO-set / LYOO-set*
Swedish for "the light"

-Makheteon [ˌmakəˈteɪɔn] – *mah-kuh-TAY-on*
Greek μαχετέον, "it must be fought, one must fight," verbal adjective of μάχομαι, "fight"

-Nautikon Ouranothi [ˈnaʊtɪˌkɔn #ˌuɹəˈnoʊθi] – *NOW-tick-on oo-ruh-NO-thi*
Greek τὸ ναυτικόν, "fleet" + οὐρανόθι, "in the firmament"

-Ouranothen [ˌuɹəˈnoʊθən] – *oo-ruh-NO-thun*
Greek οὐρανόθεν, "from the firmament"

-Photizousa [ˌfoʊtiˈzusə] – *foe-tee-ZOO-suh*
Greek φωτίζουσα, "she who gives light," f. pres. act. pple. of
φωτίζω, "give light, bring to light; instruct, teach"

-Psephos [ˈsɛfos] – *SEH-fos*
Greek τὸ ψέφος, "darkness, obscurity"

-Pyr [piɹ] – *PEER*
Greek τὸ πῦρ, "fire"

-Salainen [ˈsɑlaɪnən] – *SAUL-eye-nuhn*
Finnish for "secret, hidden; dark; esoteric; quiet"

-Selaä [ˈsɛləˌə] – *SELL-uh-uh*
Greek σέλαα, hypothetical uncontracted pl. of τὸ σέλας,
"blaze, flame, light; lightning"

-Skiai [ˈskiaɪ] – *SKI-eye*
Greek σκιαί, pl. of ἡ σκιά, "shadow, shade, phantom"

-Skiarchoi [ˈskiaɹˌkɔɪ] – *SKI-are-koy*
Greek invented compound using ἡ σκιά + pl. of ὁ ἀρχός,
"leader"

-Svarthål [ˈsvaɹthɔl] – *SVART-hall*
Swedish for "black hole"

-Synethon [ˈsɪnəˌθɑn] – *SIN-uh-thon*
Greek συνήθων, n. gen. pl. of συνήθης, "usual, ordinary,
customary"

-Tetarton [ˈtɛtɚˌtɔn] – *TEH-tuhr-tawn*
Greek τέταρτον, n. of τέταρτος, "fourth"

-Tetrachtha [tɛˈtɹakθə] – *teh-TRAHK-thuh*
Greek τετραχθά, "fourfold"

-Valonvuoret [ˈvalɔnˌvwoʊɹɛt] – *VALL-on-VWO-ret*
Finnish for "mountains of light"

-Vilse [ˈvɪlsə] – *VILL-suh*
Swedish for "lost"

Sources for word (or morpheme) meanings include:

Alanne, Severi, ed. Suomalais-Englantilainen Sanakirja / Finnish-English Dictionary. 1919.

Croghan, Vera, and Ivo Holmqvist. Teach Yourself – Complete Swedish. 2010 ed.

Liddell & Scott, eds. An Intermediate Greek-English Lexicon. 1889.

Morwood, James, and John Taylor, eds. Pocket Oxford Classical Greek Dictionary. 2002.

Online dictionaries, including dict.cc

ABOUT THE AUTHOR

Karen J. Laakko has been writing stories since age five, and she quickly gravitated to fantasy and related genres. Then, in school, she spent years studying Latin, Classical Greek, Linguistics, and classic literature. She loves bringing all of this knowledge together to develop and enhance her fictional worlds.

Karen works in a variety of language-related fields, such as editing, German-to-English translation, and dictionary analysis. In her free time she enjoys playing video games, learning new languages, watching sports, and searching for obscure bands to listen to. Like her studies, many of these interests end up feeding her writing projects, so one could say that she's always writing!

Visit https://karenjlaakkoauthor.com to learn more about the *Beyond the Hostile Sky Cycle*!

Made in the USA
Middletown, DE
08 January 2026

26786745R00158